C'est la Vie, Soldier

The Soldiers of PATCH-COM, Book V

MICHELE E. GWYNN

An M.E. Gwynn Publication

Copyright © 2023 by Michele E. Gwynn

All rights reserved.

No portion of this book may be reproduced in any form without written permission from the publisher or author, except as permitted by U.S. copyright law.

C'est la Vie and Easter Eggs

In the French language, c'est la vie (pronounced: say-la-vee) means "that's life," or "such is life." It is an idiom used to express either acceptance or resignation of a situation one can do nothing about.

The meaning I've chosen for this title is, "Such is Life." Lucien Montcourt is a realist. Whatever is beyond his control, he does not worry over. He focuses on the here and now, and what is within his grasp. He lives in the moment, and that is his charm.

Something else you'll find in this long-awaited story are two characters brought over from my crime series, the Checkpoint, Berlin Detective Series. Director Maurice Touchard of Interpol, Paris Division, is first introduced in book 1, Exposed: The Education of Sarah Brown. Back then, he was a high-ranking liaison for Interpol assigned to the offices in Lyon, France. He's obviously moved up the ranks, earning promotions since last I wrote of him.

Another character from the same series, book 3, The Redemption of Joseph Heinz, is Vladimir Brezhnev, known as The Butcher – the boss of one of the Vor v Zakone families. The Vor v Zakone also goes by the name of the Bratva, which translates to the Brotherhood. It is the Russian mafia. The Butcher is a brutal man beneath the deceptively thin veneer of a businessman. Both characters were perfect for the needs of this 5th book in the PATCH-COM series, and it was so much fun to revisit them.

If you enjoy steamy, international crime stories, please check out the Checkpoint, Berlin Detective Series here.

Thanks for adding my books to your library. Your support means the world to me.

~ Michele

Contents

La Belle Dame sans Merci: A Ballad	VII
1. Chapter One	1
2. Chapter Two	11
3. Chapter Three	23
4. Chapter Four	41
5. Chapter Five	53
6. Chapter Six	65
7. Chapter Seven	71
8. Chapter Eight	89
9. Chapter Nine	95
10. Chapter Ten	103
11. Chapter Eleven	113

12.	Chapter Twelve	125
13.	Chapter Thirteen	135
14.	Chapter Fourteen	147
15.	Chapter Fifteen	155
16.	Chapter Sixteen	169
17.	Chapter Seventeen	183
18.	Chapter Eighteen	197
19.	Chapter Nineteen	207
20.	Chapter Twenty	221
21.	Chapter Twenty-One	235
22.	Chapter Twenty-Two	255
23.	Chapter Twenty-Three	267
24.	Chapter Twenty-Four	283
25.	Chapter Twenty-Five	301
Epilogue		307
Get a FREE Book!		314
Also By Michele E. Gwynn		315

I see a lily on thy brow,
With anguish moist and fever-dew,
And on thy cheeks a fading rose
Fast withereth too.
~ John Keats

Chapter One

Lucien Montcourt followed Nastjia "Nasty" Moreno across the hall. The two soldiers quickly stepped into Senior Chief Vincent "Griz" Torres's room. Inside, Gerry "Mac" Maclean, Harold Tyler, a.k.a. Eastwood, Art "Cyclops" Diaz, Matt Rogers, Moses "the Prophet" Zigman, and Ben "Doc" Holiday stood, elbow to elbow. The small space had become their command center for planning Operation Save Moreno's Dad. Missing from their team, by design, were Jackson "Junkyard" Hicks, Carter "Woody" Ridgewood, Major Sydelle Maxwell, and the newest addition to PATCH-COM, Rick "Rooster" Ellis. Jackson had been informed, in the event the team needed a point of contact, but sidelined because the plans being made included the ability to move fast. Despite all his progress, Jackson still required a brace, and although he'd made great strides in ballet class, the extent of his injury was such that he would never be one hundred percent again. He would have a role in this operation, but it would center around his ability to coordinate quickly, quietly, and efficiently with the team for all tech-related needs.

It was decided early on that Woody would not be brought into the fold because, so far, he'd yet to join them on any missions. He had not completed rehab and wasn't battle-tested by the team. Plus, his loyalties could not yet be determined. Since what was being planned would not—could not—be sanctioned by top brass, that led to the group making the difficult decision to keep their plans under the radar of Major Maxwell. First, she would never be able to get clearance for what they intended, and second, her natural instinct to protect her team might lead her to defy chain of command and help them, which would get her into no end of trouble. No, they wouldn't do that to her.

The team presently assembled inside the room had all either been drafted in by their commanders when they were too broken to object, or they'd been offered a position at PATCH-COM on a voluntary basis—as guinea pigs for the experimental program. For one member, at least, it was a last resort.

With no official path forward, an alternate route to achieving their goal was now being meticulously plotted. It would require detailed planning, help from rogue quarters, and plane tickets.

"Fill me in," Ben Holiday said.

C'EST LA VIE, SOLDIER

It had been three weeks since his return from Moscow, from a mission that had gone sideways and nearly ended in catastrophe. Ben and Moses arrived together but got separated along the way. Zigman fulfilled the mission parameter of secreting the Russian opposition leader out of the country securing an ally for his home country of Israel. Ben stayed behind as a decoy taking a bullet for his troubles. Had it not been for the beautiful Doctor Irina Petrovna, a woman who, herself, had been targeted by the FSB, Ben might never have made it home. Much to his surprise, they'd fallen for each other.

Now that Irina's future was set, and her pathway to citizenship ensured, his life had settled into a happy routine. Together, they rang in the new year, sharing laughs, making love, and helping Jessica and Griz shop around for a new place to live. Ben's sister and the man she chose despite all his warnings, misgivings, and eventually a begrudgingly offered blessing, had decided to move in together. Still, he couldn't be happier. Especially since it gave him and Irina more room to romp naked. His beautiful personal physician had already begun putting her own stamp on the house by rearranging the bedroom furniture and dragging him out into the front yard to prep it for spring planting. They'd made so many memories already, and he spent most of his time smiling like a fool in love. But playtime was over. Duty called.

Moreno took point, turning to Ben. In short order, she filled him in on what she and Griz had discovered while he was gone, from the carved wooden bird found in the possession of one of the rescued children in the human trafficking sting to the information gathered by the senior chief's mercenary buddies south of the border. It was a lot to take in. At the end of her speech, Ben nodded, his arms crossed, and lips pursed in thought.

Beside Moreno, the French commando, Lucien Montcourt, stood, hands clasped behind his back, at ease. The expression in his eyes was anything but. He, too, was deep in thought. Still, his body language and bearing indicated to Ben, and everyone else in the room, that he was firmly with Moreno, on guard and supporting her every decision. It came as no surprise to the team. Since his arrival at Camp Lazarus and induction into PATCH-COM, the man had been drawn to the first female Navy SEAL like a moth to a flame. In the beginning, she was heartily annoyed by it. His non-stop flirtatious comments coupled with the man's characteristic snark and sarcasm had rubbed the men the wrong way, so much so that Mac had threatened bodily harm if the Frenchman didn't back off.

The rest of the team started a pool to guess how many more days would pass before Nasty gave Montcourt a beat-down. When Moreno's responses gradually changed from pissed to mildly irritated, the terms of the bet also changed: How long before Montcourt wore her down and the two ended up together? Moreno found out about the first bet, but they were sure she did not know about the second one. The reasons why were clear. If she found out, she'd exact her revenge on her teammates, and the truth of the matter was that as much as they respected her, they

C'EST LA VIE, SOLDIER

also knew how lethal she could be. No one wanted to be on the receiving end of Nasty's ire.

The only one brave enough to step up to that line had been Montcourt, and now, he was her stalwart protector. The devotion in his eyes when he looked at her was palpable. No one doubted he would guard her with his life, and had, in fact, done that only weeks before. Following the brothel sting, Nasty and Montcourt had become inseparable. They shared duties, ate at the chow hall together, and hung out in the common room each night watching movies or playing cards with the rest of the team. But when the evenings were over, Montcourt escorted Moreno back to her room, only one door down from his own, and across the hall from Griz's. It was there where the Senior Chief first noticed a change in their relationship. And that awkward moment changed everything.

On only the second night back at base, Griz came upon them standing outside the door of her quarters. He'd nodded at the two, saying goodnight, but as he turned to open his own door, he realized something. Glancing quickly over his shoulder, he confirmed it. Moreno was blushing. He'd quirked a brow in surprise, and then bit his tongue, hard. The temptation to tease Nasty for looking like she'd been caught in a compromising position was overwhelming, but he was no fool... and there were no locks on their bedroom doors. To give into that temptation meant sleeping with one eye open because Moreno would surely kill him in his sleep. Instead, he cleared his throat and turned away, stepping into his room. But once inside, he immediately texted Mac and Eastwood. That's when the stakes on their bet grew, and the betting began all over again in earnest as the pot tripled.

Ben Holiday chewed his lip, deep in thought. Finally, he looked at Moreno and said, "So, what you're saying is, we're going to Mexico for spring break?"

She smirked. "Something like that. But without the wild parties, out of control drinking, and hairy hangovers."

"Might get to kill some very bad guys though," said Eastwood, a grin on his face.

Flashbacks of a cold night and a dead Russian thug bleeding out all over him raced through Holiday's head. Prior to the mission to Moscow, Ben's career had been about saving lives, not taking them. And although he wasn't the one who inflicted the fatal wound, it happened during a terrifying fight for his life. He still had not found a way to reconcile that with his conscience. Not completely. He just couldn't be as nonchalant about it as some of the team members. Many of them had special forces combat backgrounds. Mac and Eastwood both had seen things, done things they would never discuss. And God knew what Griz had done for his country deep undercover for the CIA and DEA south of the border; even before that as a career Navy SEAL. He felt he had more in common with Rogers and Diaz, both of whom had only been lowly enlisted grunts. Now they were all getting a crash course in special forces training in this high-tech, top-secret experimental unit dubbed PATCH-COM. As far as he could

C'EST LA VIE, SOLDIER

tell, taking life would forevermore become part of his job. He needed to learn to suck it up, and fast.

"And hopefully save Moreno's father's life," he added. That part, he was down for.

Eastwood shrugged and grinned. "Of course."

Ben sighed, then looked at Nastjia. "Okay. Then I'm in."

She blinked, a sheen of tears quickly wiped away by the back of her hand before she reached out and shook Ben's. Gratitude radiated from her brown eyes. "Thank you."

Beside her, Montcourt reached out and patted Holiday's shoulder. "Yes, thank you, Ben."

"You bet. So, what do I need to do?"

Griz took over then, outlining the plan. February was the target month, second week. They had until then to secure leave for all involved. It would take some doing and depend a hell of a lot on nothing coming up between now and then from chain of command. But each of them had been at Camp Lazarus for quite some time, rehabilitating, training, and taking on missions. If anyone deserved a break, Griz figured it was this group.

"If all goes well, if my sources are accurate, and we pull this off," Griz said, "maybe we can spend a night or two actually enjoying a margarita on the beach. God knows we deserve it. Until then, no one discusses any of this outside of this room. Got it?"

Everyone nodded their agreement.

Griz stood. "Alright then, team. Dismissed."

Moreno and Montcourt waited until the rest of the team filed out, then wished Griz a good night. He patted her back and closed the door behind them.

In the hall, Lucien watched as Art and Matt ambled off to the common room. Mac and Eastwood had already left the sleep quarters to head out on a long drive home to Las Vegas. It was rough on those two having residences in the city two hours away. During the week, they stayed on base, but as soon as the weekend rolled around, Harry and Joely drove to their condo and Mac returned to Connie at their house on the northwest side of the city. Griz would be moving out on the weekends soon as well. His relationship with Jessica had progressed to the living together stage. Montcourt figured there would likely be a wedding in the not-too-distant future.

Silence intruded on his thoughts, and he looked at Nastjia. They were alone and once again, standing in front of her doorway. She leaned her shoulder on the jamb, her eyes cast down, staring at her hands as she fidgeted with her fingers. He reached out, capturing her hands in his own, his thumbs caressing her knuckles. When she didn't pull away, he smiled, looking down at the top of her head. A few stray tendrils of her dark hair curled loosely falling over her forehead. A strong urge pulled at him to reach up and smooth the curls back, just to see if they were as soft as they appeared.

But he resisted. It was enough she accepted his touch, and his heart skipped a beat at the momentous occasion. "What is it, Chéri?"

C'EST LA VIE, SOLDIER

Moreno hid a smile. The term of endearment that used to annoy the hell out of her now seemed to have the opposite effect. Somehow, somewhere along the line, Lucien had become important to her. Maybe it was saving her life, or his damnable constancy. No matter whether she wanted him around or not, he was there. He went from being a pain in her ass to a teammate who had her back, and now... something else. His warm hands on hers, his nearness, and even the deep, soothing tone of his voice when he called her "dear" in French had begun stirring feelings she wasn't sure she was ready to deal with. But she also didn't want to push him away. It was a conundrum, for sure.

"I just don't know what to think right now," she whispered.

Montcourt's heart swelled.

"I mean, so many things can go wrong, Lucien. What if my father is there because he chose to be there? What then? What am I supposed to do if my dad is really some deadbeat with cartel ties?"

Montcourt's ego deflated. He blew out a breath, which stirred her hair and recaptured his attention. With a finger, he reached up and lifted her chin until their eyes met. "Listen to me, Nastjia," he said, his voice both warm and no-nonsense. "There is no way that the man who raised you to be such an amazing young woman could be involved with garbage like the Colima cartel. We will handle anything that comes up. I won't let anything happen to you," he said, his hazel eyes locking with hers. "We will find your papa and rescue him. Do not doubt it. Do not doubt him."

She stared at Lucien. "How do you know?"

He smiled his usual cocky smile, the one that used to piss her off. Only this time, it caused another emotion. Suddenly, she couldn't seem to get enough air.

The finger under her chin stroked her jawline. "I just know. Trust me, Nastjia. You can always trust me."

Moreno swallowed, then backed up. A nervous cough escaped her lips before she reached for the doorknob. "I guess we'll just have to wait and see," she said, stepping into her room.

Montcourt's eyes followed her, a speculative gleam glowing in their depths. "Oui, we will see," he said, a smile tugging at the corner of his lips. "Goodnight, Ma Chéri."

He turned toward his own room and stepped inside. Closing the door, he leaned against the heavy wood and reached up, rubbing his temples. Sighing, he made his way to the bathroom and opened the medicine cabinet. He reached inside and pulled out a bottle, unscrewing the lid, then popped two pills in his mouth. Filling a glass with water, he swallowed them down, then left the bathroom and laid down on his bed in the dark. As the pain of the headache increased, he distracted himself with thoughts of Moreno. It wasn't a lot, but tonight, she gave him reason to hope. But what good was that, he mused? What hope did he really have?

Chapter Two

Moreno buried herself in prep work for their unsanctioned mission in between training, drills, and routine team meetings with Major Maxwell. The last were conducted regularly to keep them all apprised of the geopolitical state of the world and all pertinent information regarding current and potential conflicts for which they might be mobilized to handle should the need arise. Her only downtime was spent with Montcourt. It was those moments where she felt most at peace. Lucien seemed to know when she needed to talk, and when she just needed someone with whom to sit quietly. Alone in her room, she reflected on how far he'd come from the snarky jackass every woman encountered at least once in her lifetime to the man who now set himself up as a protective wall between her and a world intent on kicking her ass.

It was such a dramatic change that she wondered just when and why it happened. He was a different person now than he'd been those first few months. And since she no longer needed to avoid the French-fried catcalls and inappropriate comments, she noticed instead his smile when he greeted her in the hall first thing in the morning. She had to admit, it was a panty-dropper. It probably didn't help that the smile was set into a ridiculously handsome face, or that he had great hair, broad shoulders, and a deceptively muscular physique on his lean frame. Lucien wasn't as tall as most of the other guys on the team, but his larger-than-life persona made his five-foot, eleven-inch height feel like six-foot, five. Plus, she was only a mere five-foot, five inches. That put the French commando six inches taller than herself. Just about right, she mused.

But why was she noticing him now? When did this shift occur? Had he just worn her down with kind gestures, heroic rescues, and stupidly sexy French endearments? Nastjia sighed, then frowned. Maybe it was simply because it had been a long time since she'd last been with a man and he was right next door. Her mind might be having a real crisis over what to do about Lucien, but her body was increasingly betraying her. When he held her hands the other night, all she could think about was how they would feel gliding over her naked backside. The timbre of his voice when he called her, "Ma Chéri" felt like a heated caress over her neglected lady bits. Worse, she was sure he knew it.

C'EST LA VIE, SOLDIER

Far more embarrassing than Lucien knowing it was the fact that the Senior Chief caught them together during one of those moments when her mind was screaming *"No!"* while her body was leaning in, ready to pounce. Her embarrassment pissed her off and she'd glared at Griz in warning. If he'd let out one little teasing peep, she knew she would've pulled off her own left foot prosthetic and beat him with it. Thankfully, he understood the danger he'd walked into and disappeared inside his room before she found herself being court martialed for attacking a senior officer.

Part of her wanted to see if an encounter with Montcourt would be as hot as her traitorous body promised, but her brain kept tight control, not wanting to find herself in a compromising position. The team came first, and nothing fucked up teamwork like fucking a teammate.

"Dammit!" she muttered. Figuring she'd managed to talk herself out of a huge mistake, Moreno tossed off her covers, grabbed the cane she kept by the bed, and headed into the shower. After making it as cold as possible, she stepped under the spray. Montcourt would be kept firmly in the friend zone, if for no other reason than to not screw up the team dynamic. There were rules about fraternization for a reason, she rationalized. Didn't mean she had to like it, though. Grabbing the shampoo, she angrily washed her hair and promised herself when all this was over, she would treat herself to some downtime off base and away from Lucien Montcourt. Maybe she'd meet someone who could take the edge off before she started taking out her frustrations on everyone around her.

Rinsed off and wrapped in a towel, she hopped to the sink and looked at herself in the mirror. Her hair had grown a few inches longer. She really needed to get it cut and styled. It just hadn't been a priority lately. Spending most of her time on base, she simply wound it up at the nape of her neck. Hell, she hadn't even bothered with makeup probably since the Christmas and New Year's parties at the Tyler's villa and Ben Holiday's home. After brushing her teeth, she grabbed her cosmetics bag and pulled out the essentials. Today, she would make an effort. She needed to get back into the habit of giving a damn about herself. As she applied eye liner, a little mascara, and a subtle pink gloss to her lips, she tamped down the irritating inner voice hoping Lucien would notice.

And as she attached her foot prosthetic, she mentally dared that annoying bitch in her head to say something about the fact she'd actually shaved her legs for the first time in two weeks... as well as her bikini line. Not that anyone would be seeing or enjoying her silky smoothness. Not yet, at least. It was just about reforming good grooming habits. She'd been in the company of wolves for too long and had gone native. It was time to remember that she wasn't just a badass soldier in a top-secret, experimental elite special forces group. She was also a woman, and with that came certain needs. It was past time she paid attention and tended to them.

C'EST LA VIE, SOLDIER

After winding up her hair into its usual bun at her nape, she gave her body a quick spritz of her favorite scent. The light floral tickled her nose and she smiled. Then, she made the bold decision to don a lacy red thong, one she usually reserved for nights out. There hadn't been any of those in a while. Checking herself in the mirror, her mood took a bit of a nose-dive. The subtle makeup looked good, but the BDUs did nothing at all for her figure. She sighed. There was nothing she could do about that. Even so, she did look better, and she definitely smelled better. Her perfume alone set her apart from the hairy beasts she worked with, and knowing she was smooth, moisturized, made up, and wearing something lacy beneath the olive drab camo gave her a certain confidence that glowed in her dark eyes like a sexy secret. There was nothing left to do now but head out to breakfast.

She grabbed the badge she'd been issued upon arrival and clipped it onto the pocket of her jacket. Hat in hand, she stepped into the hall. It was early yet, but she'd always been an early riser. She noticed the Senior Chief's door was closed, but next to his, Matt Rogers' door was just opening. He entered the hall and, seeing Nastjia, gave her a quick smile and a nod.

"Good morning, Moreno."

"Matt," she replied. She watched as he closed his door using the robotic arm prosthetic as easily as a flesh and blood arm. He'd come a long way since his arrival at Camp Lazarus with Eastwood and Diaz. Perhaps it had to do with his age. Only twenty-three, but with the mental fortitude of a man twice his age. Still, the resiliency of his youth was most likely the biggest factor in his ability to adapt to the biomechanics that now allowed him to have a functioning arm in place of the one he lost. And he'd relearned all his firearms and weapons training as well. To Nasty, he was a real-life Universal Soldier straight out of the world of science fiction. She had nothing but respect for him.

"Heading to the chow hall?" he asked.

She nodded, then her eyes glanced one door down from her own before quickly returning to focus on Rogers. "Yeah, but I forgot something. Be right there. You go on ahead," she said, then ducked back into her room.

Matt caught the quick look she threw toward Montcourt's door and bit his lip to smother the grin threatening to erupt on his face. He knew better than to tease Moreno. They all did. Even Harry, and he was usually the first one to stick his foot in his mouth. Instead, he pulled on his hat and said, "See ya there."

Inside her room, Moreno waited until the sound of Matt's footsteps faded into the distance. When it was quiet once again, she glanced at the wall that separated her room from Lucien's. She hadn't heard the shower turn on yet. Usually, he awakened around the same time as herself. Had she missed him this morning? She thought about their goodnight nine hours ago. He hadn't mentioned any pressing business for the next day. In fact, he said he'd see her in the morning. Did Lucien oversleep?

If that was the case, he'd be late for their morning meeting, and Major Maxwell was not a CO who tolerated

C'EST LA VIE, SOLDIER

tardiness. Not wanting Montcourt to end up on the receiving end of the major's ire, she exited her room once again, this time turning right. In just three steps, she was in front of his door. Suddenly, she felt self-conscious. Biting her lip, she pushed that feeling down. She wasn't here for herself, she was here to make sure he didn't get into trouble. Raising her hand, she knocked twice.

No answer. She applied another quick knock, waited, and then turned to leave for the chow hall.

A loud crash sounded from within.

Not thinking twice, Nastjia turned back around and threw open the door. A gasp flew from her lips when she saw Montcourt on the floor.

"Lucien!" She ran inside and dropped down next to him.

He lay face-down on the concrete floor, breathing hard. A series of curses flew from his lips as he raised a hand to his forehead. Next to him, Moreno panicked.

"You're bleeding," she said, her voice strained with concern.

She gently touched his head feeling for the injury. She found it. A gash on his temple caused by the impact with the floor.

"Shit!" Montcourt muttered. "I heard knocking and got up to answer, and the next thing I knew...," his voice trailed off. He knew what happened. The medication he'd taken the night before had knocked him out cold. It was still in his system, making him groggy. He'd tried to rise and walk but the room spun and down he went. Now, he was bloodied and weak and it was not how he wanted Nastjia to see him.

"I'm okay, Ma Chéri," he said, a half-smile on his lips. He carefully rolled over and tried to sit up, but she wasn't having it.

Moreno cradled his head in her lap, one hand pressing gently, but firmly on his shoulder.

"What happened?"

Moreno's head whipped toward the open door. Griz stood there, his expression filled with concern.

Montcourt cursed beneath his breath. It was bad enough having Nastjia find him like this, but now another teammate... He ground his teeth before answering.

"I am a clumsy idiot," he said. "Got up to answer the door and tripped over my own feet."

"Can you get me a towel, please?" Moreno asked Griz. "Before he bleeds out before breakfast."

Griz took in the scene, still unsure exactly what he'd walked in on. But Montcourt was bleeding all over his hand. The Senior Chief moved quickly into the bathroom and grabbed a towel, bringing it out and handing it to Moreno. She immediately removed Montcourt's hand from his forehead and applied pressure to the gash.

"Should I get help?" he asked.

Montcourt shook his head no as Moreno responded with, "Yes!"

Griz didn't know what to do.

C'EST LA VIE, SOLDIER

"I am okay, Griz. It's just a small injury," said Montcourt. "I am in good hands. I'll get cleaned up and be fine in no time."

"You're not fine, Lucien," Moreno interjected. "And you will be going to the infirmary. Head injuries are nothing to play with. The only thing harder than your head is this concrete floor, and guess what? It won!" She gave him a no-nonsense glare, but the shimmer of tears in her big, dark eyes was what ultimately convinced him to concede.

Montcourt lifted her hand, the one still resting on his shoulder, and brought it to his lips, kissing her fingers. "If it pleases you," he said.

Suddenly feeling like a third wheel, Griz backed up. "If you're sure," he said. Neither Montcourt nor Moreno answered him. They were lost in each other's eyes. He knew when he wasn't needed. "Uh... I'll see you both later." As quickly as he arrived, he left.

"What really happened, Lucien?" Moreno asked once they were alone.

Caressing her hand, he smiled. It was meant to put her at ease, to charm her, and ultimately distract. There was no way he would tell her the truth. "I overslept, Chéri. You woke me from very sweet dreams, and I was not quite awake. I am embarrassed," he admitted. Reaching up, he wiped away a stray tear from her cheek with the pad of his thumb. "Is this for me?"

She sniffed and glanced around the room, unable to make eye contact. "Well, you scared me. I thought maybe you..." She bit her tongue.

The smile on his face turned into a self-satisfied grin. Slowly, he removed the hand holding the towel and carefully pulled it away, checking to see how much blood he'd lost. It wasn't as bad as he thought. Most of it was on his own hand, which he wiped quickly before sitting up. Montcourt faced Moreno whose eyes were looking everywhere but at him.

Seeing him rise, Moreno's attention refocused on him, her gaze finding the wound on his temple. "You shouldn't be sitting up yet," she fussed.

Montcourt chuckled. "I will be okay. See," he said, turning his face to show her the injury, "the bleeding has already slowed down. I've had far worse, Nastjia," he added, his voice now low and soothing. He wanted to take away the anxiety he'd caused her.

"You might need stitches," she said, still worried. The site was already bruised a dark shade of purple and appeared a bit swollen.

"I have what I need," he whispered, taking her hands to still their restless fretting. "Look at me," he said, leaning closer.

It was then Moreno finally noticed his state of undress. Montcourt was naked.

"Oh, my God!" she blurted, her face turning red. Her eyes bounced again to the ceiling. "Sorry, I didn't even..."

Another laugh escaped him, one that was filled with both humor and something else. "Chéri, it's just a body. My body. I have seen your body, too, remember?" he

C'EST LA VIE, SOLDIER

reminded her. "Neither circumstance is anything to be embarrassed about."

Moreno's blush deepened despite his words. It was true. He'd seen her naked. It was one of the most humiliating experiences of her life, being auctioned off inside a brothel by traffickers. She'd fought for her life, and Lucien had been there, seen it all. Not once had he mentioned it. His eyes never left hers, staying above board while he helped her back into her robe before rescuing her. He'd not mentioned it any time after that either. Not until now, and only because this time, he was the one naked and injured. They'd come full circle.

"Now we are even, oui?"

The humor of the situation sank in. The corners of her lips twitched. "I guess so. But I should leave so you can clean up and get dressed. Can't be late to the morning meeting. Plus, you really should have the doctor check that out."

"For you, I will," he promised.

Then, Montcourt leaned in and kissed her softly on her cheek, lingering for a heartbeat. It was unexpected and she felt the heat rising off his skin as his breath fanned her ear.

"Thank you for coming to my rescue."

Every inch of her body burst into flame, and it felt like someone set off fireworks inside all her lady bits. It might be winter outside but beneath her red, lace thong, it was the Fourth of July! Clearing her throat, Moreno backed up and stood, putting some much-needed distance between them.

Montcourt rose to his feet and stood before her, unabashed and smiling. It was the panty-dropper. Dammit!

"You're welcome," she replied, her throat dry. "I'll see you..." she stepped toward the door, a confused look on her face.

"In the conference room. Remember, you want me to get this checked out," he chuckled, pointing at his head.

"Right, right." Moreno made it to the hallway. She didn't mean to do it, but her eyes betrayed her as her head swiveled back around for one last look. Good Lord, why must he be so damned sexy, she thought. "Later," she mumbled, and then walked away as quickly as her legs would carry her.

Chapter Three

Montcourt sat patiently, wincing only when the staples popped into place. As it turned out, he did need stitches, except that stitches now were staples plunged into his skin before the local anesthetic injection fully took effect. Three sharp pricks left him biting the inside of his cheek. He concentrated on breathing and reminded himself he'd chosen to come to Camp Lazarus. It was either this or discharged from service. But just what would he have done after that? Sit around and wait?

No. That wasn't who he was. He'd long ago chosen the life of a soldier, much to his ambassador father's dismay. He was not one to sit around and twiddle his thumbs. He did not trust in fate or the universe or God. He trusted in what he could see, hear, do, and control. Lucien was stubborn to the bone, but also a realist. And right now, the pain of the staple gun was as real as it got.

He let his mind drift back to the moments following his hard meeting with the floor. He'd seen stars, and then... an angel of mercy. Her warm hands upon his skin, cradling his head in her lap as she bent over him in concern had been incredibly stirring. Sure, he'd often dreamed of lying naked in her arms, but nowhere in his daydreams had he been knocked senseless and left bleeding. Still, the quiver in her voice and the fear on her lovely face moved his cynical heart in ways he could not adequately describe. Over the preceding months, his feelings for Nastjia Moreno had grown from idle interest to lust to something deeper. All he knew was that the defining moment came when the CIA sting operation, inserting her into a sex trafficking bordello, went off the rails putting her in real danger of being sold to an abusive billionaire intent on enslaving her. Seeing her stripped bare, beaten, and vulnerable on the auction block sent him into a panic. His heart broke into a thousand pieces and bled out all over the floor. Lucien saw red and vowed he would kill the bastards who hurt her. To his surprise, Nastjia killed the first one. Brave and fierce, her swift actions left him not only in awe of the woman, but irrevocably in love. His shattered heart was hers, every last shard, if only she'd accept him.

But why would she? And what, he thought, could he possibly offer? A woman like his Nastjia deserved the world and then some. His Nastjia, he mused. If only... He smiled to himself as the doctor applied a bandage over the staples and advised him to come back in five days. They went over his current medications, and then the doctor

C'EST LA VIE, SOLDIER

handed him a couple of painkillers and a cup of water to help ease the discomfort from his wound. Promising to make the appointment for next week with the front desk on the way out, Lucien exited the doctor's office. Montcourt completed the appointment setup, and then headed back to PATCH HQ and the conference room, navigating the elaborate labyrinth of tunnels deep beneath the surface of Area 51 that comprised Camp Lazarus.

He chuckled as the irony hit him. Lazarus was the biblical dead man who was buried, then brought back to life by Jesus of Nazareth. Now, here he was, the walking dead. Just like Lazarus, buried underground. But there was no savior in his future. All he had was here and now. It was all he'd asked for, all he thought he would want or need. Until he met Nastjia. The joy he felt in her presence was offset by the bitterness of knowing he could never have her, never deserve her. The bitch of it was it didn't stop him from giving himself to her in any way she needed, for as long as she allowed. He couldn't help himself, despite it all. Montcourt admitted to himself what he knew he could never say out loud. He was in love with the woman.

He turned right into the hall leading to the conference room. Standing just outside the door was the angel herself. She was leaning against the wall facing the opposite direction. As he watched, Art Diaz, Matt Rogers, and Jackson Hicks approached from the other end. They led the new member, a cocky young man whose name he couldn't quite remember, Ellis something or other, along. Art caught sight of Montcourt and nodded in his direction.

Moreno noticed and turned her head to look. When her eyes met Lucien's, she smiled.

Suddenly, the sun came out deep-down inside the mountain and Montcourt's heart did a backflip in his chest. He straightened his shoulders and smiled back, the slow, deliberate smile he'd noticed made her blush. Sure enough, color bloomed in her cheeks, and a shot of desire zinged straight to his groin as his ego grew three sizes. He wished he could freeze time and stay in this moment forever. Just him and his Nastjia, eyes locked, hormones overflowing like a rain-swollen river.

A hand slapped him right in the middle of his back and a loud voice boomed.

"What the hell happened to you, Luc?"

He glanced right and tamped down his annoyance at the abrupt interruption. Eastwood stared back. The Green Beret's eyes locked onto the white bandage that stood out like a sore thumb on Montcourt's forehead.

"Headbutted something with a harder head than you," he replied.

Next to Eastwood, Mac chuckled.

"What'd I do?" said Eastwood, perplexed.

Montcourt shook his head and, reaching out, patted Eastwood's shoulder. "Nothing, Mon Ami. I am just in a mood. Had a small accident getting out of bed this morning. That's all. Three staples for my troubles."

"Well, shit," said Eastwood. "That's not the type of headbanging you should be doing in the morning, Montcourt. I thought you Frenchmen knew the difference."

C'EST LA VIE, SOLDIER

"We wrote the book on it, Harry," he said. "Trust me, I know the difference, but we are not all so lucky as you. You have Doctor Winter."

"That's Mrs. Tyler to you," Harry retorted. "And don't you forget it. She's taken!"

Montcourt smirked and Mac rolled his eyes.

"What you need, my friend, is to wake up in the arms of a beautiful woman every day," Eastwood said, waving a finger in Montcourt's direction.

The three men came abreast of Moreno and Montcourt's eyes found hers. His lips curved.

"Yes, waking up in the arms of a beautiful woman is just what I...," he paused, and his voice dropped low so only Moreno could hear, "needed."

Eastwood and Mac walked into the conference room ahead of Montcourt, both nodding Moreno's way and offering a quick, "'Morning, Moreno."

Lucien waited, one arm casually behind his back, and the other gesturing she should enter ahead of him.

"After you, Chéri," he whispered.

Moreno's big brown eyes bounced from the bandage to his eyes. The twin spots of color on her cheeks glowed and her lips were parted ever so slightly. It was all Montcourt could do not to pull her into his arms and kiss her until she begged for more. He wondered if she felt it, too, this heart-racing desire. Her blush said she was definitely aware, but his own nagging insecurity preached caution. Plus, they weren't alone. He turned his head looking into the room. The entire team sat around the table now, quietly watching them. Knowing Moreno would be mortified, he cleared his throat and took one step back, an easy smile spreading across his lips.

Moreno shook herself, then proceeded inside. As she stepped into the room, the men suddenly turned away and began talking to each other in an exaggerated fashion. At the head of the conference table, Major Maxwell sighed heavily and rolled her eyes.

"Settle down, everyone. This isn't high school." She banged the gavel, and the morning meeting came to order.

The team was briefed on current national security alerts including the continued unrest between the Russian Federation and the NATO alliance, as well as troop movement near the border of Ukraine. The major moved on to reports from the Department of Defense, DHS, and ODNI before finishing off with the daily assessment from NTAS (National Terrorism Advisory System).

"At this moment, PATCH-COM remains on standby," she concluded.

"Or, in other words," Griz sighed, "same shit, different day."

Major Maxwell blew out a breath. "Exactly." She stacked the reports and straightened, eyeing the senior chief.

Griz sat forward, an easy smile on his face. "Maybe now would be a good time to ask..." he began, "seeing as how we're not in hot demand."

"Ask what?" Maxwell took a seat.

C'EST LA VIE, SOLDIER

Griz looked around the table at the team before returning his attention to his CO. "About vacation. We do get vacation at some point, don't we?"

The other team members sat forward, all quietly waiting on the major's response. Major Maxwell eyed each one in turn.

"Why do I suddenly feel like a mother ambushed by her children?" she muttered. And then louder, "All of you?"

Griz shook his head. "Well, obviously not all of us at once, but a few of us have been tossing ideas around, just in case you were feeling generous, Mom..."

Maxwell's scarred left eyebrow shot up as she pinned the senior chief with a hard stare. The effect was as wicked and disconcerting as he remembered.

"Uh, Major," he corrected, wiping his expression free of mischief.

The major leaned back slowly in her chair and regarded the group. "So," she began, "you think you're deserving of a vacation?"

Under the weight of their commanding officer's stare, Matt Rogers was the first to drop his eyes. He reached with his uninjured hand to rub the back of his head. Art Diaz was next, swallowing hard and turning away. Moreno and Montcourt looked at each other while Ben, Jackson, Mac, Eastwood, Moses, Woody, and even the new guy, Ellis, suddenly found anywhere else in the room more interesting than the major.

Griz watched as his team, a group of battle-hardened soldiers who'd all come through catastrophic injuries and proven themselves to their chain of command not once, but twice in their careers, all clammed up like... like... clams!

Seeing them cowed simply for wanting a break from it all fired him up. For a moment, he forgot it was all a ruse, that they were secretly planning an op. They deserved time off, dammit! Each and every one of them worked harder here at Camp Lazarus than he'd seen any other operators do anywhere else, and with damned handicaps, no less!

"Now hold on, Major," he said, turning back to her. "No one has worked harder than these men," he said, then, glancing at Moreno, added, "and this woman, to serve our country. Each of us has overcome impossible odds, put ourselves through grueling, painful, and rigorous rehabilitation just to get back on our feet. Even danced around the gym on our tiptoes! And still, at the end of the day, we've answered the call to serve, and have done so without complaint and with great success, I might add." He paused to take a breath.

Maxwell held up her hand and Griz closed his mouth, furious.

"I never said you all did not deserve a break, Senior Chief," she said calmly. Standing, she addressed the room. "As your commander, no one is more aware of what you've accomplished despite your injuries. And no one is prouder and more impressed by your displays of courage and willpower, dedication and bravery."

Surprised pairs of eyes landed once again on Major Maxwell. Jaws dropped at the unexpected praise.

The major turned her attention back to Griz. "Each member of the team wishing to take a short vacation needs to submit dates and destinations to me in writing by the end of the day." She turned again to the group. "I'll see what I can do. Dismissed."

Moreno completed drills, sweat running down her face. She'd raced through Nasty Nick, the obstacle course that humbled many a SEAL candidate before Hell Week. Coming in behind her by one minute, seven seconds was Mac, who spit and cursed, then stuck out his hand in congratulations, a smirk on his lips.

"Gonna beat you one of these days, Nasty," he mumbled.

She grinned. "One of these days, Maclean," she chuckled, "but not today."

The only member of the team who'd managed to beat her time on the course tossed a towel her way, glowing admiration in his hazel eyes.

"Your athleticism puts us all to shame, Chéri."

She wiped her face and inhaled deeply, enjoying his praise. "Except for you. I still need eight seconds to beat your time." She eyed him, her expression determined. "And I will, Lucien. Just you wait," she added, pointing a finger at him.

A slow smile spread across his lips. "I have no doubt. I look forward to the day you top me," he said, stepping closer, his voice dropping low. "But you'll have to work for it. I won't make it easy for you."

A hot flash of desire burst through her body like a heatwave. The image his words conjured made all her neglected lady parts pant in anticipation. A montage of herself, slick with sweat, riding his fit, too-sexy-for-words body as she raced toward a very different finish line caused her cheeks to pinken and her lips to part as she suddenly felt she couldn't get enough air.

Witnessing the palpable chemistry between them, Mac shook his head and walked away.

Montcourt forgot about everyone else in the gym. For him, in this moment, there was only Nastjia. The look in her eyes drew him in and the sheen of perspiration on her tan skin led to dangerous thoughts. He wanted to lick the delicate groove of her collarbone revealed beneath the white tank top. His eyes traveled lower, over the outline of her pert breasts, the flat plane of her tummy, and down over the curve of her hips encased in an enticing pair of black shorts. Her scent called to him, and his body reacted. It was time to step away before everyone in the gymnasium knew how turned on he was.

He whispered close to her ear, "We shall finish this discussion later," then turned and walked away.

Moreno breathed a sigh of relief and clutched the towel to her chest to hide her suddenly painfully erect nipples.

C'EST LA VIE, SOLDIER

Cool air washed over her skin, drying the sweat, and putting out the fire in her belly.

"PT is over," Griz announced. He was standing next to Joe Poole, their company therapist. "The rest of the day is yours," he announced. "Eastwood, Mac, Rogers, Diaz, Moreno, Montcourt, Zigman, and Holiday, meeting in our usual spot in forty-five minutes. We need to get that paperwork completed."

Griz turned from them and gathered Woody, Jackson, and the new guy, Rick Ellis, in a huddle.

Moreno watched as heads nodded, wondering what Griz was saying to them. A tap on her shoulder drew her attention.

"He'll tell us later," said Mac. "Come on. Time to wash the stink off. Don't wanna be closed into the Senior Chief's room with a bunch of smelly fuckers."

Moreno laughed. "I didn't think that sort of thing bothered you, Mac." She fell in step next to him. Ahead, Montcourt walked out of the gym, Matt Rogers at his side. The two men were deep in conversation, unaware that behind them, Moreno was enjoying the view of one particular man and his firm backside.

"Just 'cuz I'm used to the stink of men doesn't mean I like it. Rather be home with Connie," he said, a smile tugging his lips.

"How is she? I haven't seen her in weeks."

"Good. Keeping busy. She adopted a cat," he said.

"What?" Moreno tore her eyes from Montcourt's backside and looked at Mac. "A cat?"

Mac shook his head. "Yeah, damned beast," he grumbled. "Big, orange furball kept coming around the house. Connie felt sorry for it and fed it. Once you feed 'em, they never leave. Now she's brought him inside."

"It's a him?" Moreno chuckled.

"Think it belonged to someone. It had a collar, but no chip. Says she checked with the neighbors, but no one knows whose cat it is. I told her to keep looking. Don't need a cat."

The look of irritation on Mac's face tickled Moreno to no end. She knew Connie now, knew the woman had a tender heart. And she knew Maclean. Despite all his grousing, he, too, had a soft heart. She'd bet a month's wages that by the end of the week, there'd be a cat bed, squeaky toys, and a cat tree at the Maclean house. That cat wasn't going anywhere.

"What's its name?" she asked, keeping her expression blank.

He sniffed. "She calls the beast Mr. Fuzzypants." He scowled. "That's no name for a male."

Moreno suppressed a smile. There it was. The first indication that there was a new member of the Maclean household.

They turned the corner. Ahead were the guest quarters where Mac and Eastwood spent much of their week away from home. The next right led to the residents' dormitory and her room. She paused at the turnoff.

"Let me know what you decide to name him," she said. "M.J. is a good name." Moreno turned, walking away.

Confused, Mac called out. "M.J.?"

Moreno tossed a mischievous look over her shoulder. "Mac Junior."

A disgusted snort met her ears. It was all she could do to hold in the laughter.

After another cold shower, Moreno dressed, taking time again to apply just a bit of makeup. She paired a black T-shirt with her BDU bottoms and boots. A quick spritz of her favorite scent, a light floral body spray called Daydream Believer, and she was ready to go across the hall to Griz's room. It was time for them to fill out their request for leave paperwork. As she stepped out into the hall, hat in hand, Montcourt was waiting.

His eyes raked her from head to toe before he approached. His nostrils flared and the panty-dropper smile eased across his lips.

"You smell intoxicating," he said.

Moreno noticed that he, too, smelled rather delicious. Somehow, their flirtation had ramped up to a dangerous level. She swallowed hard.

"Thanks."

He put out his arm, ever the gentleman she'd come to rely upon once again. "Ready?"

"Yes," she replied, taking his arm and relieved he'd changed the subject. She'd already had two cold showers today. "Do you think we'll all get the green light from the major?"

"Probably not all," he said. "It will be a toss-up to see who gets approved."

Montcourt reached out and knocked twice on Griz's door.

"Enter," came the reply from within.

Opening the door, Montcourt waited as Moreno stepped inside first. The rest of the group was already there, crowded together and filling out paperwork. Griz sat at his desk. Rogers and Diaz sat on the bed. Ben, Mac, Eastwood, and Moses were on the floor, their backs against the wall as they scribbled away on their forms. Griz held out his arm, a stack of papers and two pens in his hand.

"Here," he said, handing the forms off. "Second week of February, the tenth," he added. "Request seven days. It's all we'll have, so we need to make the most of it."

Montcourt smiled. "So, we'll all be together for Valentine's Day?"

His shoulder touched Moreno's, whether by accident inside the close quarters, or by design, she couldn't tell, but his sideways glance had her thinking it was the former.

"Why? You thinkin' of buying me flowers, Luc?" Griz asked, tongue in cheek. "You should know, I'm taken."

Holiday snorted.

"Just checking, Senior Chief." Montcourt took the forms and handed a pen and a stack of papers to Moreno. He looked around the crowded room for a place to settle.

Rogers noticed and tapped Diaz on the arm. "We'll take the floor," he said. Art joined him, leaving the bed for Moreno and Montcourt.

C'EST LA VIE, SOLDIER

The team buckled down, filling out the information required. Everyone stopped on the same line.

"What do we put for a destination?" Diaz asked.

"And why do they need to know?" asked Matt.

Eastwood grunted. "Special Operators don't get privacy, kids," he answered. "If something comes up and they need us, they need to know where we are. Or worse, if something happens..."

Griz sat up straight, his thoughts suddenly running like a caffeinated hamster on a wheel. He looked at Diaz. The man was a walking GPS. He'd forgotten about the WiFi chip installed in his new eye prosthetic. Command could see and hear everything he saw and heard anytime they decided to drop in. Well, anytime Diaz was near a cellphone tower or WiFi hotspot. If Diaz got approved, he would be an unwilling mole for chain of command. He hated the idea of cutting the sharpshooter. They could really use him in the field. But Rogers had been training right alongside Diaz and was every bit as good. The shitty part was he was bound by an NDA that made it both impossible and legally detrimental to reveal this knowledge to Diaz or anyone on the team. Only he, Major Maxwell, and Doctor Winter knew outside of the CIA and FBI. They were the ones who'd requested the upgrade before the team was sent in to The Honey Hole sting op.

Fuck! Now he needed to make sure Diaz's paperwork got lost before it ever saw Maxwell's desk. It was the only way to protect the mission. He felt bad, but under the circumstances, it was the only solution. Art would be disappointed, but it protected them all.

The other degree of difficulty was going to be keeping the ladies both safe, and in the dark about why they were all going on vacation together. They were all highly intelligent. Jessica, Doctor Winter, Connie, and Irina would get suspicious, he was sure. He sighed. One problem at a time. No one said this would be easy. Least of all, not him.

He looked at the group. "Mexico City," he replied. It was the closest tourist destination to the last known coordinates of Moreno's dad, according to his sources.

Everyone wrote it down, then Eastwood looked at Griz. "Ain't that gonna be a problem for you? I mean, you were down there a while. Your face is known to the cartels."

Griz nodded. "This face is known," he replied, his hand running over the close-cropped goatee. "But I have a plan," he said, leaving it at that.

"If you're all finished filling your forms out, hand them over. I'll take them over to the major's office." Griz waited as everyone handed in their requests for leave. He stood, then waited as those on the floor got up. "I'll meet you all in the mess hall. Cross your fingers that Maxwell is generous and greenlights everyone."

Moreno gave her papers to Eastwood who handed them to Griz. Remembering the huddle he'd been in with the rest of the PATCH-COM members, she asked, "What were you saying to Woody, Hicks, and the new guy earlier?"

C'EST LA VIE, SOLDIER

Griz smirked. "Told 'em to request leave for San Antonio. Hicks knows it's a ruse. If he gets approved, he'll be closer to us and better able to help us out with logistics or an exit strategy if we need it. Figured Woody and Ellis might enjoy the Riverwalk in the meantime. Plus, it keeps Maxwell from figuring out we're up to anything."

Moreno looked impressed. "Not bad, Senior Chief. Not bad at all."

He bowed. "Glad you approve." The room began to clear out. "See you all in a few," he said.

Moreno led the way and Montcourt followed. When they reached the hall, her hand shot out grabbing his.

His face reflected his surprise.

Her big brown eyes found his hazel ones. "It's happening, Lucien. We're going to find my dad."

He saw both her worry and hope. Squeezing her hand, he lifted it to his lips and placed a light kiss on her fingers. "It will be okay, Nastjia. I'll be with you every step of the way."

Moreno felt tears sting the backs of her eyes. Her emotions were too close to the surface, both those of worry and fear for her father, and these newer feelings threatening to burst the dam for Montcourt. She sucked in a breath and broke eye contact. She knew that soon she would need to face this thing between them. But right now, her focus had to be on her father and the mission.

"Right," she said, awkwardly changing the subject. "I wonder what they're serving tonight. Cow slop, pig slop, or chicken slop?"

Montcourt chuckled low. He could always tell when he managed to get past her guard, even if it was just for a moment. He didn't know why he tortured himself so. It could never amount to anything. Still, he was a goner the minute he laid eyes on her. It would take a stronger man than himself to resist the temptation of Nastjia Moreno. She was his one weakness, the one thing he wanted... and could not have.

Chapter Four

A week passed in a flurry of activity. The team continued rehab for some and training for others. Carter Ridgewood III, aka, Woody, and the newest patient in the PATCH-COM rehabilitation unit, Rick "Rooster" Ellis had become thick as thieves in Jessica Holiday's baby ballet class. Adding Jackson Hicks to the mix made for an hour of shenanigans from the three grown men who seemed to regress to teenagers when together. Griz watched the younger men through narrowed eyes as he now easily worked his way through the poses. He didn't like the way the new guy cracked wise while ogling his lady.

Ellis, from what he'd learned, was some hotshot Navy aviator who'd busted up his right leg in a car accident. A broken femur, tibia, and shattered kneecap were no joke. While he sympathized with anyone who suffered a catastrophic injury, that sympathy dried up when the injured party kept interrupting his girlfriend's instructions, cut up constantly, and then stared at Jessica like she was the last glazed donut at a Weight Watchers meeting. He knew then he was going to have to have a little chat with the cocky Rooster and if he didn't stop crowing, Griz would choke that damned chicken until he did.

A young private came up behind him just as the senior chief completed his final form. The soldier, one of the two who'd brought him to his quarters when he'd first arrived at Camp Lazarus, waited patiently as Griz wiped the sweat from his brow with a towel.

"What is it, Private?" he asked.

The young man stepped forward, his hand extended, holding a folded stack of papers. "For you, sir. From the major."

Griz took the papers and unfolded them, reading through. Nodding, he sighed, and then dismissed the soldier. "Received. Thank you."

The young man left and Griz headed for Jessica. After making plans to see her again on Friday after work, he sought out Ellis. The man was moving carefully to the exit using a cane, Woody limping alongside him. Jackson had long since left for his next scheduled activity for the day.

Griz quickly caught up to the two.

"Ridgewood," he said, acknowledging the younger man.

"Senior Chief," he replied, a ready smile on his affable face.

C'EST LA VIE, SOLDIER

"Good to see you doing so well. Mind if I have a word with the new guy?" Griz towered over Woody, who nodded, and moved away.

Ellis patted Woody on the shoulder. "I'll catch up to you at lunch." He turned then and focused his attention on the man in front of him. "Griz," he said.

Griz waited until Ridgewood was out of earshot before turning to Ellis. He eyed the tall man with dirty blond hair and amber eyes. There was a smugness to the aviator, a pure arrogance that set Griz's teeth on edge. He didn't like it. Which didn't bode well for the pilot, fellow Navy man or not.

Griz's eyes narrowed as he stepped in closer. "I'm Senior Chief Torres."

Ellis's lips twitched. "Yes, I know. Lieutenant Rick Ellis," he replied. "Shouldn't you be saluting me?"

Griz growled low and loomed over the tall man by a neat inch. "Listen closely, you cocky little shit. Officer or not, if you come in here again and disrespect that woman's class with your smart comments, we're going to have a problem."

The twitching stopped and Ellis bristled.

Griz smiled slowly. "And another thing," he added, now in the man's face, "if you stare at her ass again or look at her at all in any way not becoming of an officer representing this unit, I will personally break your other leg. Got me?" Not waiting for a reply, Griz quickly walked away, passing Ben Holiday, who was on his way in.

"Ben," Griz growled, nodding as he passed.

"Griz," Ben replied, looking over his shoulder at the senior chief as he practically stomped out of the gym. "Damn, who ate his lunch?"

"He's a cranky old geezer. Insubordinate, too," said Ellis.

Ben turned and faced the new guy. "Griz? What'd he do?"

"Threatened me," he replied, "and failed to salute an officer."

That took Holiday by surprise. "Threatened you with what?"

Ellis snorted, then chuckled. "Said if I disrespected the ballet teacher again, he'd break my other leg. Can't help it if she's hot, now, can I. And what business is it of his anyhow?"

Ben Holiday sucked in a slow breath, nostrils flaring, eyes narrowing. He stepped in, leaning close to Ellis's ear. "The ballet teacher is Griz's girlfriend."

Ellis pulled his head back and leaned away from Holiday. "Well, all he had to do was say so. No need to threaten me. I don't poach off another man's property."

Ben let loose a wry chuckle, now ready to throttle the man. The tight-lipped smile dropped. "She's not "property," you dimwitted fuck. She's my sister!"

The new guy's eyes rounded as he muttered, "Shit."

"And if I hear about you saying anything so damned disrespectful or dumb again, and believe me, I will know." he added, poking Ellis in the chest with a finger, "I'll be the one helping Torres break your other leg, and a few choice other body parts, too. I'm a medic. I know how

C'EST LA VIE, SOLDIER

to hurt someone. Understand?" Ben offered a mocking salute before leaving Lieutenant Ellis standing there with his mouth hanging wide.

Griz was seeing red. He wanted to turn back around and slam a fist in the cocky little chicken's beak. But he'd made his point, and he had news to deliver. He passed Eastwood and Mac in the corridor.

He held up the stack of papers. "Meeting in my room this afternoon. Three o'clock. Can you two find Moreno and Montcourt and the rest and let them know?"

Mac nodded. "Will do." He eyed Griz, noting the heightened color on his face. "You okay?"

"Yeah, you look pissed," Eastwood said. "Bad news?"

"What?" Griz asked, then shook his head. "No, no. Just some unpleasant bullshit. New guy," he said. "Not important. Just spread the word. I'll see you all later."

Mac patted his shoulder. "No worries. We'll handle it."

"Thanks, guys." Griz continued back to his quarters to shower and change.

Eastwood and Mac walked in the opposite direction and met Ben and Jessica Holiday coming out of the gym. After exchanging hellos, Ben walked his sister to the elevator that would take her back topside. Rick Ellis came out behind them, moving slowly and keeping his distance. Mac and Eastwood watched his progress through narrowed eyes. Seeing the unwelcoming looks on their faces, Ellis moved a little faster, skirting around them and heading toward the residents' quarters.

Eastwood and Mac watched him go, then looked at each other.

"What do you think the new guy did to piss Griz off?' Eastwood asked.

Mac shook his head. "Don't know, but that's no way to begin around here."

"Damn right, it isn't. We'll have to keep an eye on him. Teach him the do's and don'ts."

Mac snorted. "You were the new guy once."

Eastwood grinned, and the two continued down the hall. "Yeah, but I'm charming."

Maclean looked at him, a wry expression on his face. "Says who?"

"My wife."

Mac mumbled to himself, "Not what she said when you first arrived." He walked ahead of Eastwood.

"What? Wait! What'd she say?"

Mac kept his eyes forward and stayed two steps ahead, grinning. Needling Harry was too easy sometimes.

They found Rogers and Diaz at the indoor gun range and passed along the message from Griz. In short order, they'd located Moreno and Montcourt, and crossed paths again with Holiday where they discovered exactly what the new guy did to anger Griz... and Ben.

"Hoo-boy!" Eastwood exclaimed. "No wonder. New guy is lucky Griz didn't go all grizzly on him."

"First impressions," Mac muttered. "Hard to come back from that."

Ben agreed. "These snot-nosed kids might get commissioned, but it doesn't mean they know how to act or even deserve the rank. I hear his daddy is an admiral."

"Figures," Mac said.

"Well, Daddy ain't here, and if he's going to be PATCH, he needs to learn some respect," said Eastwood. "A team doesn't work if you can't trust the teammates."

"Help me keep an eye on him, guys. Jessica said he doesn't bother her, but no one is going to treat my sister like that. If he does it again, officer or not, he's getting a beatdown."

Eastwood and Mac nodded their agreement.

The team assembled again late that afternoon in Griz's room where he informed them leave had been granted... for everyone except Art Diaz.

"What? But... but why?" Diaz's face was a study in confusion and frustration. It reminded Griz of a kid denied by his mom to go to a birthday party all his friends were attending.

He felt badly, but it was necessary. Griz cleared his throat. "Don't know, Diaz. I think it had to do with numbers. Only a select few could be released at once."

Diaz snorted. "Not even San Antonio?" he asked. There was a hint of a whine to this last question.

"No, not even San Antonio." Griz handed Diaz's request form over to the man. "But it does say if there are no demands on the team when we come back, you can reapply."

Art took the paper and stared at it, his nose wrinkled, and brows drawn low over his eyes. He was clearly unhappy.

Griz continued speaking to the group. "Other than needing to make travel arrangements, I have nothing else to discuss with you all right now. Once we get tickets in hand, we'll meet up again." The senior chief was ready to end the meeting. He worried that even now someone could be listening in and watching them through Diaz's prosthetic eye. From here on in, Art would not be included in any meetings.

"What about Hicks?" Diaz asked. "He put in for San Antonio."

Griz glanced at him. "Approved."

"Shit!" Art threw up his hands and muttered to himself as he stood, ready to head out the door.

Griz came up behind him and gripped his shoulder. "Next time, Diaz," he said. "But while we're gone," he said, leaning in close to the man's ear and speaking low, "don't discuss any of this with anyone. Understand?"

Art nodded, but the expression in his eyes said he wasn't quite sure why Griz felt the need to remind him. "Yeah, sure."

"Good, good." Griz patted Diaz's shoulder. He turned to Moreno and Montcourt who remained behind after everyone left.

C'EST LA VIE, SOLDIER

"What was that about with Art?" Moreno asked.

Griz shuffled the remaining papers in his hand and then set them on the desk. "Nothing. Just command making their decisions. We have one less man on the ground, but we'll be fine."

Nastjia cocked her head, her dark eyes boring into Griz. "You're hiding something."

Griz stared back, amazed by her intuition, but unable to confirm. "There's nothing to hide. We have work to do." He turned his attention to Montcourt. "We need to get hold of a travel agent and get this trip booked. No using anyone inside PATCH-COM. Not Art's Miss Janeway, or anyone else. I know Natalie is efficient, but we can't risk having anyone here knowing exactly where we're going in Mexico City, when, or where we'll be staying. Understood?"

"Oui."

"You and Moreno get that started. I'll get you the info on all who are going to Mexico and Jackson's info for the San Antonio trip. It's a good thing he was approved. I'll feel better knowing we have a contact stateside, just in case."

"We'll take care of it," Montcourt promised. The French marine gestured to Moreno and she led the way out. He followed, as always.

In the hall, Moreno grabbed Lucien's hand, pulled him into her room, and shut the door.

Surprised, he spun around, a half-smile on his lips. "Chéri?" he queried, a twinkle in his hazel eyes.

"Something's going on," she said, crossing her arms over her chest.

Montcourt stepped closer, his hands casually clasped behind his back. "I am thinking so, too," he replied, his eyes traveling over her body before returning to gaze at her lips.

Heat shot through her, and Moreno pushed against his chest. "Not with us, Lucien, with the senior chief! He's hiding something."

Her shove sobered him. Taking a step back, he eyed her. "What am I missing?"

Moreno shouldered her way past him to her bed where she sat down. "Diaz. Something is going on there. Like, why was his leave not approved?"

Montcourt shrugged. "Because the major cannot let us all go at once."

She huffed and leaned forward resting her elbows on her knees. "But didn't you hear Griz's tone? It's like he was glad Diaz got denied."

He hadn't noticed, but now that he thought about it, there was something to what Moreno was saying. Montcourt ran a hand through his hair. "I do not know why he would be glad of that, Chéri. Art is as much a part of this team as any of us. He has the senior chief's confidence, and he has ours. And the major did warn us not everyone would be approved. I am sure she has her reasons."

Moreno sighed. "Maybe." Her shoulders sagged.

He watched as the fight drained out of her. She'd been keyed up for months over this whole situation. It weighed on her and he hated seeing her worry, seeing her beat herself up and blame herself for whatever peril her father

C'EST LA VIE, SOLDIER

found himself in, even before knowing the truth of his situation. In three steps he was at her side and pulling her in close. Montcourt rubbed her back and whispered soothing words in her ear.

"It will be okay, Nastjia. We're one step closer to Mexico, and soon, we'll find your papa. All will work out. We will discover the truth, and no matter what, I will be at your side. You're not alone in this." His hand found her cheek and he tipped her face up to his. "No matter what, this was not your fault. You are a good daughter, and a good woman. Never doubt it."

His assurances struck her right in the heart. A single tear slipped down her cheek, and then another. "But how do you know, Lucien?" she asked, her voice catching.

Before he could stop himself, Montcourt leaned in and gently kissed the trail left behind by her tears. When his lips hovered near the corner of hers, he whispered, "Because you are beautiful, Chéri, inside and out."

Stunned by his words, a soft gasp escaped her.

The last shred of his control crumbled. His lips found hers and slid softly and slowly back and forth. It was torture and heaven all at once. He'd dreamed of this moment, thinking it would never happen, should never happen. She deserved better. But he could not resist. One touch, one taste, and he was lost.

Moreno sighed. The sparks skipping over her skin like fireworks were better than she'd imagined, and she's imagined a lot in the last few days. Especially after seeing him naked. But what she hadn't imagined was Lucien being so gentle, as if he were afraid she'd break. The heat simmering inside her demanded more. She wanted to be thoroughly kissed, because dammit, it had been too long!

She leaned in closer, her head canting to one side.

It was all the invitation he needed. Growling low, Montcourt swept her up in his arms. One hand slid over the back of her neck, cupping her head, and the other down her spine until his palm rested on her lower back. His tongue found hers and the duel began. The taste of her mouth and the feel of her body pressed against his drove all rational thought from his mind. She was everything, and in this moment, she was his.

Every part of Moreno's body was on fire and singing hallelujah. It felt right, like it was always meant to be. But it wasn't enough. His hot palm caressed her lower back, just above the cleft of her behind. She wanted desperately for that hand to dip lower and grab her ass. She pressed closer and wrapped a leg around his waist as they fell back on her bed.

Montcourt groaned into her mouth and slid his hand lower.

Flames exploded deep inside her belly. Frustrated by the barrier of their clothing, Moreno pushed Lucien over, rolling on top. Straddling his hips, she sat up and reached for the buttons on his BDU jacket.

A knock at the door stopped her.

Chapter Five

Moreno looked over her shoulder at the door. She felt like a teenager caught with a boy in her room. A boy who was trapped beneath her and painfully erect. Her body screamed, *"Ignore the knock! Nothing is more important than this moment!"*

But the knock persisted.

"Dammit!" she mumbled, scrambling off Lucien.

Montcourt bit his own now-empty hand, the one that had been full only seconds ago of Moreno's lush ass, and stifled a groan. His pain was both torturous and exquisite. So close...

"Hide in here!" she whispered, pointing at the bathroom door.

Working around the tightness in his trousers, Montcourt eased up off the mattress and moved quickly inside the bathroom, closing the door quietly behind him.

Smoothing her black t-shirt back in place, Moreno approached the door and opened it. A private stood in the hall, hand raised to knock again. He dropped the hand and cleared his throat.

"Ma'am, your presence is requested in Major Maxwell's office immediately."

Moreno looked at him, blinking once. "Did she say why?" She reached behind her and grabbed her hat from the desk. The major had not personally sent for her before in this manner. What was going on?

"No ma'am," he replied, backing up a few steps and waiting.

It was clear he was there to escort her. Moreno stepped out and closed the door behind her. The private fell in beside her as she made her way out of the residents' quarters to Major Maxwell's office.

Moreno's bedroom grew quiet. The bathroom door cracked open, and then Montcourt stuck his head out, looking around. "Nastjia?" he whispered.

The room was empty. He left the bathroom, scratching his head. With one last yearning look at her bed, Lucien exited Moreno's bedroom, checking the hall for curious eyes. As soon as he closed the door to his own room, he sighed. His wayward man parts were almost back to normal. Almost. With a cocky half-smile, he replayed the last twenty minutes over and over in his mind. He could still taste her on his tongue, feel the heat of her body against his own, smell the scent of sex rising from that coveted place he'd only dreamed of. And just like that, his traitorous man parts surged once again. Turning, he banged his head on the wall, a groan of frustration reverberating in his throat. Maybe it was a good thing they were interrupted. What would become of them afterwards, anyhow?

Lucien glanced down. The strained olive-drab material over his crotch disagreed wholeheartedly. Glaring at his zipper, he muttered, "Just be quiet! You are not the boss of me!"

Angry now, he stripped down and marched into his own bathroom. Turning the cold water on blast, he stepped under, cringing in shock.

Moreno stopped, saluted, and waited for Major Maxwell to respond. Surprise flared in her dark eyes at the person standing next to her, arms crossed over his chest.

Special Agent Mark Peters, FBI.

"Petty Officer Moreno," Maxwell acknowledged. "Have a seat. You remember Agent Peters?" she said, continuing on.

Moreno glanced at Peters, nodding once. The agent's poker face hadn't changed. Still cold, still not giving anything away. She returned her attention to her CO.

"I know you're wondering why I called you in," said Maxwell. "Agent Peters will fill you in."

Confused, Moreno looked at Agent Peters. He wore a dark suit with a light grey shirt and dark tie. His outfit was both severe and nondescript. The short haircut, almost a military buzzcut, lent to the overall utilitarian appearance of the FBI Special Agent. He looked like a man who never smiled or experienced joy. But he'd been the one to help her and Senior Chief Torres get an interview with the two young girls rescued from The Honey Hole following the joint CIA/FBI sting operation that nearly got her auctioned off as a sex slave. It was that interview that provided information that alarmed and devastated Moreno. Her father was somehow involved with the Colima cartel and their trafficking of abducted women and children. Whether or not voluntarily had yet to be determined and was the reason she and the team were busy making plans to find out.

Peters uncoiled like a serpent and reached inside an open briefcase on the major's desk. He pulled out a file folder and meticulously set it before Moreno, turned it around, and opened it. Inside were several surveillance photos. The top-most image caught her off guard.

Agent Peters watched her reaction, saying nothing. As Moreno's horror grew, he pointed at the picture.

"I take it you recognize him."

A surge of bile hit the back of Moreno's throat and she swallowed it back down. She stared at the image, a grainy black and white aerial photo showing three men surrounding a small group of five females. It was impossible to pinpoint their ages, but one was quite small. Two of the men held AR-15-styled rifles pointed at the women, who huddled together. The third man stood back from the first two, but his was the only face looking up. It was a

C'EST LA VIE, SOLDIER

familiar face, one that emoted no detectable emotion that she could see in the pixelations. Still, she knew him.

"That's my father," she croaked, her throat dry.

Peters said nothing, but flipped the picture over, exposing the next one.

Moreno stared at two men in dark suits. One was tall, thin, with dark hair. The other one, older, his blond head balding, was shorter and stockier. His expression was bland. These two men stood roughly fifty feet from the first three and the group of women. They watched, hands in the pockets of their trousers. Behind them, a large, black Hummer was parked.

"What about these two? Know them?" Peters asked.

Moreno shook her head. "No. I don't know them." She looked at the agent. "What is this about? Why do you have a picture of my father? Where did you get this?"

Peters continued flipping through the stack of pictures. Five more, in all. The remaining three told the story of the group of women forced into a waiting van by the gun-wielding men while her father seemed to follow behind. The other two wearing suits climbed back into the Hummer.

"When's the last time you spoke with your father, Petty Officer?"

Moreno sat back. "It's been years."

"And why is that?" Peters left the photos out on display as he sat on the edge of the desk looking down on her.

She shifted in the chair. "After I joined the Navy, my dad disappeared. I haven't spoken with him since. Honestly, I didn't know where he was."

Peters raised a dubious eyebrow. "You didn't know where your own father was? How is that possible?"

She shrugged. "I wish I knew. I went home on leave, before my accident, and he was gone."

"Gone?"

"Yes, gone. Like, the house was vacant, he wasn't there, and no one seemed to know where he went. I asked the neighbors, thinking something was wrong or something happened to him, but no one knew anything. No one even noticed a whole house being packed up. So, yeah, he didn't tell me he was moving or leaving, didn't call me or write. No note, nothing."

Peters' expression remained unconvinced. "And you didn't look for him? Call a family member? File a police report?"

Moreno threw up her hands. "We have no other family, really. I mean, my dad was from Mexico, but he hadn't seen his parents in a long time. My grandfather died and my grandmother, as far as I knew, lived with her sister, my great-aunt Lupita. I don't even know if she's still alive. But to answer your question, no. I didn't look for him. I mean, he packed up the house and left without telling me. That much was clear. No need to file a police report when his actions were deliberate, or so I thought."

"So you thought, but not anymore?" he asked, pressing.

C'EST LA VIE, SOLDIER

She bit her tongue. What she thought now was that that information was on a need-to-know basis, and as far as she was concerned, Agent Peters didn't need to know. Especially now that he'd somehow found Juan Carlos Moreno and made the connection to her. She decided to err on the side of caution and wait to see what else the agent revealed.

His blue eyes bore into hers, but she gave back stare for stare.

"Granting that interview was contingent upon sharing information. Now why is it that Senior Chief Torres withheld the connection between you and those two little girls trafficked into the U.S.? What are you hiding, Moreno?"

And just like that, Peters went on the attack. Moreno felt herself bristle at the accusation, and she needed to think fast.

She breathed out slowly, controlling her anxiety. "Because he didn't know, sir."

If Peters was surprised by her answer, he didn't show it. The man had a face etched in stone. Yet, somehow, she was sure he didn't believe her. "He didn't know?" he repeated.

Moreno nodded. "That's correct. He didn't know." And now she needed to make sure Griz wiped that knowledge from his memory before Peters ambushed him into a confession. It was the only way to protect the senior chief. He'd done a lot for her. Damned if she'd pay him back by throwing him under the bus now.

"How is that possible? You were both in the room with those little girls, asking questions." Peters crossed his arms over his chest again, his head tilted forward and his eyes boring into her.

She felt a trickle of sweat slide down her spine and disappear into the crack of her ass. It was not a pleasant feeling, but she refused to acknowledge it.

Holding firm, Moreno replied, "The girls didn't know the name of the man they said tried to help them," she began. *"There, you stone-cold bastard, chew on that information!"* she screamed inside her head. No way would she not take the opportunity to put her father's innocence out there, even if she was unsure of it herself.

"One of the girls had a small carving, a bird. I recognized it, or at least, I thought I did. My dad used to make them. He gave me three. Still, I wasn't sure until I had the chance to ask the children. It was only when they described the man who gave it to them that I knew."

"And you didn't tell Torres? I find that hard to believe, Petty Officer Moreno." Peters continued to stare a hole through her head.

She really didn't like this prick.

"I did not."

"And Torres had no idea why you asked the girls about the bird carving?"

"As far as he knew, we were just seeking further information on the kidnappers. I'm sure he explained it all in his report to you," she said, rolling the dice. In truth, she had no idea what Griz told Peters, but since he was

C'EST LA VIE, SOLDIER

willing to plan an under-the-radar covert op to help her find her father, taking an incredible risk in doing so, she felt confident that the senior chief did not share critical information that would shine any light on a connection between herself and a cartel kidnapper.

Peters' eyes narrowed and he glared in silence. He knew she was lying. But about which part, he seemed unsure, if his never-changing sour expression was any indication. Moreno was pinning her speculation on his silence. He'd interviewed the two little girls himself, that much was clear. That's the only way he would know any of this. Behind him, Major Maxwell's eyes bounced between Moreno and the agent, her left eyebrow cocked at a wicked angle. Clearly, she was confused, but the major was a patient woman. She would remain quiet until the answers revealed themselves, one way or the other.

"So, you're telling me that you have not talked to your father in years, that you haven't bothered to look for him, and now that you've uncovered a clue to his whereabouts, as an inside man in a cartel trafficking ring, no less, that you've done nothing, once again, with this information?" Peters' voice was low and held an edge of accusation.

For Moreno, it felt like being in trouble with a parent who already knew what she'd done wrong but was cleverly backing her into a corner until she told on herself. But Peters wasn't her daddy, and she wouldn't give him the satisfaction.

"That's right." Moreno held firm, her ass crack a veritable swamp now.

Peters leaned in, his face inches from her own. "I find that hard to believe, Petty Officer." He stared hard for another minute before backing up and rising off the desk. "However, it doesn't change the fact that we now have credible evidence of Juan Carlos Moreno's involvement in sex trafficking into the United States. And since he's your father, we have an ace in the hole." He scooped up the pictures and placed them back into the folder, closing it.

Surprised, Moreno glanced from Peters to the major. "What does that mean? I have nothing to do with this," she began.

Maxwell sat forward, addressing the agent. "Yes, Agent Peters, what do you mean? It's clear Moreno is not part of that crime. She's been here the entire time and we monitor incoming and outgoing calls. You can check the log..."

Peters eyed the major. "No one is accusing Petty Officer Moreno of criminal activity or conspiring with criminals, major."

"Then just what are you doing, Agent Peters?" Major Maxwell asked, her voice lowering. She stood slowly, pivoting until she stood between Moreno and the agent.

"I'm assessing Moreno's loyalties... and yours, major."

"What? My loyalties?" she sputtered.

It was the first time Moreno had seen the major caught by surprise.

Peters eyed them both. "Yes. Because what comes next couldn't happen until I was sure."

C'EST LA VIE, SOLDIER

Moreno jumped up. "What the hell are you talking about, testing us? My loyalty to my team, to my country, has never been in question!"

Peters held up a hand. "Calm down, Petty Officer," he said, his cold, blue eyes revealing nothing. "Major, when I came to you today, I said it was of the utmost importance and that Petty Officer Moreno's expertise was required. That hasn't changed." He looked at Moreno again. "We need your help. Intel like this is rare, and now we have a connection to someone on the inside of the Colima cartel. This connection is invaluable after the loss of Torres' undercover identity. Busting up the U.S. side of that trafficking operation at The Honey Hole is only phase one. Phase two... that's where you come in."

Chapter Six

Moreno couldn't believe it. Operation "Save Moreno's Dad" was on. Except now, there was a major plot twist. Instead of saving her dad, the FBI and CIA wanted to use him to permanently bust up the Colima sex trafficking ring. Which didn't make sense to her because last she knew they were using Madam Gul and her Honey Hole brothel to glean information from their high-priority clientele. Why, now, they changed course, was beyond her. But she had a suspicion it had to do with the change in administration in the White House. Fucking politics. Still, in this case, it was working out in her favor.

She ran back to the residents' quarters, to Lucien. She needed to see him, to tell him what happened. After all, she'd left him high and dry. Then she would pull Griz aside and gather everyone for a meeting.

But now that she stood at Montcourt's door, nervousness overtook her. Last time she'd seen him, they'd been entangled like love-sick teenagers on her bed. There had been fevered kisses, groping hands, and a lot of grinding. Embarrassment burned on her cheeks as she stood, frozen, hand poised to knock.

The first female Navy SEAL had gone toe to toe with the best of men in BUD/S Training and triumphed over incredible odds. She'd survived Hell Week, the endless taunting of her instructors who shouted at her daily she was too soft, too weak, and would not make it. She'd told them all to go fuck themselves and had even excelled to becoming top three in her graduating class. She was determined and fearless. Until now.

Moreno's hand dropped and she turned away, walking across the hall. Three quick raps and the door swung open.

Griz stood there, a paper map in his hand.

"Moreno."

"We need to talk." She pushed past him into the room.

Griz looked up and down the hall. Seeing no one, he turned back into the room and shut the door.

"What's going on?"

She spun around and looked at him, hands wringing as the anxiety she felt standing at Montcourt's door worked itself out.

"Someone threw a monkey wrench into our plans."

Griz scowled. "Someone blabbed?" His nostrils flared.

C'EST LA VIE, SOLDIER

"No. No one blabbed, but we weren't as smart as we thought we were, and now someone knows."

The senior chief cocked his head like a dog trying to figure out what its human was saying. "Who knows? And what does this person know?"

"Special Agent Peters," she said. Moreno watched as the lightbulb came on.

Griz's eyes narrowed, then widened, then narrowed again. "Sonofabitch! He spied on us? At the detention center?" He began to pace. "I bet it was that wormy director. I shoulda done more than make him piss himself. Bastard!"

Moreno shrugged. "From what I understand, it wasn't the director. Peters went there and interrogated those two girls himself," she said. "After we left."

Griz stopped in his tracks. "So, when I submitted my report to him, he knew then I hadn't fully disclosed our findings," he muttered, distracted. "Sneaky fucking Feds. I really hate those pricks." He turned to Moreno. "But how do you know all this?"

She tilted her head. "Because I just left a meeting in Maxwell's office. She called me in," she said, anger seeping into her voice, "and Peters was there. He ambushed me."

Griz took two steps toward her, towering over the petite petty officer. His expression was both keen and worried. "And what did you say?"

Moreno held her ground, her jaw tight. "I didn't say anything. Didn't give him anything. He was fishing."

"Fishing," Griz growled.

"He had pictures, Senior Chief. Of my dad!"

His eyes widened. "What kind of pictures?"

She told him, explaining about the women and the child, and the two men in suits.

"Fuck!" Griz backed up and ran a hand through his hair. "Just what is it he wanted, Moreno? If he revealed these cards, he wasn't doing that by accident." He spun back around. "Peters does nothing without an endgame."

She sighed. "No kidding. He wants something, all right. He wants to use me and my father to infiltrate the Colima cartel. He said because your cover was blown."

Griz kicked the chair, sending it slamming into the wall. "That little shit!"

Moreno shook her head. "No, Senior Chief. It's actually a good thing. Because now we don't have to be secretive about our trip south of the border. Major Maxwell told him about the leave we were granted. He wants to use it to plan an op."

"What?" Griz looked incredulous for a moment, and then he laughed. "Well, that does change things." He walked to the chair, righted it, and sat. "Actually, that does make this a lot easier." He glanced her way. "Did he say exactly what the FBI wants out of this? And what about the CIA? There's no way they aren't involved somehow. Those two agencies can't shit without the other wiping their ass."

Moreno took a seat on the end of his bed. "You're right. They're involved too. Don't know if it's Strauss or not, but Peters did indicate interagency cooperation. Anyhow, I had your back. I told him I never told you it might be my dad. So, act surprised in tomorrow morning's meeting."

C'EST LA VIE, SOLDIER

"We're having a meeting in the morning?" Griz asked, his face a study in irritation. He knew what that meant, and he didn't like it.

"Yep. 0700 in the conference room."

Griz made a face, his brow furrowed. "The fucking Feds are taking over."

She nodded, understanding. The group had been busy making plans, with Griz coordinating with his contacts in Mexico. Parts of the plan had already been put into place, and now, the plans would change. Where that left them, they didn't know.

He snorted, and then stood. "Get word out to the group. Meeting in my room after dinner. We need to get our story straight, so everyone is prepared. I'm not letting Special Agent Peters ambush the entire team."

"Got it," she said, getting up and heading to the door.

"And, Moreno?" he called.

She stopped and looked over her shoulder. "Yeah?"

"I never thought you sold me out. You did good."

She blinked, surprised. This was high praise coming from Griz.

She nodded, and then left, seeking out the rest of the team. In the hall, she eyed Montcourt's door. Her heart pounded and the blood whooshed through her body, giving her the shakes. She wasn't ready to revisit their near-tryst. Not yet. Turning right, she left the residents' quarters. She'd find Mac and Eastwood first. Together, they would inform the team, and after dinner, they would plan. The plot had twisted, but the goal remained the same. Save her dad.

Chapter Seven

Two weeks passed in a flurry of activity. Plans previously made changed, leaving a few people unhappy. Joely, Connie, and Jessica would not be joining the team per Agent Peters' orders.

"Too dangerous," he'd stated. "We can't be responsible for the safety of civilians. Where you're going, Americans are prized by the cartels for the price they fetch on the black market. Especially women." He addressed Griz, but behind the senior chief, Mac and Eastwood sighed.

They knew they would have to break the news to their loves, and neither would be happy about it.

But one person was thrilled. Now that the FBI and CIA were in on the operation, Art Diaz was no longer sidelined. The sharpshooter would once again be on active status and paired with Matt Rogers. Diaz could barely contain the satisfaction on his face in the meetings. Across the table,

Griz noted the soldier's joy at once again being included, but he was still at odds with himself knowing that Diaz had no clue his every move, every word would be monitored and recorded without his consent.

For Moreno, the time spent prepping for the mission, both in strategy meetings and packing her carry kit, kept her so busy she had no time at all to deal with her muddled feelings for Montcourt. And despite the few spare moments he found to gaze longingly at her across the conference table, he, too, had been more than occupied with preparations. She wouldn't admit it out loud, but deep down, she was thankful the FBI intervened. She needed to focus on what was important right now. Finding and saving her father. When she accomplished that, she promised herself she would deal with this other confusing business. And then, maybe, she'd figure out just what, exactly, she felt for the cocky French commando who'd managed to slip past her walls.

On their last night at base, Griz called them all in for one last meeting separate from Peters and the major. The big man stood in the corner next to the desk, his demeanor serious.

"I think it's safe to say that the past couple of weeks have been hectic." Griz eyed the team, his gaze moving from Diaz to Eastwood, Mac, Matt, Ben, Jackson (now directly included as their comms contact), then to Moses and Montcourt, and finally, Moreno. "Much has changed, and yet, the endgame is the same. We're still going in together," he said, then glanced at Jackson and Diaz. "All

C'EST LA VIE, SOLDIER

of us now. And we're still going to find Moreno's father and get him out of whatever situation he's fallen into. As we've learned recently, the FBI and CIA have a stake in this operation. Their goal and ours do not necessarily align."

Mac and Eastwood nodded, grunting softly in agreement.

Griz continued. "They want an "in," someone who can give them intelligence from within the Colima cartel. I think it's fair to say that Moreno's dad is not the right candidate for such a position no matter how he ended up there." The senior chief reached out and put a hand on Moreno's shoulder. "We know Nastjia. We know who she is, deep down, and there isn't a person here who would ever believe the man who raised her suddenly changed from the good father who worked hard all his life, who carried on after losing his wife to bring up this remarkable individual," he looked at her, "the first woman to graduate BUD/S training, who broke the glass ceiling in becoming the first United States female Navy SEAL, could pull a one-eighty and turn into a cartel sex trafficker who abandoned the daughter he loved."

Moreno sucked in a breath. Such praise coming from Griz, a man who'd mocked her when first they met—who'd later put his job and life on the line to save her—and had come to her aid again to help rescue her father, caused a painful lump to settle in her throat. She swallowed hard and held back the tears that threatened to fall. SEALs didn't cry. Not even broken ones.

To her right, Montcourt shifted, but he did not reach out to take her hand. Moreno had come to expect these small comforts, but over the last few weeks, she'd avoided him. Now, he seemed unsure of himself, and of her. A feeling of unease settled in her gut. She'd faced danger more times than she could count, but when it came to Lucien—especially after that heated make-out session—she'd been a coward. Now, she may well have pushed him away for good. But at the moment, there was nothing she could do.

Griz gave her shoulder another squeeze before letting go. "No man who fathered this woman, our teammate, should be left in the hands of rapists and murderers," he concluded.

"Damn right," Mac muttered.

"So, how do we get around this," Eastwood asked, "and still complete mission parameters? Because last time, we really pissed the agents off. Pretty sure the major was none too happy, either, even if she did take our side. They're not going to let us buck their plans again."

Griz nodded. "I've been working on that. My merc contacts, Jack Banyon and Juan Hernandez, might have a solution."

"And what's that," Diaz asked.

Griz eyed Art. "Someone who could take over the job and save us from the wrath of the FBI. A man named Jesse Aguilar. But everyone calls him Jesus."

"Get out!" Eastwood chuckled, his expression dubious. "Seriously? Jesus is going to save us?"

C'EST LA VIE, SOLDIER

Ben Holiday slapped a hand over his face, then peeked over at Eastwood, one eyebrow quirked.

Griz smirked and rolled his eyes. "Jesus is a one-man wrecking ball. We couldn't ask for a better solution. He's been looking for an opportunity like this for a while now. I won't go into details, but the man has nothing to lose. He'll step in for Moreno's dad. We'll figure that part out. Jack and Juan are both excellent strategists. They're working out a plan. But even better, Jesus is ex-army, a former Green Beret. Once he gets in, and Peters and whoever the fuck from the CIA discover who they now have on the inside, they'll forget all about Mister Moreno."

"He's a merc?" Mac asked.

Griz nodded. "With an agenda."

"Vengeance, you mean," Mac said knowingly.

Moreno released a breath she hadn't realized she was holding. "You did all this?"

Griz turned to her, his hard look softening just a bit. "I've had help, but yeah. It was the only way. We needed someone we could swap for your dad. Otherwise, there'd be no deal."

She took two quick steps and threw her arms around Griz's neck, hugging him tight.

"Thank you," she whispered, her voice catching.

Griz stood awkwardly patting her back. He cleared his throat. "You're welcome. But we haven't found your dad and rescued him yet. Maybe save that until after we get this done."

She sniffed, smothering a smile, and stepped back. Mac reached out and took her arm, guiding her next to his side. He bumped his shoulder against hers and smiled.

"Gonna be okay, Nasty. No worries."

Moreno felt her hopes rise. Her team had rallied around her, and together, they would save her father.

"All right, everyone. That's all for now. Go spend your last hours finishing preparations and saying your good-byes to your loved ones. I have a hot date myself in the conjugal quarters."

"You could keep that to yourself, you know," Ben said, glaring at Griz. "She's still my sister!"

Griz chuckled. "Sorry. But what can I say? I love her."

"That's all you need to say, and leave it at that," Ben huffed.

Griz clapped Holiday on the back. "Go see Irina. She came out with Jessica."

"She did?" Ben asked, his spirits lifting. "She didn't mention she'd be coming here when I spoke to her last night."

"It's a surprise, brother. Act surprised, or else Jessica will kick my ass," Griz said, grabbing his gear and hoisting his duffel bag and carry kit over his shoulder.

Ben paused, thinking hard. "It would almost be worth it," he muttered.

"Don't you dare!" said Griz, pointing a finger at Ben. "Go see your woman and stop trying to cock-block me."

"Dammit, Torres!" Holiday covered his ears. "Cut that out before I save Jess the trouble."

"I'd like to see you try," Griz grinned. "But not tonight. Go on. Go to Irina."

Ben sighed, then smiled. "Only because we're short on time. But next time, I'm taking you down to the mat for those disgusting comments."

Griz batted his lashes as he passed Holiday in the hall. "It's a date."

Doctor Joely Winter Tyler exited her office. After locking the door, she checked the overnight bag hanging on her arm, rummaging in the side pocket until she located the small, black and white image. She smiled as she stared at the speck in the middle. Only two days ago, she'd confirmed what her body already knew. Joely was going to be a mother in six months. She'd waited to say anything to Harry, fearful this pregnancy might end as her first. In a miscarriage.

The smile slipped from her lips as bad memories came flooding back.

Austin was her first love, her first adult relationship. Both were in college, but Joely, being a prodigy, was far younger than Austin Evers by five years. Joely was already completing her Bachelor of Biomedical Engineering degree at the age of eighteen. Austin was still a year shy of finishing his degree in political science. Despite different career goals, Joely was taken in by the handsome young man from a wealthy, east coast family already established in the political fabric of American society. His father, Chase Evers, was the governor of Massachusetts, and a rising star within his party. Austin was expected to follow in his father's footsteps. Both Mr. and Mrs. Evers liked Joely when Austin first introduced her to them, admiring her beauty, intellect, and her ambition to start her own company focusing on helping amputees regain their mobility and independence. That admiration was short-lived. After six months of dating, Joely became pregnant. For her, the news was joyous. She was in love and the world was rosy.

But for Austin, discovering she was pregnant was a liability, not just for him, but for his parents and their re-election campaign. An unmarried son with a barely eighteen-year-old pregnant girlfriend of no social pedigree did not play well to voters. Before Joely realized what happened, Austin accused her of cheating on him, claimed the baby couldn't possibly be his, and then he left. Distraught, she tried going to him, to plead for their love, for their child. She'd borrowed a friend's car and took off in the middle of the night heading for Boston. It was right before winter exams and snow and ice covered the roads. With her eyes blurred by tears, Joely didn't see the patch of black ice. The car hydroplaned, spinning out, and crashed into a retaining wall. She awoke in the emergency room, alone, and no longer pregnant. She'd lost the baby.

The only good news came from the kindly E.R. doctor who told her that she would still be able to have children in the future. But the loss had devastated her, and for years, she'd made damn sure she never got pregnant again.

C'EST LA VIE, SOLDIER

Until she met Harry. He'd told her up front he wanted to have babies. Still, she'd hesitated over quitting her birth control. Then fate stepped in one lusty night. She and Harry celebrated the anniversary of the first time they ever met, back in London. He'd been incredibly romantic about it, even sprinkling rose petals all over their bed. She still blushed thinking about that night because somehow, she knew. It was hard to explain how if anyone had to ask, but at the moment of their third climax, as she and Harry stared into each other's eyes, she'd seen stars, and felt a oneness with him that transcended time and space. And she also forgot to take her birth control pill that day.

The smile returned to her face as she tucked the sonogram image back into the side pocket of her carry-all. Joely had hoped to be sharing this news with Harry on their trip to Mexico City, but now that it was off, and another mission was on, there was no perfect time or setting. They had tonight, in a military conjugal suite. Nothing grand or romantic about it, but she'd brought sparkling grape juice, chocolate-covered strawberries, and her most sinful lingerie. She would make do. No way was her husband going off on one more dangerous mission without knowing he was going to be a daddy.

Pleased with herself, Joely set out for the far side of the underground base.

Mac leaned back on a pile of pillows and watched as Connie Wheeler came out of the small ensuite, her dark, curly hair loose around her bare shoulders, and a midnight blue slip of a nightgown skimming her curves. He smiled his appreciation and patted the empty spot next to him on the double bed.

"Is that new?" he grinned.

Her eyebrows rose. "Of course, it's new!" she pouted. "You've seen all the old ones already."

Mac got up, reaching for her. In one smooth move, he took her in his arms, lifting her off the floor, and laid her on the bed. Connie giggled as he settled over her.

"You could wear a sack and you'd still be the most beautiful woman in the world," he whispered, his voice low. Mac angled his face and kissed her neck.

"So, I shouldn't bother buying lingerie?" she asked, then sighed as his hands slid over her body.

Teeth nipped her earlobe. "Didn't say that," he breathed. "I like this," he growled, his hands pulling the slinky blue nightie up over her hips, then further until it cleared her head. He held it out, admiring the bit of satin and lace before dropping it to the floor. His focus returned to her now naked body. "But I like this better." Mac's head dipped and his lips explored every inch of her exposed skin.

Connie moaned, then she grabbed his shoulders, stopping him.

Mac looked up. "What is it?"

"I think we should talk about Mr. Fuzzypants, honey."

C'EST LA VIE, SOLDIER

"What?" Mac exclaimed, his expression a study in confusion. "Now?"

Out in the hall, Eastwood made his way to Suite 9, and a hot date with a hotter blonde. As he passed Suite 7, he heard, *"That damned cat isn't coming into my house!"*

Eastwood paused, then chuckled, mumbling, "Note to self: Buy Mr. Fuzzypants some "welcome to the family" cat toys."

He stopped at Suite 9 and slid the key in the door. Anticipation for the night ahead filled him with a heady combination of joy, love, and lust. Whoever said the sex dies in a relationship after saying "I do" had never laid eyes, or hands, on Joely Winter Tyler. She excited him like no other and the quick reaction of his man parts when he beheld her, clothed or naked, was proof.

And she was already there, waiting.

Eastwood's body tingled at the sight of his beautiful wife lying across the rather smallish full-sized bed with the dark blue blanket tucked over the mattress in severe military fashion, corners tight. But all he saw was the gloriously near-naked woman on her side, resting on her elbow, with a glass of something sparkling in hand. Suddenly, there wasn't much room left in his pants.

"Howdy, pretty lady," he said, grinning. Quickly, he slipped inside the room and shut and locked the door. No way was he letting any stray, horny eyes get a gander at his woman.

Joely smiled slowly and patted the bed. "Took you long enough," she said.

He sat down at the desk and began unlacing his boots. "Sorry, baby. Last minute team meeting. But I'm all yours now," he said, tossing her a comical leer before kicking off his boots, pulling off his socks, and then reaching to untuck his t-shirt.

"Oh, Harry, you know all the right words, baby," she laughed. Joely sat up and reached for the second plastic champagne flute on the side table. She picked up the bottle and filled the cup. As she stood, the sheer, pale pink negligee with fine white lace edging the hem and décolleté, shimmied over her curves like a caress.

Eastwood's eyes followed the slinky material with deep appreciation. "And what did I do to deserve this? It's new, isn't it?"

Joely handed him the flute and smiled before spinning slowly and showing off the backless sheath. Hearing him suck in a breath, then growl low, she grinned. "I take it you like?"

His head bobbed. "Oh, yes. Daddy likey." Eastwood took a sip from the flute. His face immediately screwed up. "What is this? Grape juice?"

"Yes, Harry, it's sparkling grape juice."

"Was the store out of champagne? Wine? Beer?"

C'EST LA VIE, SOLDIER

"You're leaving in a few hours on a mission. No alcohol for you, Harry." Joely sipped her juice and set the flute down on the desk.

"Yeah, but you still could have..." he grumbled as she slid onto his lap. He lost the thread of his thoughts as her warm, scantily clad body pressed against his.

Joely wound her arms around his neck, and leaned her forehead against his own, touching noses. "No. I couldn't."

His warm gaze focused on her lips, so close. He watched them move as she spoke, but her words were slow to catch up to his lust-hazed brain. "What? What do you mean? I'm cool if you drink even if I can't."

She slid her fingers into his hair and caressed the short strands. "I know, baby. But it's not good for the baby."

Eastwood's eyes closed on a sigh as she massaged his head. Tingles ran rampant over his scalp, down his spine, and settled into his groin. The flow of blood now ran south, and his brain was slow to respond.

"What?" he whispered. "What baby? What are you talking about?"

Eastwood's eyes opened. A grainy, black and white picture dangled in front of his face. Behind it, his wife smiled softly.

"Our baby, baby," she said, her eyes luminous.

The meaning of her words seeped through the fog in his brain. He looked at the picture again. A sonogram. In the middle was a tiny little peanut. A baby. His baby. Their baby!

"We're having a baby?" he whispered, his jaw slack.

Joely nodded, her big eyes tearing up. "Yes, Harry. Are you happy?" she asked, suddenly uncertain.

Harold Tyler wrapped his arms around his wife, pulling her close, and kissed her for all he was worth. It was a kiss filled with so much love, passion, and joy, that by the time they pulled apart, both of them struggled to catch their breath. But Eastwood found his with air to spare. He inhaled, threw his head back, and howled with delight.

"Whoot! Baby! We're having a baby!" he said, laughing. He scooped her up in his arms and carried her to the bed. There, he laid her down gently, then turned and nearly ran to the door.

He unlocked it, yanked it open, and stuck his head out into the hall.

"I'm gonna be a daddy!" he shouted. Laughing, he closed and locked the door once again.

Joely watched as he strutted around the room, a grin on his face stretching from ear to ear.

"Oh, Harry, are you really happy about this?" she asked one last time. She needed to hear it.

Returning to her, Eastwood climbed atop the bed and pulled her into his arms. Words failed him, but his actions spoke loudly. Every single kiss and caress trumpeted his joy and excitement. Finally, he drew back and stared deep into her eyes, his own filled with happy tears.

"I don't know what in the world I ever did to deserve you, Joely, but by God, I am the happiest man alive. You make me so happy, it hurts, but in the best possible way. Hurts so good, baby. God, I love you," he said. "And I'm going to

C'EST LA VIE, SOLDIER

spend the rest of this night showing you how much," he whispered.

Suddenly, he paused, staring at her with concern.

"What is it, Harry?"

"It won't hurt the baby, will it? I mean, poking around in there?"

It was all Joely could do not to laugh. Her big, strong Green Beret, who could kill a man with his bare hands, was worried sex would harm their little peanut. She smiled and touched his face.

"Oh, Harry. I love you so much. No, sweetheart. It won't hurt the baby, I promise."

The tension eased from his face and was replaced with love and heated passion. There was no more need for words.

Eastwood reached for the bedside light and turned it off. In the darkness, hands and lips explored and desire flared sending them straight to the stars.

In the residents' quarters, Montcourt lay in bed, alone with his thoughts. The past couple of weeks had been difficult. He'd barely seen Nastjia, even though her room was next door. She'd been avoiding him, coming in late and leaving early. He could only conclude it had to do with him, with the kisses they'd shared. Had she been turned off? What went wrong? Even if that were the case, and his ego couldn't accept that possibility, they were still friends, weren't they?

He'd replayed their passionate encounter over and over again as he lay there in the dark. No way had she not responded to his kiss, to his touch. He'd felt her heat, tasted her desire, and he could still recall the scent of sex rising from her perfect body. No, she enjoyed him every bit as much as he'd enjoyed her. So, what was going on? She wouldn't even talk to him. And now, there was no time. In a few hours, they would be on a transport to Mexico City, heading into danger. Again.

He hated knowing she would once again be walking right back into cartel territory. After the brothel incident, he didn't know if his heart could take it. Seeing her stripped, beaten, and put up for auction had damaged his soul. Since that moment, he'd silently declared himself her protector. Without a doubt, he would put himself between her and anyone intent on doing her harm. He would kill them gladly. But would she even allow it now? If she didn't want him around anymore... who would save her?

Montcourt shook himself. He knew that last thought was patronizing as hell. Nastjia was a strong, capable woman. She was well-trained and could take down men twice her size. He'd witnessed that, too, at the auction. She had, after all, beaten and killed the man who'd dared to lay hands on her. He smiled. That was the moment he knew he loved her. The image of her naked, fierce, and lethal was one he would never forget. Truly, she was magnifique! But still, she'd ended up in a bad situation, and it could happen again. Montcourt didn't know if he could survive if something happened to her and he wasn't there to save her. It wasn't patriarchy or machismo, as the Spanish say. No, it was deeper. It was the protectiveness one feels for someone they cherish more than their own life.

This mission was important to her, and he understood why. She needed to save her father. Guilt and love drove her despite the danger to herself. Montcourt vowed that he would do all he could to shield her from harm and to help her reunite with her papa. Even if it was the last thing he did.

He glanced at the red numbers on the digital clock at his bedside. Two a.m. He sighed. Only two more hours before the alarm would go off. He shut his eyes, and rolled over, praying that no headaches plagued him in the days to come, and that his body wouldn't choose an inopportune time to give out.

Chapter Eight

The plane landed in ass-crack, Texas, otherwise known as a small border town where the military ran transportation between the U.S. and Mexico. Here, the team switched off to an unmarked chopper that could fly below radar. Like their previous journey into Mexico, it was the only way in where they could bring in the weapons necessary for the mission. No commercial airline would greenlight the guns, the ammo, and the other paraphernalia, and the mission was not one where permission was sought from the Mexican government.

At least this time they wouldn't have to jump. The chopper landed in a fallow field outside of Mexico City, one that belonged to Griz's merc contact, Jack Banyan.

Moreno followed the Senior Chief out to a clear point a safe distance from the rotors. As soon as the entire team had disembarked and unloaded their gear, the chopper took off again. It was mid-morning on a cold, overcast day and now the work would begin.

A gruff, older man with long silver hair tied at the back of his neck stood by one of two old vans painted in a dark shade of green. His face was weathered, and his expression remained stoic until Griz approached. Then the man's lips split into a crooked smile revealing two teeth missing up front, one on top and another on the bottom.

"Looking good for a dead man, Griz," he cackled, reaching out and pulling the senior chief in for a one-armed hug and a pat on the back.

Griz snorted. "At least I still have all my teeth," he replied.

Jack Banyan laughed, then coughed. He pounded his chest until it subsided. "Yeah, you do. You still have that government healthcare. A bit harder to find a good dentist out in these parts," he explained. "At least, one I'd trust anywhere near my mouth."

Griz chuckled. "You only need two good teeth to gnaw a steak, Jack."

The older man patted his widening girth. "And I ain't missing any meals. Rosita keeps me well fed." Banyan cast his squinty gaze over the team. "This them?"

Griz nodded. "Yep. This is them."

Banyan placed his hands on his hips and stared hard at each member of the team. "Son of a bitch, the rumors are real."

"The rumors are real, but that's not important right now, Jack. We need to get going. I'll introduce you to everyone as soon as we get settled. I assume you have more news for me?"

Banyan nodded and turned, opening the side door on the old van. "Got some updates for you. Juan will be here in about one hour. Jesus, too."

Their gear was loaded into the back of the vans leaving scant room for the team. It would be tight.

Moreno listened to their exchange as she climbed in. It smelled like old sneakers and piss inside. Mac and Eastwood got in behind her, but the two men moved to the opposite side leaving room for Montcourt to sit next to her. Ben joined them leaving Matt, Art, Jackson, and Moses to ride in the second van. The driver, an old Mexican man, waited patiently as each tossed their bags inside and squeezed in where they could.

Griz got in on the passenger side riding up front with Banyan. The old merc took off at breakneck speed down a dirt road hitting every rock and pothole along the way.

Moreno was bounced repeatedly into Montcourt who did his best to keep his distance without letting her fall over his lap. On the other side of the floor of the van, Mac, Eastwood, and Ben watched, confusion lighting their eyes before they reined their curiosity in. Eastwood glanced at Mac, one eyebrow quirked as if asking, *"What's going on with them?"*

Mac's head shook imperceptibly, his eyes warning, *'Not now!'*

Thankfully, the ride was short. The van pulled to a stop and Banyan shut off the engine. Moreno scrambled out quickly ahead of Montcourt followed by the rest of the team. To her surprise, they'd arrived at a villa nestled among tall oak trees that seemed to go on and on inside the valley where they originally landed.

The villa was three stories tall with a tiled courtyard just inside a twelve-foot wall that ran around the perimeter of the structure. Banyan led the team through the gate, his arms stretched wide.

"Welcome to my little hacienda."

Two Pit bulls came running from the back of the house, barking.

"Sit!" Banyan ordered. The dogs stopped short and sat, tails wagging and tongues lolling. The man grinned. "These are my boys, Heckle and Jeckle. Don't mind them. They're very well trained." He reached out, patting both their heads.

"Looks like you've done okay for yourself, Jack," said Griz. "Last time I came around, you had a shack sitting here on the land."

Banyan nodded. "Well, yeah. It's been more than six years, Torres. I've done a little remodeling."

"Merc work is paying you well," Griz added, looking around.

"I dabble, too," Banyan chuckled. "Stocks, bonds. I play the market."

Griz eyed the man, his expression deadpan. "Sure, you do."

A woman came out of the house, approaching them.

C'EST LA VIE, SOLDIER

The first thing Moreno noticed about her was that she was at least twenty years younger than Banyan, and that she carried a baby boy on her hip. The toddler looked no more than a year old, with curly brown hair and big brown eyes in a cherubic face. The baby smiled at her, and Nastjia found herself smiling back at the tike.

The young woman approached Banyan who reached out for the boy, taking him in his arms.

"This is my youngest, Patrick Michael. Named him after my father," he said, showing the boy to Griz. "Patty, this here is the meanest, ugliest son of a bitch you'll ever meet. But you can call him Uncle Griz."

Griz eyed the baby boy who stared up at him, seemingly unsure what to make of the big man. A moment passed and the baby gurgled, then laughed, pointing at him.

Moreno snorted, saying, "Guess you passed the baby test, Senior Chief."

Griz cut his eyes in Moreno's direction, then looked at Banyan. The man nodded, understanding Griz despite no words being spoken.

"I know what you're thinking, Torres. But there's no safer place than here. Just look," he said, pointing toward the wall surrounding the villa.

Griz followed Banyan's line of sight and saw, for the first time, outposts along the wall. They were twenty feet apart and hidden from the outside, but inside, hardened men armed to the teeth kept vigil over the property. No one uninvited would get near the entry to the villa without getting mowed down by heavy fire.

"Didn't see them coming in, did ya?" Banyan asked.

Moreno, who stood next to Griz, shook her head. The team, assembled behind her, noted the military-grade weapons the mercenaries carried.

Eastwood let out a low whistle. "Good thing we were invited."

Griz replied, "Nope. And should've." He turned to the team. "Time to get our head in the game. Pay attention, because from here on out, there won't be any second chances."

Banyan chuckled. "It's like riding a bike, Griz. You just needed to fall off it first. Now dust your ass off and let's get inside. Rosita has been cooking all day. You and your team can freshen up. By that time, Juan and Jesus should be here. We'll eat, then strategize."

Griz nodded and motioned for the team to follow Banyan's wife, who smiled and led the way inside. Banyan brought up the rear, Patty in his tattooed arms.

Chapter Nine

The crying broke his heart. It always did, and there was nothing he could do to stop it. He'd tried many times, but the words of comfort, of reassurance he offered were, despite his best intentions, lies. It wasn't going to be all right. It was never going to be all right again for these young women. And the little girls...

Juan Carlos Moreno choked on the sob threatening to erupt from his own mouth. He swallowed it down and carried a tray of bread and cheese and bottled water into the small, stuffy room. It was his task to see to their needs while they were here, a task he hated but suffered in silence. He'd attempted to help the women brought here before to escape and had been beaten viciously for it the first time. The second time was far worse.

The two men in suits made sure he never interfered with their business again. Instead of having him beaten the next time, they ordered a couple of the Colima soldiers to tie him to a chair, stuff a dirty rag into his mouth, and then watch as, one by one, they raped the women in front of him.

Juan Carlos had raged, screamed, and even shut his eyes, but one of the enforcers forced him to look. And then they brought in the child, no more than eleven years old. It was then that he broke down and cried. The horror of that moment haunted him every day. Since then, he'd done their bidding and taken care of watching over the women and girls brought in, making sure they were fed and had the basic necessities provided until they were taken from the compound and run through the pipeline.

His hatred for the cartel and what they did to these victims was deep, but the hate he felt for the two suits ran deeper.

They were the reason he was here.

After his wife, Nadia, died in a car wreck all those years ago, he knew it was only a matter of time.

But time had ticked by uneventfully, and his daughter had graduated from high school, then joined the Navy. He'd been so proud of her, and knowing she was in the military, surrounded by soldiers, her comrades in arms, he'd felt reasonably safe. Maybe the threat had passed, he thought. Maybe everything would be okay.

How wrong he'd been.

On a Tuesday morning, they'd broken into his home. He'd awakened to the nozzle of a Kalashnakov in his face. It was the last thing he saw before his hands were zip-tied

C'EST LA VIE, SOLDIER

and a dark hood was shoved over his head. He'd kicked and screamed and was knocked out by the butt of a rifle for his efforts. He remembered no more until the moment the hood was removed.

It was then, after God knew how long he'd been out, that he realized how much danger he was in. And Nastjia...

In the first few months he'd been interrogated, beaten, starved, waterboarded, and repeatedly threatened with worse. Juan Carlos could not imagine worse than he'd already suffered himself, and eventually, the two suits who'd overseen his torture figured that out. When he wouldn't give them the information they demanded, their threats turned more sinister.

But he held out. Despite the pain and anguish they, and their cartel flunkies, inflicted, he refused to answer their questions.

No, he did not know the whereabouts of his daughter. He'd stuck to that story, insisting they had a falling out and she'd fled their home after graduation.

Through one particularly long stint in an underground room with no windows, no fresh air, and barely any water or food to survive, he'd been grateful for the one smart move he'd made shortly after Nastjia went off to basic training. He'd taken every single picture of her from the walls and put them into an album... which he'd buried beneath the floorboards in the kitchen.

It was an odd thing to do, he knew, but he couldn't shake the bad feeling that his luck would run out, like his wife's had that fateful day. He knew then that the crash was no accident. There was no reason why Nadia would've been traveling in the opposite direction of home that night. Not unless she was desperate to lead someone away from her family.

It was a secret spoken between them only in the early days of their marriage, and then, never mentioned again. But it was always there, lurking like the monster of a nightmare just waiting for the dreamer to step one foot out of bed.

Juan Carlos and Nadia took pains to protect their identities and that of their daughter. Nadia and her mother had changed their names when first they came to America. And marrying Juan Carlos further muddied that trail when Nadia became a Moreno. For a while, it seemed as if they were safe. Juan Carlos had prayed it was so. He loved his wife and his daughter more than anything in this world. Time moved on, with both of them successfully building a life and raising a child.

And then one night, Nadia didn't come home. It wasn't until the state troopers showed up on his doorstep that he knew what happened. Still, he had to lie, even if by omission. No, he didn't know where his wife was going or why she'd traveled north instead of home to the south. No, she wasn't meeting anyone that he knew of. No, she wasn't having an affair (because one officer raised that speculation). He had to wait out the investigation, which eventually ended when no clues presented any possibility other than Nadia Moreno had lost control of the vehicle.

C'EST LA VIE, SOLDIER

The fatal wreck had been ruled an accident, and the investigation closed.

After it was over, he grieved, but never in front of Nastjia. He waited until she was at school or asleep, and then he would close himself up in his bedroom and weep into the pillow Nadia slept on throughout the years of their marriage. When it finally lost her scent, the last remnants of his heart shattered. Part of him was dead inside, but another part of himself knew he couldn't shut down and continued on. Nastjia needed him.

Because soon, they would come.

Juan Carlos balanced the tray of bread and cheese, and shifted the bag filled with water bottles up around his wrist so he could unlock the door.

He slipped the key into the lock and turned the knob. The crying inside instantly ceased. He swore he could hear them suck in lungsful of air out of fear of who was coming into the room. When he poked his head around the door, the three women inside exhaled in relief, but the tears began to flow once again.

Still, they were grateful for the sustenance, and in his quiet way, he attempted to make their captivity a little more bearable with kindness. He answered their questions truthfully when they asked what would happen to them. And he explained, with both heartache and shame, why he couldn't help them escape. Then, he reached into his pocket and pulled out a small, carved bird, handing it to the youngest of the group, a girl no more than nine years old.

He'd whittled it only yesterday, thinking of his own daughter and the little carved wood birds he used to make for her. He wondered if she still had them, if she thought about him. Tears had blurred Juan Carlos's eyes as he whittled away. By now, he figured she would believe he was dead. Too much time had passed, and no matter how much he wished he could see her again, it was best he didn't. Because that meeting would lead the suits to her.

The young girl took the little bird carving and clutched it to her chest. The look of gratitude in her big, brown eyes was mixed with fear. It tore him up inside. As the women ate their bread and cheese, he sat down next to the girl, handing her some food, and told her stories from his own childhood. Some were true, others, made up. He kept them light, hoping to ease the terror of her situation, even if just for a little while. When he told her about his pet chicken, Hortencia, she smiled. It was a small smile, but it was a big deal, as far as he was concerned. It brought a hint of joy to his battered heart, and even the other women shared in the moment.

The door banged open and two of the cartel soldiers entered, guns in hand.

The women screamed, one of them grabbing the little girl and pulling her into her arms.

"You, get up!" the first one ordered, pointing at Juan Carlos. "The bosses want to see you, now!"

Juan Carlos scrambled to his feet, eyes down. He moved quickly out the door, not wanting to keep the soldiers waiting and giving them an excuse to either beat him or

C'EST LA VIE, SOLDIER

linger inside the room. To his relief, they followed on his heels. But his heart pounded, wondering what fresh hell the suits had cooked up this day.

One of the soldiers prodded his back with the rifle, steering him toward the main house on the property. It was a grand estate, one which might feature on some reality television program showcasing elegant mansions in exotic parts of the world. From the outside looking in, no one would suspect what went on inside the heavily fortified walls of this Mediterranean villa in the mountains. It was well situated with only two roads leading in, and both were guarded day and night by Colima soldiers. There was a helicopter pad on the property by which the two suits often came and went. This, however, was not their house. The owner was the current head of the Colima cartel, but he'd somehow lost control over his own property, probably when he'd made whatever deal with the Russian devils who ran the roost.

He stumbled up the outside steps and through the inner courtyard. He'd lost weight since his abduction, and the beatings had taken a toll on his fifty-year-old body. He felt like an old man now, with one foot in the grave, and the other on a banana peel. He just hoped his death would be quick.

A hand shoved him the last few steps into the study on the right. There was wood paneling and rich brocade wallpaper on the walls. Frescoes graced the ceiling, and deep green velvet, overstuffed wing chairs flanked the ornate mantle of the fireplace. The two suits were waiting, one leaning on the mantle, the other sitting in a wingback chair, one leg crossed over his knee. Juan Carlos had dubbed them the two "Ivans" when he'd first seen them. Their names were irrelevant to his way of thinking. Only their boss's name mattered. But he did know theirs.

Anton Kadyrov and Anatoly Zadornov. The enforcers.

Zadornov was the one sitting, staring at him as he entered, with a cold smile on his thin lips.

Juan Carlos stopped in the middle of the carpeted floor and waited. The smile on Zadornov's lips was not a good sign. The man never smiled, and the cause of it worried him.

"Señor Moreno, come, come." Anatoly Zadornov unfurled and sat forward, his elbows now resting on his knees.

When Juan Carlos refused to take another step forward, Zadornov sighed, then chuckled.

"As you wish then." He stood. "I have some very good news for you."

The suit walked closer, casually shoving his hands in his trouser pockets. When he stood within two feet, he delivered a bombshell.

"Your daughter is in Mexico, and I have it on good authority she is coming to find you."

The bottom fell out of his world and Juan Carlos Moreno felt his heart stop. It was unfortunate it chose the next moment to beat again, and then gallop out of control.

Nastjia, no!

Chapter Ten

Nastjia was shown to a small room at the end of a long hall. The wing Banyan provided for their stay was at the eastern side of the villa. There were six rooms here on the second floor, three on one side, three on the other. At the very end of the hallway was a spa-like bathroom for guests to share that included a large sunken tub and a shower that was half in and half out on a private patio surrounded by high stucco walls, complete with potted exotic plants and palms. She eyed it longingly, feeling the dirt and grit of travel on her skin. Back inside on the opposite wall were three bathroom stalls set up like the fanciest hotel she'd ever seen. If she didn't already know she was here on a mission to find and rescue her dad, she'd think she was on vacation at a posh retreat.

After setting her duffel bag and carry case down in her room, she washed her hands and face and headed back down to the main house. Banyan had told them all to join him for dinner followed by a meeting to plan out next steps.

As she entered the hall, Montcourt stepped out of his room.

He paused, his expression uncertain.

Moreno could see Jackson just beyond Lucien picking out his bed in the oversized room. There were two beds in her own room, but she would be the only occupant. Griz had already divided the men up into the other five rooms. Mac and Eastwood chose the room next door to her. Ben and Moses were in the first room on the right, next to Mac and Eastwood. Across the hall, Matt and Art shared a room, and Griz, like Moreno, had a room to himself.

It would take no time at all for everyone to get ready for dinner. No one was unpacking. They would be heading out at first light.

Montcourt cleared his throat. "After you, Ma Ché ... eh, Petty Officer Moreno." His voice dropped low, and his gaze skipped over her head, avoiding eye contact.

The formality stung. She'd grown used to his endearments and their easy camaraderie. She missed it, but knew it was her fault that the comfort was now lost in their relationship. She'd left him hanging and then ignored him, all because she was a coward. At first, she'd rationalized that her father came first, that the mission was paramount, and it was. But that was an excuse. Had she just said so to begin with, Lucien would've understood. He'd gone out of his way to be understanding, and patient,

C'EST LA VIE, SOLDIER

and kind, and sexy. And she'd screwed it all up. Now she didn't know how to fix things between them.

"Lucien," she began.

"Hey, Montcourt, which bed do you want?" Jackson called from inside the room.

A look flashed in Montcourt's hazel eyes before he called over his shoulder. "I don't care. Pick one."

Moreno sucked in a breath and moved past him, cowardice winning the day yet again. "I'll let you two get settled."

"Nastjia, wait..." Montcourt said, reaching out, his hand stopping short of touching her arm.

"Is that Moreno out there?" Jackson came to the door.

She paused, just out of Montcourt's reach. "Just on my way down to dinner."

Jackson grinned. "Oh, good. Hope you remember the way. This place is like a maze," he said, joining her in the hall.

The two walked ahead, leaving Montcourt to follow. She glanced once over her shoulder, her eyes connecting with his.

Moreno felt her heart skip a beat in that split second. Montcourt looked away and moved quickly past the slower Jackson, practically running down the stairs. Moreno watched him go, not hearing anything Jackson said. She'd automatically moved to Jackson's opposite side allowing him the rail to steady himself as he navigated each step.

"Moreno, are you okay?"

A hand touched her shoulder. She blinked and glanced up at Jackson.

"What?"

Jackson's brown eyes reflected concern. He threw a quick look at Montcourt's retreating back before the man disappeared around the corner. "I know it's not my business, but if you need someone to talk to, I'm here," he offered.

Nastjia nearly spat out a retort worthy of her nickname, but she bit her tongue instead. This was Jackson, and he'd been her teammate since the beginning of her service at PATCH-COM. The man never pried, and he wasn't prying now. He was simply being a steadfast friend.

She shook her head. "Thanks, Jackson, but the mess is all mine. I have to clean it up myself."

He nodded, and took the first step down, his free hand holding onto the banister. "Okay, but I'm rooming with him. If you want, I can wait until he's asleep and then stick his hand in a glass of warm water."

Moreno cocked her head, a confused look on her face. "What in the world good would that do?"

Jackson Hicks chuckled. "Won't fix your problem, but it'll make old Luc wet the bed."

She stopped, staring at Jackson's back as he took another two steps down the staircase. Her lips twitched, followed by a loud laugh.

He turned and grinned at her. "Plus, it made you laugh. Seems like you needed that."

C'EST LA VIE, SOLDIER

"You're a sneaky little shit, you know that?" Moreno chuckled and hopped down two more steps gaining his side. She linked her arm through his, and together they descended the stairs. When they reached the bottom, she looked up at him.

"Thanks for that. I'll let you know if it becomes necessary."

"Here to help, Moreno," he said.

"Now let's go find the others. This damn place is way too big. You just know that Banyan character is into some very illegal nonsense to own a home like this."

Jackson's eyes bounced around the walls and the ceiling. "Best not to ask, Moreno. Pretty sure we don't want to know."

"Plausible deniability, they call it," she smirked.

"Exactly."

As they made their way through the maze of hallways, Jackson added, "but I hope you and Montcourt work it out. I like him. And he really seems to care about you."

Moreno felt tears prick the backs of her eyes and looked away.

"Yeah. Thanks."

He nudged her shoulder as they turned the corner. Here, they found the formal dining room. The team was already there, plus two new players.

Montcourt watched her enter the room, Jackson at her side. Their ease with each other struck a nerve, one he was not comfortable with at all. He knew was ridiculous, because it was Jackson, his teammate, and for the next ten hours, his roommate. Yet the sharp stabbing pain to his heart and his pride persisted. To admit he was jealous was an understatement. There was also an undercurrent of anger. It was, perhaps, unfair to be angry with her, he knew. But after the passionate moments they'd shared, to be cut off without explanation stung, even if he knew it was best for her in the long run.

He struggled with the anger far more than the jealousy, but the two were intertwined, as they had been that afternoon in her room, on her bed, before she'd been pulled away. He could live with whatever reason she gave for her about-face, as long as she gave him one. The not knowing, not understanding what had happened was killing him. And that thought brought a humorless sneer to his lips as he watched Jackson pull out her chair. She smiled over her shoulder at him, and Jackson's hand reached out to touch her shoulder before he plopped into the open seat next to her. He'd never wanted to punch Hicks in his face before now, but by God, he was considering smothering the man in his sleep tonight for that liberty.

Ever since the op at The Honey Hole outside of Las Vegas, he'd been the man at her side, the one to hold her chair, the comforting hand. It should be him on that side of the table, not stuck out in left field next to Mac and

C'EST LA VIE, SOLDIER

Eastwood, and the rest of the team. As he glared, he felt eyes on him, then a throat cleared.

"Is there a problem, Montcourt?"

Lucien's eyes pulled away from Moreno and collided with Griz's. Torres pinned him with an inquiring stare, one eyebrow quirked.

Montcourt shifted in his seat and gave a small shake of his head. "No, Senior Chief. My apologies."

Griz continued to eye Montcourt before his gaze bounced to Moreno, then back to the head of the table. "Sorry, Jack. You were saying?"

Jack Banyan nodded at one of his mercs, who stood by the large, carved wooden door. That man quickly closed the door leaving Banyan, the team, and the two new arrivals inside the dining room.

He turned his attention to the group. "Before we enjoy the great meal Rosita and my kitchen staff have prepared, I wanted you all to meet Juan Hernandez here." He reached a hand out to grip the man's shoulder to his left. "Juan, Griz, and I go back a ways. Griz had just infiltrated the Sinaloa family the hard way, taking a beating that nearly killed him. Juan's brother, Pedro, was the doctor that treated him. They broke his ribs and messed up that pretty face something awful, but he survived, and passed along the news of his initiation through the doc to Juan, and up the line to the DEA and CIA. I was doing some contract work with them at the time and was asked to make contact with this ugly old cuss and keep an eye on him. Juan, too. Insertion was precarious and Griz's cover could've been blown at any time. But we underestimated the bastard. He not only got in, he excelled up the ranks. It got harder and harder for us to stay under the radar and still keep him in our sights. But Juan, he took the biggest risks by taking contract jobs for Sinaloa. It was the only way we could get in after the badger took you into his confidence," he said, looking over at Griz. "Anyhow, I digress," he grinned.

Griz rolled his eyes, but a smile touched his lips. "You always did talk too much, Jack."

"Yeah, that's why I'd make a shitty spy. I'm a people person."

Juan snorted. "And a lying sack of shit."

"Embellishing sack of shit, Hernandez. Get it right!" Banyan chortled. Then his face grew serious. "But this gentleman right here," he began, looking at the newcomer next to Juan Hernandez, "is by far the toughest, scariest sonofabitch I've ever met. And I mean that as a compliment," he added. He looked around the table at each team member. "Kids, this here is Jesus." His eyes stopped on Moreno. "And he's about to become your savior."

Moreno looked at the man. Jesus, or Jesse Aguilar, as Griz had explained before they left Camp Lazarus, was a very big man. Taller than Griz by at least two inches, she guessed by just his stature sitting in the chair, and with arms and shoulders that made Griz's look like a Pooh bear instead of a grizzly bear.

His hair was black as night, long, and tied back at his neck, and although he was handsome by any woman's standards, there was an intimidating aura surrounding him along with a murderous glint in his dark eyes. His bare arms were covered in tattoos, and he wore a black leather cut over a white tank t-shirt. This was not a man a person would want to run into in a dark alley. And his name was Jesus. It suddenly struck her as absurd, and she smothered a smile. Moreno didn't want to appear ungrateful to the man who'd agreed to help rescue her father and take his place in captivity. That would just be rude.

"Nice to meet you, Jesus. Thank you for helping with my dad." She meant it, wholeheartedly.

Jesus gave her a brief nod, and his expression softened. "I should thank you. I've been waiting a long time for this opportunity."

Moreno cocked her head, a question in her eyes, but any chance to ask was cut off by their host.

"Now that everyone is here, let's eat. Then we'll go over the plan. And it'll be an early night. We move out before dawn."

Banyan turned in his seat and hollered toward the kitchen. "Rosie-baby, Estamos listos para comer!"

Chapter Eleven

Montcourt waited in his room while Jackson utilized the sunken tub in the bathroom down the hall. He was the last, as far as Montcourt could tell. Everyone else had already cleaned up in preparation for their pre-dawn departure. However, no one had jumped into the tub except for Hicks. Soaking his legs in hot water was better than just about anything for his stiffness and pain after a long journey. And although he would be staying on here at the villa as a their point of contact, Montcourt gave him the greenlight to get his soak on. He wanted time to think, not that he needed to torture himself any more than he already had.

There was too much on his mind, the sheer volume of which that just wouldn't leave him in peace.

He'd promised Nastjia he would help her find her father, that he would be there to protect her no matter what. Now that she'd distanced herself, he didn't know where that left him, or his promises. He was not one to go back on his word, but he also did not wish to force himself on her if his help was not welcome. Then there was the matter that this was a team effort, one now sanctioned by the FBI, CIA, and DEA, in addition to their command. Which meant following orders, something ingrained in him. Nastjia was a teammate, and a soldier always had his teammate's back. The problem wasn't that he didn't know how to be a teammate to her, but rather, how to treat the woman who owned his heart as just another soldier. That was the rub.

His instincts regarding protecting her were not the same as how he would back, say, Mac or Eastwood. Sure, he would have their backs in the heat of battle, but Nastjia was different. His focus in a firefight would be less about mission and more about her safety. And that would piss her off. She would consider it an insult to be the object of his primal urge to protect her when she was perfectly capable of protecting herself, and others around her. He knew this, but it didn't quell the bone-deep need to shield her from danger.

Until recently, she'd begun to accept this side of him, even welcome it. That is, until their passion bubbled over into the best few moments of his life. He still questioned whether it was possible these feelings were one-sided. In the next moment, he discarded the notion. He might not know everything, but he knew when a woman wanted him, and everything about Nastjia Moreno that afternoon confirmed she was as attracted to him as he was to her. Her abandon, her heat, her scent, and her taste on his tongue were all one hundred percent positive responses to his touch, his desire.

No. She definitely and clearly showed her interest. But what happened after? That was the mystery. And it was killing him.

"It's all yours, Luc."

Jackson entered their room wearing a blue robe. Montcourt eyed him, noting the brace on his leg visible beneath the robe's hem. Jackson's injury was such that a brace would always be necessary despite the progress he'd made at Camp Lazarus. It was why he could no longer do field work, but his skill with computers and previous mission work led to his training as team point of contact and group coordinator. In addition, the man was generally affable and well-liked among their team. His easy-going manner, proven reliability, and even his ability to entertain them all with song on his guitar made him a favorite, even for Montcourt. But that was before he'd seen his interaction with Nastjia earlier.

Now, all Montcourt could think about when he saw Jackson was punching the likable fucker in the face. It wasn't fair to the man, but there it was.

Montcourt grunted and got up, grabbing his toiletry bag and clothes. Unlike Hicks, he would not be sleeping tonight in the nude, as per usual, or in pajamas, as Hicks seemed to be slipping into now. He would be combat ready at first light wearing his fatigues, with only his boots lined up at his bedside, and his carry case and weapons bag next to them.

He moved past his roommate leaving Jackson staring in confusion at his back.

In the hall, he glanced briefly at Moreno's door, shaking his head in frustration before entering the bathroom at the end of the corridor. He looked forward to trying out the indoor/outdoor shower hoping the hot water and exotic setting would help clear his thoughts and aid him in getting a few hours of much-needed sleep.

Montcourt stopped at the sink to brush his teeth. The soothing sound of the water feature he'd noticed on the outdoor patio earlier drifted past his ears along with night sounds from whatever nocturnal prey was on the hunt beyond the villa walls. He rinsed and spit and placed his things back inside his toiletry bag before pulling out a bar of soap and his two-in-one shampoo with conditioner. Stripping down, he carried his items with him through the archway to the secluded terrace.

The sound of the water grew louder, and he smiled as he ducked into the tiled alcove where the shower was located. The smiled died on his lips and his jaw dropped.

Moreno screamed.

"Get out!"

A bar of soap flew and struck Montcourt's chest.

Moreno stood before him, a washcloth clutched to her breasts with one hand, her other hand desperately trying to grip the wall as she balanced on one foot. Shock and anger blazed in her dark eyes.

C'EST LA VIE, SOLDIER

He spun around too late. The image of her nakedness was burned into his brain. Tan, wet, supple, perfect. But his feet wouldn't move.

"I'm sorry, Ma Chér...er, Nastjia. I did not know you were in here."

"Why are you still here?" she asked, outraged. "Go, Lucien!"

He bristled at the command, furious, and then a laugh tugged at his lips. With his back still to her, he replied, "I don't know. You looked so..."

Moreno's nostrils flared and her eyes narrowed. "I looked so what?"

He could hear the warning in her voice, and instead of sending him running as it should have, he fought to smother the laugh. It came out in a muffled snort.

"I was going to say *unstable*." He looked around to his left and right, finally spotting her prosthetic next to her robe on a nearby chair. "Do you need help?"

"Are you laughing at me?" she asked, her outrage escalating.

Much to his shame, Montcourt lost it. Laughter bubbled up inside him and rolled out. He slapped a hand over his mouth, but it would not be contained. Finally, he sucked in a deep breath and blew it out, gaining control over his inappropriate outburst.

Glancing over his shoulder, careful to keep his eyes level with hers, he sighed. "No, not at you. Never at you."

Her narrowed eyes pinned him as she hopped once to readjust her stance. "Then what are you braying like a donkey about?"

He shrugged. "Us. This situation. It's utterly absurd." He turned then, and she rotated sideways in an attempt to shield her nudity.

Her hand slipped on the mosaic tile wall, and she pitched sideways.

Montcourt lunged, catching her.

"Are you okay?" he asked.

Moreno nodded, her jaw tight with anger—at him for laughing and for interrupting her shower, and at herself for overreacting and causing the entire awkward situation.

"No, I'm not okay," she said through clenched teeth.

His eyes widened with concern, then inspected her for injury. "Where does it hurt? I didn't see you hit anything."

She pushed at him, trying to put some distance between them. It was an impossible task while trying to hold her wash cloth in place and balance on one foot. Plus, he wouldn't let go.

"I didn't," she said, "hit anything, that is." The will to continue fighting died. Deflated, she looked up at him. "I'm sorry, Lucien."

He froze. This was not at all what he expected to hear. Insults, he expected. Possibly violence, but not an apology.

"For what, Nastjia," he asked, his voice soft now, as if he feared spooking her.

C'EST LA VIE, SOLDIER

She couldn't look at him. With her eyes cast down, she replied, "For leaving things unclear between us. I... I didn't run off that day. I was called into Major Maxwell's office. I had to go."

He knew what *"day"* she meant. *That* day. The day everything changed between them. He nodded. "Yes, I know this."

The silence stretched between them as he waited for her to continue.

"But I didn't seek you out afterwards. I just, you know..." Her gaze bounced everywhere avoiding him.

Montcourt's hands gentled on her arms, and he stepped closer. Reaching out, he lifted her chin until their eyes met.

"You were scared," he said.

Moreno stared into his hazel eyes, unable to breathe. Saying sorry was hard enough. Saying it while naked in front of an equally naked, ridiculously sexy French marine was the hardest thing she'd ever done in her life. And she was the first female Navy SEAL!

Montcourt wanted to smile but thought better of it. Explaining why he suddenly felt so happy might send her running. Instead, he offered a confession of his own.

"I, too, was scared, Ma Chéri. Still am," he whispered.

This surprised her. "What are you afraid of?"

"Of losing you." His intense gaze bore into hers. "Don't you know how much you mean to me by now?"

A loud boom, boom, boom filled her ears, and Moreno realized it was her heart beating out of control.

He caressed her cheek. "Nastjia, whatever this is between us, I ask only that you give it a chance. It can be as little as friendship, or as much as lovers," he said, hope in his eyes, his lips now inches from her own. "Whatever you want, but please, don't ever feel like you must shut me out. That is the only thing I cannot take."

Heat combusted between them; erotic flames dancing along frayed nerves, igniting their passion like a single spark on dry kindling.

Speechless, she dropped the washcloth, wound her arms around his neck, and kissed him.

It felt like a nuclear explosion, and Montcourt willingly and wholeheartedly weathered the blast.

The feel of her lips pressed against his, the taste of her on his tongue sent him spiraling. He wrapped both arms around her waist, pulling her naked body against his own. The tips of her breasts teased his chest, and the softness of her mons pillowing the hardening length of him forced a guttural grown from his throat.

Carefully holding her upright, Montcourt moved her under the spray as he plundered her mouth. His hands glided sensually over her back and down to cup her backside. The action caused a delicious friction and he wanted more.

"Lucien, please," she whispered, as his tongue licked a line down her neck, nibbling in between.

He smiled hearing the plea in her fevered words. He'd longed to hear his name on her lips in the heat of passion, dreamed of it.

"Please what, Ma Chéri?" He whispered the question in her ear before sucking the tantalizing lobe.

When she didn't answer, his hand slid up over her ribs and palmed her breast, squeezing. When she sucked in a breath, he caressed the hard peak with his fingertips.

"That," she said, her head thrown back, and eyes closed.

He looked down into her face, marveling at her beauty. He was consumed in her fire, and still, he wanted to burn.

"How about this?" he whispered. Then his head dipped, and he sucked her nipple.

Moreno whimpered and the sound caused him exquisite pain as he grew harder. He felt sure he would soon explode, but he was lost in the absolute ecstasy of giving her pleasure.

He moved to her other breast, lavishing attention upon both. She tasted so sweet, but the sweetest was yet to come.

Montcourt backed her against the shower wall, then knelt before her.

Startled, Moreno looked down. "Lucien, what are you—"

"Sssh," he said, a wicked glint in his hazel eyes. "This is a dream, and I don't wish to awaken."

Before she could reply, he pressed his face against her softness and his tongue flicked, finding her nub.

"Oh, my God!"

Moreno reached out to the side wall with one hand, and she clenched his hair with the other. It was all she could do to remain upright as Montcourt's mouth made love to her. She swore he licked lengthy, sensual French poetry into the very pulse of her womanhood. Her eyes closed and her lips parted, panting.

Just when she thought she'd lose her mind, he slid two fingers inside, caressing her slick walls.

"Lucien!" she breathed.

"Let go, Mon Amour," he growled. "Let yourself go. So beautiful," he murmured between nibbles and licks.

Her thighs trembled and her belly tightened. Each flick of his tongue brought her closer to the edge. She was so swollen now, and she wanted more of him, more than his mouth and fingers.

"Lucien, please," she squeaked, and then her world exploded into a million stars.

The sounds of her climax were music to his ears. He held her hips with both hands now, his tongue lashing slowing down, but not yet stopping. He smiled watching her ride the waves of ecstasy. It was the most beautiful sight in the world.

The little devil on his shoulder begged him to continue the sensual assault. Unable to resist, he latched onto her nub and suckled hard, his teeth teasing and his tongue not the least bit tired of tasting her honey. When her breathing hitched, he went all in, working her hard and fast until a second orgasm wracked her luscious body. This time, her knee buckled, and she slid down the wall into his arms.

He held her gently under the spray, grinning with pure male satisfaction.

C'EST LA VIE, SOLDIER

Moreno's eyes fluttered open, and she stared at him, satiated.

"What did you do to me?" she asked, a surprised look on her face.

He kissed her lips then, taking his time, before pulling back.

"What I have dreamed of for so long."

Breathless, she glanced down between them noting his hard length.

"But now it's your turn," she said, reaching for him.

He gripped her wrist, stopping her.

"No," he said. "Not tonight. Tonight is about you. We will have time for me later, after we find and rescue your father."

She touched his face. "But that's not fair, Lucien."

He kissed her knuckles. "All is fair in love and war, Mon Amour. Tonight, it was love. Tomorrow, it is war. And we only have a few hours left. You need your rest. Come," he said, sitting up.

He stood and reached for her, pulling her up beside him. When she was stable, he found the washcloth on the shower floor and bent to pick it up.

"Let us finish here, and then get some sleep." He lathered the cloth and began washing her, his hands once again sliding over her skin, igniting sparks. But he didn't immediately make a move to put these out. Instead, he grinned as she wiggled her backside against him, tempting him shamelessly. "When this is over, Nastjia," he whispered, his lip hovering over her ear, "make no mistake, we will make love. Fully," his hands glided over her breasts, "thoroughly," his hips rubbed against her backside, "and deeply." With those last words, his soapy fingers slid between her legs, teasing and exploring.

Moreno leaned against him, her thoughts scattering as her body heated again from his touch.

"Why didn't you tell me you were this talented?" she moaned.

A low chuckle rumbled against her neck.

"You would not have believed me, Mon Amour. And I do not brag."

She grinned. "Yes, you do."

His fingers worked her over once again. "Only when it's true."

He turned her face to his and took her lips in a sweet, soft kiss.

As the pleasure rolled through her muscles and bones, making her feel all gooey inside, Moreno thought, *"Why in the world did I wait so long?"*

CHAPTER TWELVE

Moreno rolled over and glared at the clock on the nightstand. It was 4:00 a.m. The team would depart at 5:00 leaving her not much time to throw herself together. She sighed, closing her eyes. Five more minutes, she told herself. A smile touched her lips. She might have only had five hours of sleep, but they were the best five hours of sleep ever. Memories of the night before played out in her mind. A steamy, X-rated shower scene like nothing she'd ever experienced before had happened, and she still couldn't believe it.

Lucien was something else. She'd been with other men before. She wasn't a virgin, but the few times she'd experienced sex, it always seemed to go quickly. Not that she hadn't enjoyed it, but her two exes had not shown a tenth of the control her French lover did last night. And neither had ever given of themselves so much, focusing solely on her, like Lucien. She didn't know if that was a French thing or just a Lucien thing. Whatever it was, she liked it.

Just the thought of what he'd done to her brought a blush to her cheeks. She was glad she was alone, in the dark, where she could unpack this monumental event and try to make sense of it all. Much had changed in a short period of time. She wasn't *'Ma Chéri'* anymore. Somewhere between her first and third orgasm, she'd become *'Mon Amour'*.

"My love," she whispered. "Am I?"

It was a lot to think about, and there was no time. Packing her memories and ponderings away for another time, Moreno got up and dressed.

He said they would discuss things after the mission was over. It was what she'd wanted all along, but at least now, there was no tension.

She grinned as she put on her prosthetic. "Well, there's a different kind of tension now, the good kind." she muttered.

Before saying goodnight, he'd told her in no uncertain terms exactly what he would do to her when all was said and done. Dear Lord, if their shower together was any indicator, she was surely going to die by orgasm, speared by his magnificent cock.

Seemed as good as any way to go, she thought. And she couldn't wait!

The smile wouldn't leave her face, but she forced it back. No way did she want to clue her nosey teammates in on what was going on with her and Montcourt. Especially

C'EST LA VIE, SOLDIER

Mac. He'd been overprotective of her from day one. Most noticeably after Alex Pavluk. Not that she minded much. Mac was family, as far as she was concerned. But she definitely didn't want Maclean to kill Lucien before she figured out what was going on between them.

With her ablutions complete and her bags packed, Moreno hoisted her duffel over her shoulder and picked up her carry case, slinging it around her neck. She had everything she needed for the field, weapons and all. It was time to head down to the dining room for a quick bite, then off to find her father.

She hoped the plan Banyan, Griz, Juan, and Jesus concocted worked. It was risky at best, suicidal, at worst. But it was all they had.

She left the room and met Mac and Eastwood in the hall. The other rooms were already empty, doors wide open.

"Mornin', Nasty," Mac mumbled.

"Mac," she replied. Then she looked at Eastwood. He had a spring in his step today. She glanced down. Only one boot. "New prosthetic, Harry?"

He nodded. "Leaving the original with Jackson. This one's one of Joely's first designs."

He pulled up the pantleg of his fatigues and flashed the streamlined design. It was a curved arc of carbon fiber.

Harry grinned. "It's my blade runner. Lighter and faster in the field. I've been using it on all my track runs. Shaves a lot off my running time. Can't hide weapons in this one, but it has this."

With the pantleg still lifted high, he smacked the palm of his hand on the metal knee. A slicing sound rent the air and sharp knives popped out the outside of the carbon blade, about three inches in length, each, fully extended. In a fight, Harry had a secret advantage. One sweep of his leg anywhere on an opponent's body and they would be sliced and skewered.

Moreno's brow quirked and her lips twitched. "Nice. Think Dr. Winter could upgrade my foot?"

Harry slapped his kneecap again and the blades retracted. He dropped his pantleg and straightened. "Pretty sure she was already working on an upgrade for you, but don't tell her I told you. It's supposed to be a surprise."

He smiled and walked ahead.

Mac fell in step beside her.

"He's like a kid with a new toy," he said.

Moreno shrugged. "Yeah, but as toys go, it's a good one."

"Yeah," Mac said, a half-smile on his lips. "I still like my guns though."

She patted her duffel. Inside were her two favorite rifles and several handguns. "Yep. Me, too."

"The arm prosthetic machine gun was cool," Mac grunted, referring to the test model created for Alex Pavluk when he'd first arrived at PATCH-COM.

"Hey, what ever happened to that? Seems like something Matt could use."

Mac shook his head. "Dr. Winter pulled it after Pavluk died. Not sure if command nixed it after the schematics ended up in Russian military hands, or if they're revising it or what."

That was a long speech for Maclean, and Moreno chewed on his words quietly as they descended the stairs. She tried not to think about Pavluk. He'd caused her too much trauma while he lived, and then had really screwed her head up by delivering a post-mortem apology via Joely Winter. He was an asshole, but an asshole who'd finally apologized. An asshole who had, in his last hours, done the right thing for his team and his country. He'd saved Joely, and that counted.

She was about to remark on that when they turned the corner and arrived in the dining room.

Mac stopped dead. She ran into his back.

"What the ever-loving hell?" he muttered.

Moreno peeked around him, seeing the entire team assembled inside. Harry was already there and he, too, was standing frozen with his mouth hanging wide.

She followed his line of sight, finally seeing what had everyone's attention. A snort escaped her, and then a giggle.

"Don't you dare, Moreno!"

Griz glared at her, his meanest scowl plastered on his face. He was pointing at finger at her, and then the grizzly glare pinned each member of PATCH-COM where they stood.

"No wise-ass words from any of you!"

Next to Griz, Jack Banyan slapped a hand over his mouth, his shoulders shaking, desperately trying not to laugh. He was failing miserably.

Griz stood near the head of the table, no more goatee on his clean-shaven face. But it was his hair that had everyone gawking. Some time between last night and this morning, the senior chief had cut his black hair short, and bleached it out. And it hadn't gone well.

Moreno coughed, then took several deep breaths. She cleared her throat. "Did you do that yourself?"

Banyan lost his shit and guffawed. Bending over and slapping his knees, he laughed outright. Between chuckles, he filled in the blanks.

"Rosita offered to help. She told him his hair was too dark, that it would take more than one round to strip out the color. But, you know, we're in a time crunch, and he said he could handle it."

Griz growled. "It ain't funny, Jack!"

Next to Jack Banyan, Juan Hernandez bit his lip, but his mouth kept stretching into a grin.

But it was Eastwood who spoke the words out loud best left unspoken.

"It's so... so...," he choked on laughter, "orange!"

Moreno winced, waiting for Griz to explode and beat Harry to a pulp.

Montcourt came around the table quietly and bravely stepped in front of Eastwood. "It is a very good disguise, senior chief," he said, trying to defuse the volatile situation.

C'EST LA VIE, SOLDIER

"Yeah," said Art Diaz, "no one in Mexico will recognize you like that."

Mac tugged Eastwood's jacket and yanked him back out of range of Griz's arms. Montcourt remained in the line of fire. He glanced back once and caught Moreno's eye.

She mouthed, *"thank you,"* to him for rescuing Harry from the consequences of his own foot-in-mouth disease.

"He's right," Moreno added. "You're unrecognizable. I wondered what you were going to do about that considering the cartel soldiers know your face, and you're supposed to be dead."

Somewhat mollified, Griz grunted. "It'll do." The wind went out of his sails, and he cast his eyes to the tiled floor. "Just don't know how I'm going to explain this to Jessica when we get back."

Ben Holiday choked, snickering. He swiped tears from his eyes, but by some miracle, managed not to poke the bear further. Next to him, Moses Zigman looked around the room, everywhere except at Griz., whistling to himself.

"If everyone is done having their little fun, we need to get ready," Griz said. "Eat quickly. You got fifteen minutes, then we head out."

Rosita and her kitchen staff had set out breakfast on the buffet. Eggs, bacon, toast, coffee, and juice waited for them.

As the team lined up, three mercs from Banyan's employ joined them. Moreno recognized the driver from yesterday, and the other two were much larger in size and more intimidating. One was Mexican with tattoos down his arms. The other was Caucasian and had a burn scar down the left side of his face.

Banyan introduced them.

"These men are three of my best." He pointed at the driver. "This is Gil." Banyan nodded at the tattooed, Mexican merc, "This big fucker here is Marcos." Finally, he faced the last man. "And this is Massey."

The three men eyed the team but remained quiet. Moreno gave a brief nod to the first two, but the white giant of a man with the burn scars gave her pause. He held her gaze, staring a hole through her. She glanced at Banyan who was now in conversation with Griz over a plate of eggs. Neither seemed to notice or offer a clue as to why the merc was eyeballing her.

Next to her, Mac handed her a plate and nudged her toward the buffet line.

"What is it?" he asked, keeping his voice low. He followed her line of sight.

Moreno shook her head and moved in behind Jackson who was already filling his own plate.

"Nothing, I guess. He just gives me the creeps."

Mac watched her face and cut his eyes back at Massey. The man had turned away, talking with his own men while the rest of the team served themselves. Massey said something to the one called Marcos and the two glanced back in their direction, their gazes skimming over Mac before landing on Moreno. He didn't like it.

C'EST LA VIE, SOLDIER

To her, he replied, "Mercenaries are like feral animals. Good to have on your side in a fight, just don't ever trust 'em."

Mac glared in silent warning at both. Marcos turned away, but Massey returned the look, undeterred.

Behind Mac, Montcourt watched the exchange and his hackles rose. He stepped closer to Mac and Moreno and reached back tapping Eastwood on the shoulder. Sensing something amiss, Harry joined Mac and Montcourt as the three of them sent a silent, but clear message. *Moreno was off limits!*

"Ten minutes, team," said Griz. "Get some food down because it'll be the last you have for hours."

Massey turned away and Moreno's three protectors softly grunted in unison.

"Anyone want to tell me what that was about?" Eastwood asked.

"Not sure," said Mac.

"If he comes near her, I will kill him," said Montcourt.

Eastwood threw Mac a sideways glance. "I definitely missed something."

Mac stepped up in line and handed plates back to Montcourt and Eastwood. "Whatever his interest in Nasty, it ain't going nowhere. We stay close to her."

"Agreed," said Montcourt, who began spooning eggs onto his plate.

"No one messes with our Nasty." Eastwood grabbed two slices of toast and some bacon. He looked at Montcourt. "Nice to have you back in her corner, Luc."

Montcourt regarded Eastwood. "I never left." He walked away, taking a seat with Ben and Moses.

Eastwood quirked an eyebrow at Mac, who shrugged.

The team finished off their breakfast in record time, and moved out, assembling in the dark courtyard. After piling into the backs of three repurposed army jeeps, they were on their way, heading southeast into Colima territory.

Chapter Thirteen

Two hours later, the jeeps slowed, and turned right onto a dirt road. Nasty noticed they began to climb, and the going was both slow and treacherous. The view out the backside of the vehicle through the canvas flap showed muddy tire tracks partially obscured by the dense jungle overgrowth on each side of the narrow path. She glanced to her left.

Mac stared out at the same view, his expression grim.

"What's wrong, Mac?" she asked.

He shook his head. "Don't like it. No place to turn around. No exit."

Eastwood grunted. "Not like the deserts in the Middle East. Nowhere to hide there, but at least you got room to maneuver, and you can see what's coming a mile away."

"Exactly," Mac agreed. "Can't see a damn thing through these trees." He leaned up and lifted the flap, peering out.

Moreno considered his observation. This operation was planned down to the last minute, a strategy devised between Griz and Banyan. It was timed out from the travel it would take to get to their destination, to extraction, and then the getaway. Everything hinged on the intelligence gathered by Banyan's men from inception until early yesterday. He'd sent Marcos and Massey to assess the roads, finding the one least monitored. From the looks of it, she understood why. Although a semblance of a road existed, it was being taken over by the jungle and it was obvious it hadn't been used for some time. Every bump and rut, and the slow speed at which they moved, proved that.

Even so, a backup plan and a contingency plan were also developed. The backup plan split off from them at the main road right before the trucks turned onto the hidden path and began to climb. Moreno heard the motorcycle continue on, carrying Jesus to another destination, one not hospitable to the jeeps. He was on his own now. If all went well, they would not see him again, and the man would face an uncertain future as he inserted himself into the Colima cartel following the extraction of her father. This plan was the path of least resistance. A snatch and grab.

The contingency plan involved some high-powered explosives and emergency extraction of the team that would be run by Jackson, but only if the greenlight was given by Griz. Jackson Hicks knew if he heard from the senior chief, it meant everything had gone wrong. It would then be his job to inform Special Agent Peters, who, through

C'EST LA VIE, SOLDIER

inter-agency cooperation with the CIA, had an emergency transport chopper on standby.

But plan A was the goal. Rules of engagement were set based on the assessment made by Banyan's men about the spatial situation of their destination, and the number of men believed to be on the premises as well as their firepower. No casualties unless absolutely necessary, and even then, consider an alternative. The CIA and FBI didn't want to stir the anthill too much. Neither did the team. Peters was clear he wanted to establish contact and communication via Moreno. His plan was to have Moreno inform her father that the U.S. government was aware he was with the Colima cartel, had evidence of his participation in international sex trafficking, and would offer him immunity for any intelligence he could provide. Blackmail via usury was their plan. The team's plan differed in just who, exactly, would be on the inside and cooperating with the FBI and CIA. Their plan was to simply extract one ant and insert another, then get the hell out.

She felt they'd covered all the bases. But the best laid plans could easily go awry, as Mac just pointed out. Still, she felt good about their preparedness and knew that Mac and Eastwood were just being who they were trained to be, as they were all trained to be. Good soldiers. Be alert, assess the lay of the land, find all the entries, the exits, the choke points. If anything, the fact that her teammates were actively engaged made her more confident that they would be successful in finding and extracting her dad.

And Lucien promised her nothing would stop them from reuniting father and daughter. It was the last thing he said before kissing her goodnight and slipping from the exotic villa bathroom back to his own room shared with Jackson before anyone caught them together. She recalled the sincerity in his words, the earnestness in his hazel eyes. Her French marine did not make loose promises. When he told her he would protect her with his life, he'd done so. And she believed him now. Lucien would never let her down.

Mac glanced over his shoulder. Eastwood was staring out through a hole in the canvas, his expression concerned. Moreno gazed out over Mac's head, an absent smile on her lips.

His brows rose, and he was about to ask what she was smiling about when Gil, their driver, slammed on the brakes, sending them flying.

Shots fired, and all three scrambled up off the floor of the jeep, rifles in hand.

"Get down!" Mac shouted at Moreno and Eastwood. "Eyes on the trees! Find the snipers!"

Eastwood and Moreno both fell into position on the floor of the truck bed, M4s aimed out beneath the flap of the canvas.

Moreno searched the tree line on her side as shots continued to rain down. Bullets pinged off the body of the jeep. Several pierced the canvas, one too close for comfort near her leg.

A voice interrupted the chaos, one that hailed through her comm.

"Mac, Moreno, Eastwood, anyone got a location on the snipers yet?"

It was Griz. Mac answered.

"Negative. Searching now. What happened up there?" Another round of bullets had them returning fire.

"Trench in the road, hidden. Our goddamned jeep is nose-first in the hole. We barely got out intact. Keep your eyes peeled. They're all around us. Banyan sent his men out to recon. Rogers and Diaz are still in the second jeep. Montcourt, Holiday, and Zigman are in the bush with me. We're going to make our way around to you. Wait for my signal."

"What's the plan, six?" Mac asked.

"No way to get back out with the two remaining vehicles until we find whoever is ambushing us. We put them down first, then reassess the backup plan."

"Do we still have a chance?" Moreno asked, glancing at Mac.

He shook his head, unsure.

Griz replied, as if reading her mind. "Tell Moreno to keep the faith. It ain't over yet. Six out."

"Fuck!" Eastwood grunted. "Two in the treetops, my ten and two!" He took aim and focused.

Mac scrambled to his side. "Nasty, you got our backs," he said, indicating she should continue covering the opposite side.

"Roger that," she answered. Keeping low, she scanned the thick vegetation, looking for anything that either reflected or moved.

Behind her, Eastwood softly exhaled and fired. That shot was followed by another from Mac.

The jungle went silent, and no one dared to breathe.

Eastwood whispered, "I know I got him. But Mac?"

"Yeah?"

"I don't think they were alone."

As soon as Eastwood said it, a fresh volley of fire came from all sides.

Moreno could see them now, coming out of the trees. An army of men in camo, faces painted black. They rushed the vehicles, and she opened fire.

All hell broke loose.

"Dammit!" Mac spat. "We need to get out of here. We're sitting ducks!" He turned to Eastwood. "Lay down cover fire, Harry. I'm getting us out of here. Moreno, on my six!"

Over their comms, Griz shouted orders.

"Rogers, Diaz, take out as many as you can. Holiday, Banyan, get out past the horde! We need to penetrate their lines and gain ground, attack them from behind. We'll distract them from here. Get everyone out on my signal!"

"What signal?" Eastwood muttered.

C'EST LA VIE, SOLDIER

The first of three explosions rent the air. Screams indicated one of the grenades hit its mark.

Harry grinned. "Oh, that signal."

Mac slipped out the back of the jeep and laid down fire. Moreno jumped out behind him and dropped low.

"That way," Mac said, his head nodding to the right of the jeep just north of the first explosion. "Harry, pull out!" he shouted over his shoulder. "This way!"

The second explosion went off on the left side of the jeep, and it was immediately followed by a third. A tree fell and a cloud of smoke mushroomed into the air.

The comm link crackled and Griz's voice ordered, "Head due north, the path is clear. Over."

Eastwood retracted his M4 and rolled, sliding out the back of the jeep.

Matt Rogers and Art Diaz leapt out the back of the second truck. The three of them moved out, following Mac and Moreno. They just made the trees when the second attack began.

Three Colima soldiers came at Eastwood's left.

Rogers and Diaz swung around and fired. Two went down, but the third jumped Eastwood.

Yet another group of cartel soldiers rushed them, this time from behind. Rogers and Diaz spun, dropping low and firing into the crowd.

Behind them, grunts and curses flew. Eastwood punched the man's grease-painted face, a satisfying cracking sound filling his ears, but his enemy kept coming. The thug was large with a chest like a barrel and arms that would make an Olympic weightlifter jealous. If he got those massive guns around Eastwood, he'd be a goner. But as big and solid as he was, all that mass moved slowly. Backing up a step, Eastwood waited, keeping his balance on his good leg. When the thug feigned left, Harry slapped the 'knee' of his prosthetic, and swung his body around delivering a roundhouse kick to the man's head. There was a sickening stabbing sound followed by a string of curses as Eastwood struggled to stay upright.

The deadly blades on his prosthetic leg sank deep in the thug's skull, getting stuck, and the man was going down, his eyes fixed.

"Shit!" Eastwood spat as he repeatedly banged his hand on the prosthetic's 'knee'.

A scraping/sucking sound rent the air as Harry hit the ground, but his leg was free.

He glanced down at his pantleg. The material was ripped and bloodied.

"This modification needs work, Joely," he muttered, then jumped up and grabbed his rifle from the weeds.

"You okay, Eastwood?" Diaz called over his shoulder.

"I'm good. Just kill those bastards so we can get out of here!"

Rogers aimed and fired one bullet at a time with singular precision. Next to him, Diaz, too, switched to single fire, and the two took down the group behind them like two good old boys at a carnival target shoot.

When the last man fell, the three took off north through the trees.

C'EST LA VIE, SOLDIER

As they gained the jungle, they kept their heads on swivel.

"Which way, Eastwood?" Art asked.

"Straight ahead, Cyclops. Stay alert. Rogers," he said, glancing back, "you got our six."

"No one's getting past me, Sarge," said Matt.

The deeper they traveled, the quieter it became. Eerily quiet.

"Fuck, they can't be that far ahead of us," Eastwood mumbled.

"Should we hail the senior chief on the comm?" Diaz whispered.

Eastwood shook his head. "If our guys are this quiet, there's a reason. Stay low. No talking from here on out until we find them."

Moreno and Mac moved through the jungle underbrush carefully. They kept a northerly push, but still hadn't found Griz and the rest of the team.

She glanced behind her, searching for Eastwood. It was dark this far in. The trees grew over sixty feet high, and the density of the growth blotted out the morning sun. The heat and humidity sucked the moisture from her skin and soaked her BDUs leaving the material clinging uncomfortably. Her face coverings didn't help the breathing situation. She swiped her arm over her eyes and looked ahead at Mac.

He picked his way through the low ferns and hanging vines making a path for her to follow. At a fallen tree, he stopped, holding up a fist.

Moreno crept up behind him.

"Where are they, Mac?" she whispered.

He shook his head. "Dunno, but I don't like this."

"How the hell did they even know we were here?" she asked. "That wasn't just a few guards, that was an ambush."

Mac nodded. "Yep."

"Too risky to reach out by radio," she said.

A twig snapped and Mac put a finger to where his lips would be beneath the camo bandana covering the lower half of his face. Moreno went silent, her eyes bouncing around them searching for the source of the sound.

Ahead, the ferns parted, and Mac and Moreno took aim from their blind.

Massey stepped out followed by Marcos. Even with the lower part of their faces covered, she recognized them.

Mac exhaled, his rifle lowering. He mumbled, "About damn time."

He stepped from the blind and indicated Moreno should follow.

Massey approached; his rifle still aimed.

Mac paused, his eyes darting around Banyan's two men at the group of hardened Colima soldiers emerging behind them, and all around the enclosure.

C'EST LA VIE, SOLDIER

Mac raised his M4, alarmed, but was too late. The butt of a rifle came down on the back of his head. The last sound he heard was Moreno screaming, "Mac!"

Chapter Fourteen

Montcourt followed Senior Chief Torres, Jack Banyan, and Gil. They'd decided to double back when the others failed to catch up. Behind him, Ben Holiday and Moses Zigman kept pace.

Banyan was on edge and Griz was on high alert, head on swivel, as the two led the way through the thicket of trees.

"They were right behind us," he whispered.

Griz grunted. "Something isn't right, Jack. The cartel was ready for us."

Banyan nodded, then cast Griz a sideways glance through narrowed eyes. "We'll get to the bottom of it, I promise you. Let's find my men, and yours."

"Mac!"

The scream sliced through the density of the jungle, and straight into Montcourt's heart.

He jumped, and his pulse raced, and before anyone could stop him, he bolted in the direction of that scream.

"Mon Amour!" he croaked as he took off running.

"Montcourt, wait!" Griz whispered harshly, then he, too, began to run.

The group followed, all of them fighting their way through the branches and vines at a fast clip.

When they reached a clearing, they found Mac on the ground, and Marcos standing over him, gun in hand, finger on the trigger.

Griz aimed his M4.

Next to him, Banyan shouted, "Freeze!"

Marcos turned, and seeing Banyan, Griz, Gil, and the others fanning out behind them, each having him in their sights, dropped his gun and threw his hands up.

"On your knees, Marcos," Banyan barked. "Hands on your head. Now!"

"Moses, Ben, secure him," Griz ordered.

The two men ran up behind Marcos and made quick work of zip-tying his wrists.

Mac groaned.

"Shit, Mac, are you okay?" Griz dropped down at his side.

Mac spat, then cursed, rubbing the back of his head. "Where's Moreno?"

"Not here. We heard her scream."

"Fuck! It was Massey," Mac grunted, sitting up. His head spun.

C'EST LA VIE, SOLDIER

Ben Holiday left the prisoner in Gil's and Zigman's hands and went to help Mac. "Easy, Maclean. Your head is bleeding. Stay still."

"It can wait. Gotta get Nasty. He's with them. Massey is with the cartel."

"Jesus!" Montcourt exclaimed. "Which way did they go?"

"Montcourt, stay calm!" Griz ordered, pointing at him.

"Which way did they go!" he screamed, his eyes wide with horror.

Mac locked eyes with Lucien. He knew the look of a desperate man in love. And this was Moreno, their teammate and friend. He pointed beyond the enclosure.

"Go get her," Mac said.

"Goddamn it, Maclean!" Griz said, turning to stop Montcourt, but it was too late.

The French commando had already taken off through the dense trees, moving northwest.

"Fuck!" Griz spat. He looked at Moses. "Follow him, and report back as soon as you find him. I'll need coordinates."

Zigman nodded and released the prisoner into Banyan's hands. The Israeli intelligence officer moved fast, disappearing into the jungle.

Griz shouted after him. "And don't do anything until I say so!" He barked a slew of orders, pissed. "Mac, hold everyone here. I'm going to find the rest." He turned to leave, then paused, eyeing Jack. "And if I find out you had anything to do with this clusterfuck, I'll kill you!"

Jack's face remained fixed, but regret filled his eyes. "I understand. But for the record, I didn't betray you, and never would." He glanced sideways at Marcos. "We'll get to the bottom of this, my friend, I promise you. And there's going to be hell to pay.

Montcourt's feet flew like the Roman God Mercury. He'd immediately searched for tracks in the direction Mac had pointed. He found them, many of them. The problem was, they were hit and miss in the overgrowth of the jungle floor. But there were other signs the group Maclean indicated had passed through. Broken and bent vines and branches were hard to hide, especially when a group was travelling fast. One pair of boot prints were deeper than the others.

Those would be Massey's, pushing deep into the soil from carrying Moreno.

And since there were no signs of a scuffle, he had to assume Moreno was unconscious. That thought made Montcourt see red.

He moved swiftly, now at least a mile from where he began. A twig snapped, and he stopped dead, dropping low.

Ducking back between the long branches of dark green ferns, Montcourt scanned the jungle. He heard no other sound and was about to re-emerge from hiding when a man ran out along the path he'd taken. The denseness of the tall trees blocked out the sunlight and darkness shadowed the man's face. Aiming chest high, Montcourt waited, finger on the trigger.

The man was almost upon him, still running and unaware of the certain death waiting for him in the verdant foliage.

"Mon dieu!" Montcourt cursed, lowering his face cover.

The man spun and aimed but caught himself before firing.

"Dammit, Montcourt!"

Moses Zigman pointed his M4 to the ground, his brows drawn low. "I could have killed you!"

Moncourt stepped out of the ferns. "I had the drop on you first. Why are you here?"

Zigman snorted. "Why do you think? To keep you from doing something stupid."

"Senior Chief sent you," Montcourt concluded.

"And now I have to inform him I've found you." Zigman reached for his two-way.

Montcourt stopped him. "And then what? Wait? Not happening, Mon Ami."

"You can't just charge in by yourself, Lucien. We have a plan."

"Which is blown!"

"And a contingency," Zigman continued. "We follow orders."

"Fuck orders! They have Nastjia! She may not be one of your men, Captain, but she is my teammate, and my..." He bit his tongue.

Zigman's brows quirked. "Your... what?"

Montcourt blew out a breath. "I will not wait, Moses. I'm going after them, and when I find Massey, so help me God, I'm going to kill him!"

Zigman stood quietly, assessing.

Lucien pleaded. "I promised her. I promised her I would not let anything happen to her. That promise is broken. I have to save her!"

Zigman remained quiet, studying Montcourt. His orders from Griz were clear, inform him immediately when he found Montcourt and don't let him do anything stupid. But the French marine was chomping at the bit. There was no feasible way to restrain Lucien short of tying him down, and Moses was sure he would not go down quietly. No, he'd fight, and the two of them would end up beating the hell out of each other, and that wouldn't help anyone. Plus, it was common knowledge among the team that Montcourt was in love with Moreno. He'd already seen the lengths his teammates would go for the women they loved. He'd heard about Harry and Joely after arriving at PATCH-COM. Mac raced headlong into dangerous cartel territory to save Connie, and then had to deliver a beat-down to her ex. And then he'd seen Griz, of all people, lose his shit to save Jessica when she was kidnapped. Then there was Holiday. He'd witnessed Ben's fall from bachelorhood firsthand. Seems it happened pretty much from the moment he'd first laid eyes on Irina. From what he'd observed, restraining battle-hardened men who'd been shot in the ass by Cupid's bow was an exercise in futility.

C'EST LA VIE, SOLDIER

The senior chief's orders were clear. Inform him the minute he found Montcourt.

He sighed. "Seems I haven't yet found you."

Montcourt blinked. "What? What are you saying..."

Zigman turned facing ahead. "I'm saying I haven't yet found you, but I'll be on your tail. Still gotta keep you from doing something stupid. Because you might need help."

Montcourt flashed a wicked grin and clapped Zigman on the shoulder before pulling his face covering back up. "I won't forget this, Moses. Now keep up!"

Montcourt took off again, running like the wind. Captain Zigman ran behind him, shaking his head and hoping like hell his knee wouldn't give out, and that his momentary burst of compassion wouldn't get them, or Moreno, killed.

Chapter Fifteen

It took nearly an hour on foot to follow the trail to the compound. The climb grew steadily, and the track became more treacherous. The humidity of the thick jungle trees gave way to cliffs packed with rocks and debris. But the breeze above the jungle floor was welcome.

Montcourt and Zigman caught sight of the wall a third of the way up. And they spotted two guards walking the wall near the end of the path. There was no way to approach without being seen beyond the next bend.

They ceased moving forward and concealed themselves behind shrub-covered boulders.

"We need to call the senior chief now," Zigman said.

A heavy sigh passed Montcourt's lips. He peeked out, scanning left and right. He watched the two guards heading away from where he sat behind a stack of boulders. It took them three minutes to complete their walk to the far end of the wall. Then they turned and began the return sweep, long rifles in hand. These were snipers, trained to take out threats before they could reach the stone wall, that much was obvious. The return sweep took another four and a half minutes.

Montcourt eyed the wall, finding the footholds. There were enough to make it to the top, but not in time without being seen. The guards would have to be taken out, and doing so without raising the alarm would require help. And that meant waiting, something Montcourt did not have the patience for. There was nothing more he could do alone. The alternative was getting caught or killed before he could get inside and find Nastjia.

He turned to Zigman.

"Make the call."

Moses retreated a hundred feet back and contacted Griz. Montcourt could barely hear the senior chief cursing from where he sat.

"Where the hell have you been? Send me the coordinates of your location now and sit tight!"

Within moments, Zigman returned to his side.

"He sounds pissed," said Montcourt.

"He is. He'll get over it. We stay put until they arrive."

"Dammit. What's their ETA?"

"Forty minutes if all goes well."

"Shit. She could be dead in forty minutes."

Zigman eyed Montcourt before glancing up at the wall. "She could be dead already, Luc."

C'EST LA VIE, SOLDIER

Quick as a flash, Montcourt grabbed Zigman's shirt and pinned the man to the ground. He brought his face within an inch of his teammate's.

"Don't you say that!" he whispered harshly.

Zigman remained still. He understood why his words upset the man. Cautiously, he patted Montcourt's shoulder.

"It's just a statement of fact, Luc. And so it this... they didn't take her to kill her. They have a reason. Whatever that reason is, there's a long game at play. They won't hurt her. Calm yourself. When the team gets here, we'll figure out how to rescue Moreno."

Montcourt glared at Zigman, his eyes spitting fire. With a frustrated grunt, he released him.

"When we find Massey, he's dead. I don't care what Griz says!"

Zigman sat up, dusting himself off. "Agreed, but we may have trouble from Banyan."

"Fuck him," Montcourt spat. "How do we know he didn't have something to do with this?"

"I guess we don't, but I'm sure we're not the only ones thinking along that line. He may be an old friend of the senior chief, but Torres is no fool. We'll know more when they get here."

Montcourt knew they had no choice. They would have to wait for the rest of the team to arrive.

But it chafed. The pain ripping at his heart, his soul was tearing him apart. *Mon Amour*, he thought, *I will save you. Hold on!*

Nastjia awoke to a pounding headache. Her tongue was glued to the roof of her mouth, and her hands refused to cooperate when she tried to lift them to touch her aching jaw. Slowly, she opened her eyes. As things came into focus, she realized she was inside a small, windowless room. A light shined overhead, the fluorescent bulbs buzzing. In the far corner, a small table was placed against the wall. Carefully, she rolled to her side. That's when she realized her hands were tied behind her back, and she'd been stripped of her weapons.

She was on the floor, a palette of old blankets beneath her. Sitting up, her hands began to tingle immediately as the blood rushed back to each digit. The stabbing pin pricks were excruciating, and she wiggled her fingers in an attempt to speed the process along of regaining her circulation. While she did this, she took in more of her surroundings.

Across the way was a door. Although she was sure it would be locked, she knew she needed to get up and investigate. It took all the energy and concentration she had to get her feet beneath her, using her shoulder against the wall for support.

A wave of nausea hit when she stood, but she took several deep breaths, standing still, until it passed. She exhaled slowly. The side of her face felt hot. It was then she remembered that Massey had punched her several times, knocking her unconscious. Her eyes narrowed.

When I find him, I'm going to kill that traitorous sonofabitch!

Taking a step, she found her balance and walked to the door. Up close, she could see it was solid wood, probably oak. With nothing to use to break it down, she'd have to find a way to spring the lock, but she'd need her hands free for that.

Moreno turned and walked around the perimeter of the room searching for anything sharp she might use to cut through the bindings around her wrists. As far as she could tell, they were zip tied. Finding nothing of use, she turned her search inward trying to think of how to get free. Only one thought presented itself. She stared down at her boots. It wouldn't be easy, but she had one advantage.

Bending forward, she began shimmying her hands down over her butt. It took many attempts despite being slim through the hips, but she finally managed to get her hands low enough and past her bum. Now she needed to bend her knees and sit back down.

She half fell, but the hard landing on the slate-tiled floor was the price paid to get one step closer to freedom.

With her bound hands now beneath her thighs, and her knees pulled up to her chest, she began kicking at her boot, the one covering her prosthetic foot. Being unable to untie that boot made it hard, but she kept stomping down on it and pulling her leg back, trying to pull her stump out of the prosthetic socket.

Sweat beaded on her forehead and dripped into her eyes. Moreno shook it off, cursing at the sting she couldn't yet wipe away. She blinked rapidly, muttering to herself and plotting Massey's brutal death with each pull.

It hurt like hell, but she refused to give up. Taking another deep breath, she pushed down with all her might with her good foot, tugging back with the opposite leg.

With a sharp pain, her stump popped out of the prosthetic cup. Another tug and her leg was free of the boot.

Taking a quick minute to catch her breath, Moreno worked her hands down as far as she could while curling that leg up to her chest as high as she could manage. Twisting and grunting, she finally slipped her leg through her hands. With one leg out, she was able to free the second.

Working quickly now, she pulled the laces loose from one side of her boot and then stuck the loose end in her teeth, biting down hard. The Kevlar laces were strong and wouldn't break. Pulling the lace taut, she began cutting the zip ties on the material. Sawing back and forth, Moreno worked until the ties broke, and her wrists were free.

With no time to waste, she reattached her prosthetic and laced up her boot.

On her feet again, she approached the door, this time intent on finding a way to pick the lock.

As she jiggled the knob, the sound of footsteps filtered through the wall. She backed up, searching for anything to use as a weapon.

There was nothing.

Moreno moved to the side of the door. The best she could hope for was to clobber whoever came in before they realized what hit them, then run.

The handle jiggled as a key was inserted into the lock from the outside. The clicking sound was loud in the silence.

Sweat dripped down her back as she took slow, deep breaths, readying herself to attack.

The door swung in, and a figure appeared.

Moreno stared at the back of the man's head, waiting until he stepped fully inside.

Then, she pounced.

Her arms wrapped around his neck and her legs around his waist. She squeezed for all she was worth.

The man bucked, then fell sideways, choking.

"Nastjia! Mija, stop!"

The weak voice rasping her name stopped her cold.

She loosened her hold and fell back, scrambling to the wall.

The man exhaled loudly, coughing, then turned to look at her.

"Papa?" she whispered.

Moreno stared at the man who sat before her, his hands rubbing his neck as he wheezed. It had been a long time since she'd last seen her father. Then, he'd been happy and healthy, perhaps a few pounds overweight, but not overly so. He'd always kept his hair cut and his clothing neat, his shirt tucked into his pressed pants. The man before her bore the resemblance of her papa, but he was a shell of his former self. Gaunt, dirty, bedraggled. This man's hair had grown long and gray, his eyes, once filled with good cheer, reflected shadows and defeat. This was not the Juan Carlos Moreno she knew.

This man appeared for all the world as a prisoner barely surviving, barely alive.

Guilt ate at Nastjia. She'd spent so long being angry, thinking he'd abandoned her based on so little evidence. It seemed obvious at the time, but now, she knew it never was.

Tears slid unbidden down her cheeks.

"Papa?" She inched closer. "Papa..."

Juan Carlos Moreno sniffed, his sunken brown eyes pooling. He threw his arms wide and, just like when she was a little girl, Nastjia launched herself into them, burying her face in his collar.

"I'm here, mija. I'm here," he crooned, rocking his only child as she sobbed.

Moreno clung to him, feeling the bones of his ribs through the fabric of the tattered blue button-down shirt he wore. He'd wasted away in this place while she'd gone on with her life. It was more than she could bear.

She squeezed her eyes shut and took a deep, calming breath before pulling back and looking up into his face.

Juan Carlos Moreno's gaze took in all the changes since last he'd seen her, and then his eyes noticed the bruises on her jawline and the swelling. Pain lanced through his heart followed by fury.

"Nastjia, my sweet girl, why?"

C'EST LA VIE, SOLDIER

The question confused her.

"What? Why what, papa?"

He reached out to tuck a strand of hair behind her ear.

"You should not have come. You shouldn't have tried to find me."

She sat back on her knees, aghast. "What do you mean I shouldn't have come? You've been missing for several years," she began. The guilt nearly choked her, but she continued. "I had to find you, papa. And I'm sorry it took so long. I didn't know. I thought..."

He gently cupped her face in his bony-fingered hands.

"You thought I left you, that I abandoned you," he whispered, his voice raw with grief. "I know, mija. I know. They told me what they did. It was part of their plan. I'm so sorry... so sorry. I wish you'd stayed away. Knowing you were safe far away from them, from him, was the only thing that was important, that gave me peace. Now it's too late."

Confusion and anger filled her. "What? What are you saying, papa? Who told you? What plan? What are you talking about?"

"He is referring to us."

Moreno whipped around.

Two men entered the small room. Two men in expensive suits. Two men she recognized instantly from the pictures Agent Peters had shown her not long ago in Major Maxwell's office.

The shorter of the two cast his cold eyes upon her, a smirk tugging at his thin lips.

"Or rather, to our boss." He smiled fully then, but it did not reach his cold eyes. "It is good to finally meet you, Nastjia Moreno. Or should I say, Nastjia Elena Nikolayeva? My boss will be very pleased." The man sighed, a smug look on his face. "He is most eager to meet his granddaughter."

Moreno's mouth gaped as her heart pounded. She looked to her father for denial and found in his expression only pain and confirmation. Juan Moreno had shrunk in on himself, cowed in the presence of these two men. Fear radiated off him and it sickened her. Pushing her guilt down, Moreno embraced the anger she felt at seeing her father in such a state.

She rose to her feet and planted herself between the two suits and her father. Squaring her shoulders, she straightened her spine and glared at the shorter Russian.

"Who the hell are you and what the hell are you talking about?"

"Forgive my manners," he said, offering his hand. "I am Anatoly Zadornov. and this is my associate, Anton Kadyrov."

Moreno eyed the man's extended hand like it was a snake about to strike. She ignored it and glared hard.

Zadornov chuckled and dropped his hand. He cast a sideways glance at Kadyrov. "Fearless, da?"

Unlike Zadornov, Kadyrov did not find Moreno amusing. "Foolish." He moved closer to her, his gaze raking her up and down. His eyes focused in on the bruises on her jaw. "Who did this to you?" He reached out, gripping her jaw.

C'EST LA VIE, SOLDIER

Moreno quickly slapped his hand away. "Don't touch me!"

Behind her, Juan Carlos uttered a distressed, *"Don't anger them, mija!"*

Kadyrov's reflexes were fast. He grabbed Moreno by her neck, lifting her until she stood on tiptoes.

Fury and defiance flashed in her dark eyes.

"Let go of me!" she sputtered.

Kadyrov leaned his face close to hers, ignoring her objection. He stared at the injury, noting the purpling along the edge of her jaw. His thumb absently caressed the bruised skin, a sick smile edging his thick lips.

"The one who did this will be dealt with, I promise," he said, his eyes finding hers. "The boss does not want you harmed."

Moreno could feel his hot breath on her face. She didn't like the look in this one's eyes, nor the liberty he was taking by touching her.

Her eyes narrowed and her fists bunched at her sides. Before he could blink, she headbutted him.

Blood spurted from his nose as he thrust her away, his hand flying first to his face, then raising high readying to strike.

"Anton, no!"

Zadornov stepped in and grabbed Kadyrov's arm, stopping him before he could land the hit.

"The boss will kill you! Get yourself under control!" He pushed Kadyrov toward the door. "Go clean yourself up." Zadornov stood now between Moreno and his associate.

"The fault is yours. You were warned of her disposition, yet you chose to ignore it and got too close. She is his granddaughter, after all."

Kadyrov's nostrils flared as his gaze skipped past Zadornov and found Moreno's. A smirk graced her lips even as her terrified father wrapped his spindly arms around her in a vain attempt to protect her. Her eyes mocked. His promised retaliation. With Zadornov once again pushing him out the door, he left.

The man turned back to Moreno and her father. He couldn't quite hide his amusement, but beneath it was a steely resolve.

"You should not have done that, Nastjia Nikolayeva. He will not forget, and I will not always be there to stop him from indulging his dark side."

"Stop calling me that," she hissed.

His eyes widened. "Why? It is your name."

She gently pulled away from her father's arms.

"My name is Moreno, after my father."

Zadornov chuckled. "You are more like your grandfather than you know. The bravado you display now is pure Nikolaev." He pointed at Juan Carlos. "Look, Nastjia, your father cowers in fear while you brave the lions. You are better than him." He smirked, satisfied. "Yes, your grandfather will be most pleased." He glanced at the bruise on her jaw. "Anton was right, though. The one who did that must be dealt with. Tell me, please, who did this?"

Flashbacks of her fight with Massey filled her. She had no sympathy for the man who betrayed them all and hurt

Mac, hurt her. What became of him as a result was no skin off her back."

"Massey, the traitorous bastard who brought me here."

Zadornov nodded. "Thank you. You need not worry about him again." He turned and walked to the door. "Now, come with me. We must take you up to the house. You meet your grandfather today."

Shocked, Moreno looked at her dad.

He kept his eyes cast down, but his hand reached for hers.

"Papa..." she began.

"I'm sorry, baby. I should have told you..."

"Told me what, papa? What's happening? Who is this grandfather?"

Juan Carlos raised his head and looked straight into his daughter's eyes. A tear slid down his cheek and a world of sorrow emanated from his haggard face.

"He is Oleg Nikolaev... the boss of the Russian mafia."

Chapter Sixteen

Moreno's world turned upside down. *The Russian mafia? Her grandfather was the head of the fucking Bratva? What? How?*

"Your grandmother, Nadia's mother, was his second wife. She fled St. Petersburg with your mother to get away from him. You see, the marriage was forced upon her. She never wished to be part of that world, but Oleg is not a man to be refused. They came here and your grandmother Elena changed her last name back to her maiden name. For a time, it worked. Elena and Nadia were safe. Then we met and Nadia became a Moreno and your grandmother passed. She told me all this and we thought she would be safe, that you would be safe, until..."

Moreno shook her head, putting the pieces together. "Until they found mama and killed her." Her voice wobbled. "It was never an accident."

Her papa nodded. "No, it was no accident. Your mama was trying to lead them away from us, from you. That's why they found her so far from home."

From behind them, a voice interrupted. "That was a mistake. We never meant to kill her, but she foolishly fled, then her car spun out of control."

Moreno whipped around, remembering Zadornov was still there; waiting, watching, listening.

"You motherfucker!" she screamed, rushing toward him with murder in her eyes.

Zadornov pulled a gun from the holster inside his jacket and pointed it at her face, stopping Moreno dead in her tracks.

"Calm yourself, little Nikolayeva. You don't want to end up like your mother."

Furious, Moreno fumed. But then she remembered.

"You won't shoot me," she said, her tone confident. "You said it yourself, my grandfather doesn't want me harmed. And if you do, he'll deal with you." She smiled, but it didn't reach her eyes. "I'm betting yours would be a slow, painful death... da?"

Zadornov kept the gun aimed, his face neutral, but Moreno could tell he was thinking hard.

Finally, he dropped the gun and chuckled.

"Da, it would. But make no mistake, Nastjia Nikolayeva, there is an army of Colima soldiers outside this door who will not hesitate to shoot you. And I would let them and let the chips fall where they may. Now, are you willing to get yourself and your father killed, or will you follow me like a good girl and have a pleasant family reunion?"

Put like that, she knew she had no choice. She would have to follow him and meet this brutal next of kin. Then, and only then, could she figure out how to get herself and her father out of here. Pulling herself together, she nodded.

"Lead the way, Ivan."

"It's Anatoly," he corrected, his words sharp.

She smirked, knowing she had struck a nerve. "Whatever."

The bright sunlight blinded her after being inside the windowless room. Moreno squinted and blinked rapidly while holding her hand up to shield her eyes. She glanced around taking in the lay of the compound. It was actually quite sophisticated and richer inside the walls than expected. It was obvious that the cartel and their Russian counterparts put a great deal of their resources toward comfort. The outer buildings, like the one she exited, were simple structures with no perks. The wall surrounding the compound was made of thick stone and at least ten to twelve feet tall. There were lookouts at every corner with heavily armed soldados on guard. Even so, it wasn't impenetrable. Especially after dark. All it would take was stealth, rope, grappling hooks, and of course, the quick deaths of the wall guards in the quietest possible manner. Once inside, however, it was a different story.

One would need to know the basic layout, where the interior guards were stationed, how many, and their firepower. Fortunately, she was inside the walls, and her father had been here long enough to have gathered all that intel. She just needed a moment alone with him to brainstorm an escape plan, and hope her team would be on the same page, working on Plan B or C.

She still needed to get through whatever the hell Ivan the Terrible was dragging her into. Moreno had no desire to meet this mysterious grandfather. She still did not know how her father ended up here, but his appearance and his reaction to seeing her presented a lot of clues. He was definitely not here on his own accord, and he'd been treated terribly. Juan Carlos Moreno was a shell of his former self. This both angered Nasty and caused a great deal of guilt. She had, after all, thought he'd left her behind, without a word, and on purpose.

Tears stung her eyes as she silently berated herself. How could she have ever thought her papa, the man who'd loved her and raised her and protected her all her life, would just up and leave?

Yeah, sure, he was gone, the house empty, and no note, no phone call, nothing.

Dammit! Moreno shook her head, then reached out for her father's hand, holding it tight.

He squeezed back, his eyes finding hers.

C'EST LA VIE, SOLDIER

She couldn't keep doing this, not right now. There would be time later for explanations and apologies.

They arrived at a large villa in the center of the compound. Zadornov led the way inside the courtyard and then into a large, tiled hallway. He kept going and turned right into a room with a high ceiling and rich, brown paneled wainscoting. The walls above were decorated with brocade wallpaper. It was a masculine room designed around a marble fireplace and a very large oak desk.

A man sat behind that desk.

His tanned skin, dark hair and eyes, and Latin features marked him as Mexican. The fine linen of his white suit and authoritative bearing showed he was a cartel higher up, if not the leader.

Zadornov walked straight to the desk.

"We need the room," he said, his tone indicating he expected immediate obedience.

The dark-haired man's eyes narrowed, but he did not move otherwise.

"You realize this is my home?" he asked casually, but there was an undercurrent of annoyance.

The Russian glared. "And you realize you owe Vor v Zakone Nikolaev for all you have, since it is his protection that keeps you alive after your predecessor turned rat for the United States, da?"

The men glared at each other, neither blinking. Finally, the Mexican stood, pushing his chair back with force until it bounced off the wall behind him.

"I grow tired of the reminder, Zadornov." His eyes raked over Juan Carlos and then settled on Moreno. "My men helped deliver his long-lost familia." His gaze flashed back to Zadornov. "And the cut he takes from my businesses more than pays for his *protection*." He spat the last word.

The Russian enforcer took slow, deliberate steps toward the Mexican until they were face to face.

"Shall we see how long you last without our help, Victor?"

Moreno watched them, picking up quickly on both the animosity between the two and the name of this new player. She recognized that immediately. Victor Jimenez, Oscar Fernandez-Ochoa's successor. Ochoa's deal with the American government had fallen through not long after Mac and her teammates brought him in. As it turned out, he was too "hot" to put back into play, and coward that he was, he refused to be cut loose and deported back to Mexico. So, he managed to disarm a guard and then shot him. Killing a U.S. citizen while in custody was a no-brainer prison sentence, and Ochoa now enjoyed a cell inside a federal facility where he was fed three meals a day and allowed to continue breathing.

Still, Moreno figured it was only a matter of time before someone connected to the Sinaloa cartel got to him, even on U.S. soil, inside a maximum-security federal prison.

She felt her father's hand squeeze hers, as if saying, *"Don't move, don't speak!"*

She squeezed back and watched intently to see who would back down first.

Finally, Jimenez emitted an annoyed snort and stepped around Zadornov.

"I have work to do." He walked to the door, his eyes bouncing off Moreno once again, a speculative gleam reflected in their dark depths.

She didn't like it. At all. It triggered memories of her captivity inside The Honey Hole and the guard who'd stripped her down, punched her, and threatened to kill her. In that moment, she fervently wished Lucien were here. He'd become her safe place, the protector who unfailingly stood between her and a dangerous world.

"Nastjia Nikolayeva, please, come sit here." Zadornov interrupted her thoughts. He stood at the desk and gestured toward the seat vacated by Jimenez.

Her spine went rigid. "It's Moreno," she corrected.

He smirked, then pushed the chair back from the wall where Jimenez left it. "Please," he repeated.

She looked at her father. Juan Carlos nodded, but there was fear in his eyes.

"It's okay, papa," she whispered.

Nasty moved to the desk and sat in the chair. She kept a close eye on Zadornov the entire time.

The Russian enforcer then opened a laptop on the desk and typed on the keyboard. The screen changed and revealed a window. Inside the window, a green phone icon appeared. Zadornov clicked it and waited.

The window opened and a face appeared, a much older man's face with hard lines and cruel eyes. Those eyes locked with hers and the rigid set of his lips relaxed into the semblance of a smile. It was chilling.

He stared at her, assessing. Then finally, he spoke. "Hello, my granddaughter. We finally meet."

Montcourt was losing patience. His knee bounced as he kept low and out of sight, but his agitation was clear. Next to him, Zigman shook his head, silently pleading for Griz and the rest of the team to hurry before Montcourt did something stupid.

"Putain de merde!" he muttered. (*For fuck's sake!*)

"Calm down, Luc," Zigman whispered.

"What is taking them so long?" Montcourt rubbed his sweaty palms on his pants.

"It takes as long as it takes."

"It will be too late. Nastjia will be..."

Zigman gripped Montcourt's shoulder and gave it a shake.

"I told you, they won't harm her. They took her for a reason."

"But we don't know what that reason is, Moses." Montcourt snorted, then ground his teeth. "Every minute we delay is another minute they could be..." he made a disgusted face, then spat.

"I know. But I don't believe that's why she was taken. It was too specific, and Massey risked everything to get to her, plowing through Mac like that, which you know is damned difficult. Maclean isn't easy to take down. No, something else is going on here."

Something moved in the tree line off to their right.

"Sssh!" Zigman hushed Montcourt and pointed.

In the dark canopy of the jungle, giant fern and palm fronds undulated, then slowly parted.

Montcourt and Zigman aimed their M4s at this new threat at their back. Keeping low behind the bushes, they waited.

Barely discernable, the business end of a high-powered rifle emerged, sweeping left and right.

Montcourt's finger tightened on his trigger as he prepared to exhale.

A head came into view.

Zigman grabbed Montcourt's wrist and tugged, his whispered words low.

"Hold. I think that's Diaz."

The two men waited, watching.

The figure in the jungle stepped forward leaving the darkness of the canopy. He was followed by another, a man with shocking orange-blond hair.

A half-snort, half-chuckle escaped Zigman's lips. "That for-shit bleach job is going to get Griz killed."

Montcourt was not amused, but rather, impatient. He glanced up toward the compound wall checking for the sentries. Seeing none, he half-stood and waved.

Diaz spotted him and pointed the location out to the senior chief. Griz signaled behind him, and the rest of the team emerged from the trees quickly making their way up to Montcourt's and Zigman's position.

"It's about time," Montcourt said.

Griz shot him a look. "When this is over, we're having a little talk about chain of command and insubordination."

Montcourt bit his tongue, though it pained him. He knew Griz was right in pointing out his actions in failing to wait for orders, but for Nastjia, he'd do it again. The senior chief was the highest ranking officer of their group and subsequently, had the most experience. He was in charge and Montcourt knew he was out of line by taking off without permission—even if Mac had silently agreed. Maclean was not their CO on this mission.

Banyan arrived behind Griz and Diaz followed by Mac, Eastwood, Matt Rogers, Ben Holiday, and Banyan's man, Gil, who was pulling Marcos along by a rope tied around the man's body. The other man, Juan Hernandez, was not with them. Montcourt could see they'd already zip-tied the traitor's wrists at his back. With hands secured and his arms tightly bound to his sides, Marcos wasn't going anywhere.

Montcourt spat on the ground, eyeing Banyan. "And what about him, Griz? It was his men who took Nastjia."

Griz's nostrils flared as he held his temper in check. He understood Montcourt's anger and frustration. He shared those feelings. But now was not the time for this discussion. He glanced at Banyan.

C'EST LA VIE, SOLDIER

"Right now, Banyan is a warm body, and we need every one we have." The look in his eyes told his old friend that he would brook no argument.

Banyan gave a brief nod of acceptance.

Griz continued. "And we have a plan."

Eastwood stepped up next to Montcourt.

"Don't worry, Luc. Plan B."

Montcourt shook his head. He remembered Plan B from their pre-planning, but there was no way that would work now. They'd lost the element of surprise for both Plan A and B.

Eastwood saw the confusion in his eyes and patted his shoulder.

"A new Plan B. With a bang, buddy."

Frustration simmered in Montcourt's hazel eyes as he waited to be enlightened.

Griz spoke. "We're going over the wall and getting Moreno back."

Montcourt began to swear under his breath, each word sounding prettier in French than had he spoken English. But everyone present knew he wasn't spouting poetry.

The French marine raised his arms out in an all-encompassing posture as if to say, *"Well, of course! Why didn't I think of that?"*

"There are snipers on the wall who pass every four and half minutes. That is not enough time for all of us to get up and over, and if we take them out from down here, we'll set off the alarm and be overwhelmed before we can breach the damned wall!"

Griz grinned.

"Why the hell are you smiling?" Montcourt asked, astounded.

"Because of Plan B, Luc. Even if you'd already hightailed your insubordinate ass over the wall, the rest of us would still need a plan. Harry and I finagled the old Plan B."

"And just what is this finagling?" Montcourt asked, suspicious.

A loud explosion ripped through the jungle shaking the ground beneath their feet. Up on the wall, guards ran the length, their focus away from the team hiding in the overgrowth on the mountainside as they looked inward. The two guards Montcourt and Zigman had been watching screamed something to someone on the ground inside. Then, they ran off, disappearing from view.

Griz whispered orders to Mac, Zigman, Holiday, and Eastwood. "Get those grappling hooks up now!"

The men moved quickly, pulling spiked hooks attached to long lengths of rope. They got to the foot of the wall and began swinging. Up and over, they went. After giving them a tug, and making sure they were anchored, the ascent began.

Griz tapped Montcourt.

"Follow Diaz up. You two take two of the lines down the other side and secure the perimeter." He looked at Matt Rogers. "You stay down here with the prisoner. Keep this side secured."

"Roger that," Matt replied. He took the lead from Gil's hands and pulled Marcos down into the thicket of bushes

C'EST LA VIE, SOLDIER

and trees where he tied the rope around a sturdy trunk. Before Marcos could object, Rogers pulled a bandana from his pocket and shoved it into the man's mouth.

Montcourt was already up the wall, with Diaz clearing the top behind him, when a second explosion rocked the compound. They could see several buildings in the back ablaze and cartel soldiers running frantically in that direction, guns drawn.

"Quickly," Diaz said to the team before he and Montcourt dropped their lines over the other side and descended into the chaos within.

Chapter Seventeen

Moreno stared at the computer monitor, at the face of the man claiming to be her grandfather. She recognized nothing about him. The cold eyes and cruel twist of his lips bared no resemblance to the warm brown of her mother's own eyes nor her ever-present smile. She had no idea what her grandmother looked like having passed before Nastjia was born, but she felt sure that any woman in her family who fled a man like Oleg Nikolaev could not be so cruel or cold.

Her eyes narrowed. "What do you want?"

Oleg chuckled, amusement briefly lighting his dark eyes.

"You have your grandmother's fire." His chuckle died and he sat forward, his face serious once again. "I tried to beat it out of her, but an ember smoldered. She never could see the advantage of being my wife. A shame, really. She was quite beautiful but came from nothing. One would think the life I offered would make the woman happy. She wanted for nothing. Still, she ran, taking my daughter with her. My heir." His lips twisted with derision as his fist pounded the desk in front of him.

Outrage for the grandmother she never knew filled her. Moreno mimicked his posture, leaning forward until her face filled the inset screen on the FaceChat call.

"Maybe she didn't like being beat," she said. "Or maybe it was just you, you vile sonofabitch," she added, her voice dropping low as she replied in perfect Russian.

Behind her, Zadornov gasped. She could see her father out of the corner of her eye wringing his hands and shaking his head at her with vigor, his lips mouthing, *"No!"*

Grandfather and granddaughter stared at each other, neither blinking.

A sly smile spread across Nikolaev's lips.

"It is good you speak our language. But I suppose you learned it more from your American military than at your mother's knee. You asked what I want," he said, his tone deceptively calm.

"Yeah?" she replied, her face neutral.

"I want my heir," he answered, leaning back into his leather chair. "And since she is dead, thanks to sheer incompetence," he added, his words clipped and obviously directed at Zadornov standing behind her, "my granddaughter must now take her place. You, Nastjia Nikolayeva, will be brought here to Mother Russia, and you will take your place at my side. You will join the Vor."

Moreno's eyes flew wide, and she fought to keep her jaw from dropping into her lap. She had not been expecting that.

"The fuck I will!"

"And you will learn respect for your elders!" he barked. "One way, or the other. The choice will be yours how hard the lesson."

She pushed back from the desk and stood, ready to run.

"Zadornov, stop her!" Nikolaev shouted through the screen.

The henchman pulled a pistol from his holster and aimed at her head.

"Sit back down, Little Nikolayeva, or I will put a bullet in your skull!"

Thoughts raced through her mind a mile a minute.

"Great way to eliminate your last heir, *grandpa!*" she hissed.

"You will NOT kill her, Anatoly! If you do, you will suffer... and so will your family. Just detain her! I want her on a flight tonight. Get her to the jet!"

"Yes, sir," Zadornov replied. "And what about her father?" He eyed Juan Carlos.

Oleg Nikolaev could not see the man but guessed his placement in the room from the direction of Zadornov's stare.

"We do not need him anymore. Kill him."

"No!" Moreno shouted, then leaped into action, grabbing Zadornov's wrist as he moved to shoot her dad.

The two wrestled for control of the weapon with Moreno digging her nails into his skin as she kicked his knee.

The Russian screamed in pain and swung at her with his free hand.

"Subdue her, you fool!" Nikolaev shouted.

Seeing the henchman's intent, Juan Carlos found his courage and rushed the man.

An explosion rattled the windows, sending plaster flying from the ceiling all around them.

"What was that?" Nikolaev screamed, his face filling the screen, trying to see what was happening.

Zadornov's attention shifted toward the window. Moreno took advantage of the distraction and jammed an elbow into his ribs with a satisfying crack. She followed with a punch to his genitals, then ripped the handgun from his grasp. She rolled away quickly, shouting orders.

"Freeze, Ivan, or I will kill you!"

Zadornov clutched both his side and his crotch, tears welling in his eyes as he shot a hateful look in her direction. Her father still had the Russian's legs.

"Papa, get up! Move away!"

Juan Carlos released Zadornov and scrambled backwards, then found his feet.

"You will not get away, you know," Zadornov wheezed. "There is nowhere you can hide. Your grandfather will find you."

"Nastjia? Nastjia?"

C'EST LA VIE, SOLDIER

She looked at the computer as Oleg Nikolaev called her name. She stepped closer and turned the computer around until he could see her. Rage radiated from the face of the monster through the monitor.

"If you come looking for me, you will only find death," she hissed. "Yours!" Then Moreno pulled the trigger, putting two holes through the screen.

She turned back to Zadornov. "Get up!" She moved close enough to kick his side. He grunted, sucking in a breath. "I said get up or I'll break more of your damned bones!"

The Russian turned, getting on his hands and knees before slowly rising. He winced in pain, but his eyes shot daggers at Moreno.

"Now what, little bitch?"

She shook the tip of the gun toward the door. "Now you walk out ahead of us. If you try to run, I'll shoot you in the back of your head."

"You'll never get out of here alive," he huffed. "We will hunt you down."

"I'm not even going to point out the contradictions in those two statements, Ivan. Just walk."

Zadornov led the way out of the room back into the long hallway. As they reached the door to the outer courtyard, another explosion shook the ground sending debris flying.

Moreno was thrown down, as was her father. Seeing his chance, Zadornov ran.

Ears ringing, Moreno rolled and rose quickly looking for the Russian. He was gone, and chaos ensued all around.

Cartel soldiers ran toward the backside of the compound shouting instructions at each other. The only words she could pick out of the noise were *'attack'* and *'Americans'*.

She grinned and turned to grab her father's arm, pulling him up.

"I think help has arrived," she said, leading him away.

At the back wall, another explosion blew large stones in every direction. The barrier was breached. To her surprise, two men slipped inside before those thrown to the ground could recover. They quickly blended into the crowd of confused soldados. Even with dark bandanas covering the lower halves of their faces, she recognized them. Banyan's friend, Juan Hernandez, and the savior himself, Jesus.

"Looks like they went to Plan C," she muttered.

Jesus ducked and ran further into the compound with Juan at his six. For a brief moment, their eyes locked.

The big Mexican took in the man at her side and then nodded at her as he quickly pointed to the front of the compound.

She understood and turned to run, dragging her dad along. As they drew closer, she caught sight of men dropping down the inside of the wall from ropes.

Lucien!

Moreno's heart sped up and she pushed harder to reach them.

Shots rang out from behind her and in the direction she was heading. More cartel soldiers swarmed the interior of the compound realizing the new threat at the front door.

C'EST LA VIE, SOLDIER

She was nearly to Montcourt and Diaz when an arm shot out, clotheslining her. Her body jerked back hitting the ground hard, and she reached for her neck instinctively, choking and fighting for air.

A loud cracking sound filled her ears. Bone on bone. She whipped around in time to see her papa go down, his eyes dazed. Standing above him was the man responsible for the bruise on her jaw.

"Massey, you motherfucker!" she screamed, rising.

Massey smirked then let his hand fly, smacking Moreno before she could launch an attack.

Blood flew from her lip and her face stung as she stumbled, trying not to fall again.

Behind her, a spine-chilling war cry sounded.

The smirk on Massey's face died as he looked over Moreno's head.

Running at him at full speed was a man possessed. Rage mottled Montcourt's handsome face as he leapt not ten feet from Massey, landing on the man, his hands going around his neck.

The two men hit the ground hard, fists flying. Massey's large, beefy arms swung wildly and Montcourt's punches found their targets in Banyan's man's ribs, kidneys, and the sides of Massey's head.

Around them, Griz, Banyan, and the team strategically took out anyone who came near the two men fighting, creating a deadly perimeter. From behind, Jesus and Juan herded the remaining cartel soldiers toward that perimeter where they hesitated to go further. Eventually, the battle died down to just the two men beating the hell out of each other on the ground.

Moreno helped her father to his feet. Ben arrived and steered them both clear of the danger zone.

Once her father was in Holiday's hands, she tried to get to Montcourt, but Mac and Eastwood stopped her.

"No, Nasty. Leave off. He's got an ax to grind," said Mac.

"But he'll kill him!"

"And he'll deserve it," Eastwood said.

She eyed Harry with shock. "Lucien doesn't deserve to die, Harry!" she shot back, trying to yank herself from his hold.

Surprised, Eastwood turned to her. "Not Luc," he said, shaking his head, "Massey. Do you really think that big fucker can win against our boy? He's fighting for the woman he loves. Shame, shame, Moreno. Have a little faith in your man." He grinned.

Mac snorted. "He went berserk the moment he discovered you missing. Beat us all here. Yeah, he's gonna kill him alright."

Moreno turned her attention back to the fight. Her team and several cartel members were watching with sick anticipation. It was like a giant cock fight, but in this case, she had a vested interest in keeping her rooster alive. But how? Her heart pounded in her chest as Massey flipped Lucien over and punched him in the face.

She gasped!

Before she knew it, Montcourt throat-punched Massey and slipped out from beneath the overgrown traitor, then behind him, his arm coming around the mercenary's neck as he quickly unsheathed a large, sharp dagger from his hip. The French commando brought that wicked blade to Massey's neck as the crowd around them began cheering and egging him on to kill him.

A loud shot rang out over the jeering crowd.

"Stop!"

Banyan stepped forward, rifle in hand. He locked eyes with Montcourt. Behind him, Griz tensed, his own M4 now pointing at Banyan, his dark eyes fixed.

"The moment of truth, Jack," said Griz, his voice deceptively low.

Banyan froze. On the ground, Massey glared at his boss through swollen eyes in a bloodied face.

Griz continued. "He kidnapped Moreno. Either he was operating on your orders or..."

"He's a traitor," Banyan finished, then spat on the ground. He eyed Massey. "What the fuck were you about? Why?"

A slow smile split Massey's face, showing no remorse. "The Russians pay better."

Banyan's eyes narrowed. "And Marcos?" he asked, referring to Massey's partner.

The merc gave a tight shrug, still locked in Montcourt's deadly embrace.

"Easy enough to recruit. Like I said, the Russians pay better."

"Fuck," Banyan whispered. He stepped back and turned to Griz. "I'm sorry, friend. This wasn't my doing, but he's one of mine and I take full responsibility." Then he glanced over his shoulder at Montcourt. "We both have a reason, but yours seems greater," he added, glancing at Moreno. He looked at Massey one last time, then nodded at Montcourt. "Go ahead. Kill him."

Montcourt sneered.

"With pleasure," he replied. Leaning closer, Montcourt whispered, "This is for laying hands of the woman I love!" Then, he jerked the blade across Massey's neck.

Blood sprayed out drenching the hardpacked soil. Massey gurgled, his hands uselessly flying up around his neck as he choked. The life drained from his eyes as his lids fluttered and closed, his body slumping to the ground.

Montcourt stood, panting, and wiped the bloodied dagger against his pants leg. Before he could get it sheathed, Moreno ran to him, throwing her arms around his neck.

"Lucien!" she whispered into his neck, tears stinging her eyes.

Montcourt wrapped his arms around her and held her tight. "Mon Amour." He buried his face in her neck and breathed in her scent. "I am sorry I was late," he said. "Forgive me."

Moreno kissed his cheek and pulled back to rest her forehead against his. "I knew you'd come."

"I will always come for you."

Mac and Eastwood looked away. Diaz coughed and swiped at his good eye. Ben Holiday cleared his throat and looked toward their leader.

C'EST LA VIE, SOLDIER

Leaving his face cover in place, Griz gave his men orders and then addressed the Colima soldiers.

"We're taking the woman and the old man. Anyone who tries to stop us won't see the sun set this day."

One of the cartel men stepped forward, the one Moreno met in the villa earlier. His white linen suit was now wrinkled and splattered with blood. Someone else's, apparently.

Victor Jimenez cocked his head and eyed Griz. "And who the hell are you to come into my home and bark orders, eh?"

Griz stepped to the man, looking down into his face. Deliberately, he spoke in English, although Moreno knew Griz spoke fluent Spanish.

"I'm your worst fucking nightmare. But don't get your panties in a bunch, Jimenez," he said, his American accent exaggerated.

Victor Jimenez tensed.

"That's right. I know who you are. Oscar's little bitch. Guess you got a promotion. Doesn't matter. We're taking the woman and the old man. I don't give a rat's ass what deal you have with the Russians, but I do have something to offer in exchange."

The crowd parted as Jesus joined them.

Jimenez looked up at the big Mexican who casually uncovered his face.

"Who the hell is this?"

Griz nodded at Jesus, then eyed Jimenez. "This is a present. He'll fill you in. Let's just say if all goes well and you cooperate, he's gonna save your ass from the badger," Griz chuckled. "Because Sinaloa isn't finished with Colima, and those Russians won't forget you lost their prize." Griz glanced at Juan Carlos.

"He wasn't the prize, gringo," said Jimenez. "She was."

Surprised, Griz blinked, but kept his eyes neutral.

Jimenez remained quiet, thinking hard. Finally, he nodded and looked from Jesus to Griz.

"I will hear you out," he said to Jesus. Jimenez turned back to Griz. "You, take your men and get out of here, and don't ever come back!"

"Gladly," Griz replied.

He signaled the team to move out.

Montcourt steered Moreno ahead of him just behind Mac and Eastwood. Holiday, Zigman, and Diaz brought up the rear.

Moreno looked over her shoulder, catching Jesus's eye. Quietly, she mouthed, *"Thank you."*

As they all slipped through the now open front gate, she could see Rogers in the distance, Marcos tied to a tree next to him. She had no idea how far they were from the trucks or even if any of them were still operational, but she didn't care. She'd made it out alive and they had saved her father. And once again, Lucien had come to her rescue. Despite everything she'd learned this day, it was the best possible outcome.

She turned and reached a hand back for Lucien, her eyes catching his. He grinned, reaching out. Then the world slowed down.

C'EST LA VIE, SOLDIER

Her father's face twisted in alarm as he shouted, pointing off to the side.

From the trees, Rogers cried out, "Shooter!"

Her fingers brushed Montcourt's but then his hand fell away. Shock filled his eyes and to her horror, blood bloomed across his chest spilling from a hole in his upper right side.

Moreno screamed and ran to him.

"Lucien! Lucien!" She tried to cushion his fall, wrapping her arms around his body.

All around her, shots rang out.

Griz, Mac, Eastwood, and Zigman located the shooter and fired.

Moreno spotted him, recognizing the second Ivan. Anton Kadyrov was turned into Swiss cheese before her eyes.

Ben Holiday ran to her, dropping down at Montcourt's side. He was working fast on Montcourt and calling out to her, but she couldn't make heads nor tails of what he was saying.

Holiday pulled something from the medical bag he carried and began packing powder around the wound before applying battle dressing. She watched, feeling helpless as Ben then removed a syringe from the bag and plunged it into Montcourt's arm.

She looked down into Lucien's face now cradled in her lap. He was trying to lift his hand, but failed.

She grabbed it and held on for dear life.

"Don't you die on me, Lucien Montcourt! Don't you dare!" she cried.

"Call in an evac now!" Holiday shouted.

Banyan called his standby while Griz contacted Jackson by SAT phone.

The world around Nastjia Moreno faded away to nothing. All she heard were the words that fell from Lucien's lips.

"I... love you, Mon Amour. It's okay," he said, his hazel eyes glazing over. "You are safe now."

Her vision blurred in a storm of tears.

"Lucien!" she screamed. "Please! God, please! Don't you die. I love you!"

Chapter Eighteen

Moreno sat in the quiet room, bent forward, her head in her hands. She was angry, relieved, and terrified. Angry at herself because it was her family drama that led to this moment. Relieved that by some miracle he was still alive. And terrified that this was only a short reprieve after learning exactly why Lucien was sent to PATCH-COM in the first place.

The monitor beeped assuring her that Lucien's heart continued to beat in proper rhythm. But his heart wasn't the problem. His heart was true and strong.

The problem, the threat, was his head. A cerebral aneurysm. And according to Ben Holiday, inoperable due to its location, information she'd nearly had to beat out of him. But she'd witnessed the fallout his condition caused. Lucien was on a blood thinner medication. Getting shot in his right anterior shoulder almost caused him to bleed out before they made it back to a hospital in Mexico City. If it weren't for the fact that Holiday was up to speed on Montcourt's condition and had the necessary items on hand to help his blood clot, she'd be sitting next to a casket instead of a hospital bed. Quick thinking, Prothrombin powder, and a Vitamin K shot saved his life. So did the Kevlar vest. Another bullet hit dead center of his chest. But it was her that Kadyrov had been aiming for.

As soon as he was deemed stable, they flew Montcourt, with Moreno by his side, back to Camp Lazarus and the state-of-the-art medical care provided by the DOD and medical contractors. The rest of the team were enroute behind them.

She rubbed her temples and looked sideways at him. His face was at peace and his breathing even. She took his hand in hers and kissed it, fighting back tears. There had been no opportunity to speak to Lucien since his injury. To make sure he didn't move and reopen the wound, causing a bleed out, doctors kept him sedated. And she had so many questions, like why he never told her about his condition, and why he agreed to come on this mission, or any mission knowing that the smallest wound could end him or a blow to the head could be the killing blow.

Moreno sighed, clutching his fingers. In her heart, she knew at least one of the answers. He'd come on this last mission for her, to help her find her father, and to protect her. He'd said so a number of times, and she'd ignored the deeper meaning because she wasn't ready to face her feelings for this aggravating, insane, annoying,

C'EST LA VIE, SOLDIER

loyal, sweet, and amazing man. In the beginning, she'd literally wanted to throttle him for his unwelcome teasing and unwanted attention. She'd dealt with enough of that nonsense with Alex Pavluk. But she'd never been attracted to Alex.

Lucien was different from the start.

As annoying as he'd been, she had to admit he was handsome. Something in those hazel eyes drew her in, and despite the words coming out of his damned mouth, his smile warmed her. The accent didn't hurt either. He'd followed her around like a puppy with its tongue lolling out. But when push came to shove, that puppy morphed into a guard dog that attacked anyone who threatened her. Montcourt stayed by her side and helped when she needed him and when she didn't, he kept her high on a pedestal, his penchant for saucy catcalls gentling into flowery and sincere compliments.

That's when everything changed. That's when she really noticed him. Or rather, her body noticed him, and her heart followed.

Lucien was the one constant in her life, and now he lay broken, wounded, perhaps beyond repair. And it was her fault.

Tears spilled unchecked down her cheeks, as she shut her eyes tightly, trying to hold them back. Pain filled her heart and squeezed the breath from her lungs. She couldn't lose him.

"Mon Amour, please... don't... cry."

Moreno gasped and her eyes popped wide.

Montcourt was awake, his hazel eyes slightly unfocused as he turned his head to look at her. The hand she held pulled free and lifted to her face wiping the tears away.

"Lucien! Oh, my God," she whispered, leaning her face into his hand as she covered it with her own. She sniffed, trying to control her emotions. Joy bloomed at the sound of his voice. "I'm sorry. I didn't mean to wake you."

A half smile tugged his lips. "Seems I've done nothing but sleep. Don't be sorry, Nastjia. I am happy to awaken with you by my side," he said, his voice groggy.

She didn't know whether to laugh or cry. Her body decided for her with an awkward watery chuckle.

Montcourt patted the bedside. "Come, Mon Amour, come here. Lay with me."

His softly spoken words insisted.

Moreno situated herself on his left side, careful not to jostle him. She stretched out on the small space and laid her head next to his on the pillow.

Montcourt wrapped his good arm around her and kissed her forehead, sighing.

"Much better. Now tell me, why are you crying?"

She didn't know where to begin, or how to put her thoughts into words; a conundrum for someone usually so forthright.

She chewed her lip, while he patiently waited for her answer.

"I thought I'd lost you," she said.

Montcourt gazed into her dark brown eyes. He could see the vulnerability pooling there, and the courage it took

C'EST LA VIE, SOLDIER

for her to admit that to him. His heart swelled. They'd come so far since their first meeting, and then a bullet had almost ended their story. When he'd first arrived at Camp Lazarus, he knew all the risks of this experimental spec ops unit and had accepted them. His life would end, one way or the other, and sooner than he wished. Then he met Nastjia and his world tilted on its axis. He'd found a reason to live, a reason to care. But his circumstance had not changed. He was still a ticking time bomb. It wasn't fair.

So, he'd done the only thing he could do and dedicated whatever time he had left to this beautiful, sweet, smart, feisty woman. In so doing, he'd fallen head over heels in love with her. Which was fine, he figured. Only he would suffer when all was said and done. But that is not how life works, he discovered. At first content to love her silently from an emotional and physical distance, he stood between her and the world. That resolve changed over time. The more he was with her, the more he wanted to be with her—in every way. He wanted so much more than to be a ghost at her side. He wanted to hold her, kiss her, make love to her, have babies with her, and live happily ever after. He wanted it all.

It was torture, and yet he condemned himself to suffer alone. Then he noticed a change in her too. She began seeking out his company, she blushed when he complimented her, and her body warmed when his gaze skimmed her curves. He could see her interest, sense her desire, and his own body screamed for more. The devil on his shoulder encouraged the connection, and now... Now she, too, was suffering.

His heart broke even as it soared with the joyful knowledge that he meant this much to her, that she would shed tears worried over losing him.

For once, the fast-talking French marine did not know what to say. Humbled, all he could manage was the only thing that mattered.

"I love you, Nastjia Moreno. And I am so sorry for worrying you. But you need to know..."

"I already know," she said.

One eyebrow cocked as he regarded her. "What do you know?"

Moreno splayed her fingers gently over his heart. "I know about your head, Lucien. I had to practically beat it out of Ben. I just wish you'd told me yourself."

Montcourt chuckled and closed his eyes. "Poor Holiday."

Anger flashed in her eyes. "It's not funny, Lucien."

He snorted. "No, not really. But you have to understand, Mon Amour. When I came here, I knew already the eventual outcome. I was at peace with it. And then I saw you..."

She leaned up on her elbow, looking down into his face. "And?"

He opened his eyes and smiled, shaking his head. "And I was a goner for sure. How could I not fall in love with you?" He reached up, caressing her cheek.

The heat of his touch seeped into her soul. "You should have told me. You should never have come to Mexico City—"

C'EST LA VIE, SOLDIER

"That's why I didn't tell you, Nastjia," he said, cutting her off. "You needed me. You needed me in your corner, at your side, between you and any threat. And not because you could not handle it. I know better than anyone how capable you are, Mon Amour. It's why I love you so much. But that is also why I had to come, because I love you so much. For as long as I have breath, I will not let anything happen to you, and for as long as my heart beats, you will have me in your corner, and at your side, standing between you and this world... if you will let me," he said, his hazel eyes growing suspiciously moist.

His words took all the hot wind out of her sails. What could she say to that? And why would she? Never in her life did she expect to find someone who loved her enough to put his own life on the line for hers. It was the stuff of fairytales she'd never bothered to read. He was her very own Prince Charming, but for how long?

That thought was like a bucket of cold water brutally thrown in her face.

"There has to be a way to fix your head, Lucien. Some kind of surgery..."

He sighed, his hand cradling her cheek. "No, Mon Amour," he shook his head sadly. "That was the first thing the doctors addressed when the aneurysm was discovered. I'd just come back from a mission with a concussion. I had an MRI, and it was then we found this ticking time bomb in my brain. There were more tests, more imaging. It's in a precarious spot. To get to it is already dangerous. To remove it without rupturing the artery is impossible.

I would die on the operating table, and that is not how I wish to go."

Moreno squeezed her eyes shut trying to block out the pain of his words. Of course, that is not how Lucien Montcourt would die. The man was larger than life, a true friend to those around him, a teammate, a warrior, a hero. Her hero. And she couldn't imagine losing him.

"But it's not right. I just found you. I love you," she said, her voice catching as a fresh round of tears filled her eyes.

Montcourt pulled her close and kissed her with every ounce of love in his heart, stealing her breath. She loved him. She'd said it. This amazing woman loved him. It was more than he could have hoped for in this miserable life. Him, an accomplished flirt, an occasional scoundrel, a rebellious soldier son of an unfaithful ambassador father. She loved him. He could die a happy man right now, but it was the last thing he wanted.

The kiss turned heated, and although vital parts of him were not injured and happy to rise to the occasion, the part that was injured began to complain with a sharp, jabbing pain. He pulled back and kissed the tip of her nose, smiling.

"You have made me the happiest of men, Nastjia Moreno."

Overcome, Moreno sighed. "You make me happy too. But what do we do now, Lucien? I mean—"

"I know," he whispered, placing a finger over her lips. "We live, Mon Amour. It is all we can do. And I have an idea."

C'EST LA VIE, SOLDIER

"What?"

He grinned. "Looks like I will have some time off," he said, glancing at his bandaged shoulder.

Moreno let her free hand sink into his hair as her fingers caressed around his ear. "More than a little, I'd think."

The tingles in his scalp spread down his spine. "Once I am on my feet again, what do you say we get away from here for a while? I'm sure Major Maxwell would approve leave time for you considering all you've been through."

She liked the sound of that. "Where will we go?"

Montcourt gazed into her eyes. "To my home… to France."

Chapter Nineteen

The third weekend after Moreno and Montcourt returned to Camp Lazarus, Nastjia left base with Mac. He and Connie had taken her father in following his debriefing with the FBI and DEA. Juan Carlos Moreno no longer had a home in New Mexico, and after all he'd been through, had no desire to return. She didn't want him to leave either, so with the help of her teammates, a temporary solution was decided upon. Mac offered to take Mr. Moreno in, declaring he and Connie had a spare room, and Connie was home so she could help Moreno's dad settle in. Ben Holiday and Irina checked in on him to monitor his health and aid in getting him back to peak physical condition beginning with putting on some weight.

Moreno was beyond grateful. It brought a lump to her throat seeing how her new team at PATCH-COM had, somewhere along the way, become her family.

Although she knew he was in good hands, he was still her father, and she needed to check in on him and do whatever she could to get him settled into his own place soon. Especially since she would be leaving for Paris in ten days.

Major Maxwell had approved hers and Lucien's leave for two weeks. She found she was excited about the trip having never visited France. She would see Lucien's home, a place he described as the most beautiful place on earth.

So, she needed this time with her father to reconnect.

The past few weeks had been brutal. Between the agony of Montcourt's seemingly slow recovery from the gunshot wound to the ass-awkward and uncomfortable grilling she sat through—for eight hours—with Agent Peters going over every detail of her newly-discovered relation with Oleg Nikolaev, she just wanted to run away and hide. Where better than Paris with the man she loved?

Still, even she wasn't naïve enough to think she would be one hundred percent safe anywhere she traveled now that Russian mafia granddaddy had found her. Agent Peters and his contacts in the CIA speculated that Nikolaev had not known until three weeks ago that Moreno was in the United States military. His interview with her father seemed to confirm that. Juan Carlos had refused to tell the two Ivans anything about his daughter. He'd done all he could to protect her, which is why they held onto him for so long. He was bait. Since they had no leads to find her beyond a public birth certificate, they figured she would eventually come looking for him. As time passed, that hope grew dim, and their prisoner was forced into servitude.

It was a stroke of luck when their double agent, Massey, reported that a U.S. spec ops team was enroute to Mexico to rescue a man named Juan Carlos Moreno from the Colima cartel. And when he shared one of the team members was Moreno's daughter, the Ivans immediately informed Nikolaev.

That information was beaten out of Marcos by Banyan and passed along to Griz.

What happened to Marcos after, well, Banyan said only that the man was "out of commission," whatever that meant. Moreno didn't want to know. It no longer mattered.

But she was aware that a new threat existed in the world aimed in her direction. She'd pissed off one of the most brutal monsters in the underworld. Her tenuous genealogical relation was probably not enough to save her from retaliation should he ever get his hands on her. He'd all but said so—before she put two bullets through that computer monitor.

Her main goal now was to protect Lucien. Whatever time he had left would be spent living, laughing, and loving. She sniffed back a tear and smiled. How she could be both happy and sad at the same time was a mystery. But it was the median she found herself occupying for now.

When Mac pulled his truck into the driveway, Moreno found she couldn't wait to see her dad. They had a lot to discuss, but now, she just wanted to throw herself into his arms like she used to as a child.

Mac clicked the button on the garage door opener and pulled inside.

Moreno got out and pulled her weekend bag from behind the seat.

Mac pulled a bag of dirty laundry from the bed of the truck and shouldered it as they headed for the door to the kitchen.

Inside, the house smelled like cumin and chili and corn. It smelled like her dad's chicken tortilla soup. It smelled like home.

Tears stung Moreno's eyes as a smile spread across her face.

"Mija, you're here!"

At the sound of his voice, she turned. Dropping her bag to the side, she flung herself into his open arms.

"Papa!"

Mac watched father and daughter reunite before greeting Connie with a grin and a searing kiss.

"Miss me?" he murmured.

Connie's cheeks pinkened as she hid her face from Nastjia and Mr. Moreno. "Of course, but honey..." She glanced at their guests.

Mac chuckled low and whispered in her ear. "You can show me later." He nipped her neck and squeezed her butt before letting her go.

"Gerry Maclean!" she squealed. "Go put that in the laundry room," she said, pointing down the hall, "and then get cleaned up. Juan Carlos made us dinner."

"I figured," Mac replied. "Smells damn good." He waved at Mr. Moreno and then headed down the hall.

Connie turned to Moreno and gave her a big hug. "How are you, Nastjia?"

"I'm good now that I'm here."

"And Lucien? How is he?" Connie asked.

Moreno bit her lip and sighed. "It's been slow going but he's much better," she replied. Nastjia knew Connie was asking in regard to Lucien's gunshot wound. No one outside of a handful knew his real condition. At present, those in the loop were herself, Ben Holiday, Mac (because he had to pull her off Holiday after the heart-stopping drama of the medical evacuation from the cartel compound), Major Maxwell, Doctor Joely Winter Tyler, and the medical staff at Camp Lazarus. She wasn't sure about Griz, but she hadn't brought it up in front of him, and he'd kept quiet, only inquiring often about the injury Montcourt sustained in the field.

Lucien hadn't wanted anyone to know, didn't want his team to treat him any differently. She was trying to honor that while navigating what she now knew were his needs to cope with an aneurysm.

"In fact," she continued, "we're taking leave in ten days and going to Paris." Moreno looked back at her dad in the kitchen as Connie gasped, her delight obvious.

"I knew it! I knew you two would get together eventually." Connie leaned over and hugged Nastjia again. "Oh, sweetie, how exciting!"

Juan Carlos put the big spoon down on the counter and regarded his daughter with worried brown eyes.

"Mija, I don't think it's wise—"

Moreno threw her father a quelling look and a quick shake of her head. He closed his mouth and turned back to the pot, staring down into the soup.

"I mean, who is this man you're going off with?" he said, changing the subject.

Nastjia got up and went to stand beside him. "You met him at the compound. He's the one who stopped Massey."

Juan Carlos took a deep breath. "The one who killed him." He picked up the wooden spoon and began stirring the soup once again. "He's violent," he mumbled.

Nastjia reached for his hand, stopping him.

"You don't know him, papa. Lucien didn't just kill that man for giggles." She sighed, then looked her father in the eye. "Massey nearly killed Mac to kidnap me. He beat me unconscious then took me to the compound, all because he was working for those Russian monsters. He had no honor, papa. He wasn't a good person. And in my line of work, monsters get taken down."

Juan Carlos blinked at the moisture stinging his eyes. "He was the one who put those bruises on your face."

"Yes."

Fury filled her father's eyes. "Then I am grateful to this Lucien. But mija, going off with him, it's unseemly."

C'EST LA VIE, SOLDIER

Moreno stifled a laugh. It was the first genuine moment of humor she'd experienced in a long time. Here she was, a grown woman, the first female Navy SEAL, and now a member of an experimental spec ops unit for wounded warriors, and her dad was chastising her for wanting to take a vacation with a boy. It was downright funny.

There was no arguing with him. Her dad was her dad and no matter how old she got, he would probably always see her as his little girl. It was absurd, so much so she grinned and threw her arms around his neck, hugging him tight.

"Oh, papa, I love you so much." She sniffed back tears and chuckled. "I've missed you so."

Mac returned to the kitchen in time to see father and daughter embracing and laughing. He looked at Connie, about to ask what was going on, only to see tears running down his woman's face even as she smiled. He knew better than to ask then. Instead, he took Connie into his arms and kissed her cheek.

When the silence became awkward, he cleared his throat. "We gonna eat dinner or what?"

Moreno laughed and pulled away.

"Yes, Mac. Where are your bowls?"

"I'll get them. You sit down. You're our guest," Connie said, moving past Moreno and reaching into the overhead cabinet.

"At least let me get the drinks," Moreno insisted.

"Beer is in the fridge, Nasty," said Mac, pointing. "Koozies in the drawer next to it."

"Perfect! Papa, you ready for a cold one?"

"Thank you, mija, yes."

Moreno grabbed the drinks. Her father and Connie filled bowls with his homemade chicken tortilla soup topped with crispy baked corn tortilla strips and a dollop of sour cream, and together, they enjoyed the food, the drinks, and the company of friends and family. For tonight, at least, Moreno could forget that a murderous Russian mafia thug was still looking for her, could forget that monster was her grandfather.

After Mac and Connie retired for the evening, Moreno changed into her pajamas and brushed her teeth. When she came back into the living room, the sofa bed was already pulled out and made up for her. She climbed in, removed her prosthetic, and pulled the covers over her legs, leaving her foot out for temperature control. The pullout wasn't bad. Moreno adjusted the pillow beneath her head and stared up at the ceiling. She'd yet to turn off the lamp on the side table.

"Mija, are you asleep?"

Her father's voice came from the doorway of the spare bedroom.

She sat up. "Papa? No, I'm still awake. Are you okay? Do you need anything?" she asked, turning to get up.

C'EST LA VIE, SOLDIER

"No, no." He stepped into the living room and walked to the easy chair next to the sofa. "I was hoping we could talk. Just me and you."

Moreno nodded and scooted up, sitting with her back against the sofa cushion.

"Sure. What is it?"

Juan Carlos sat on the edge of the dark gray easy chair, looking down at the carpet, collecting his thoughts. The prosthetic foot caught his eye and he reached to pick it up, turning it in his hands. A sad smile touched his lips.

"I can't believe this happened to you."

Moreno nodded. She couldn't believe it most days, either. She'd been riding a high, one that made her both cocky and a bit careless. Being the first woman to pass BUD/S and SQT, and then making it all the way to receiving her Trident, being designated a United States Navy SEAL, had boosted her ego to the stratosphere. Then, on her very first mission, she lost it all. She was the last operator to climb into the Zodiac as her team narrowly escaped capture by a Pakistani Special Services Group off the coast of Karachi in the Arabian Sea. The boat was already moving when she swung her right leg up. She couldn't get her grip quick enough before her body slipped back in. Her left leg, still hanging down in the water, was pulled toward the motor. If her teammates hadn't reached down to haul her in, she would certainly have died then and there.

As it was, the rotors nearly cut her left foot off. When the Zodiac rendezvoused with an American carrier near Oman, she'd been first stabilized, then air-evac'd out to the closest medical base where doctors finished the job the boat rotors started.

Moreno sniffed, swallowing the memory. "I got through it."

Juan Carlos clutched the 'foot'.

"I should have been there. I should have been there no matter what." He looked at her. "You needed me."

The lump in her throat threatened to choke her. The tears she held back began to fall.

"I did. I did need you, papa. I'm so sorry. I was so angry. I should have looked for you sooner!"

He dropped the prosthetic and went to his daughter, wrapping his arms around her.

"I'm sorry, baby," he crooned, kissing the top of her head. "None of it was your fault. I'm sorry for all of it. You shouldn't have gone through that alone. You're so brave, mija, so strong. I'm so proud of you."

Father and daughter held each other, healing tears flowing.

Finally, her papa began to speak.

"I need to explain so much, but first, I need to tell you what happened." He looked down into her eyes. "I never abandoned you, Nastjia. I would never leave you. Never!"

He told her the tale, about coming home from work one afternoon and finding the two Ivans in the house. They'd wrecked the place in search of any clues to her whereabouts, and when they didn't find anything, they tortured him for hours. He'd suffered terribly but refused to tell them what they wanted to know. Instead, he'd told

C'EST LA VIE, SOLDIER

them a lie, that his daughter had left long ago, a troubled girl after losing her mother, and he'd not seen or heard from her since.

At first, they didn't buy his story, but decided to take him with them and use him as bait.

The Ivans had his house packed out and his things taken away after, a detail Juan Carlos had not known until Nastjia told him. But one thing he did know was that they never found the photo albums and personal items he'd hidden years before beneath the floor in the kitchen.

Moreno turned to her father. "Do you think all that stuff is still there?"

Juan Carlos shrugged. "Unless whoever lives there now tore up the flooring, probably."

"Mama's pictures," she whispered.

Her father nodded. "And all the photos of you from the time you were a baby."

She knew then she needed to get those back. How was another dilemma. It would be really awkward to knock on a stranger's door and ask to dig up their kitchen floor. But right now, she was just glad she had her father back, safe and sound.

"I don't think it would be safe to go back there, papa. Not yet."

"Agreed. Those Russian thugs won't stop looking for you, not while old Oleg is alive and determined to have his heir."

She shook her head. "Well, Zadornov, anyhow. Kadyrov is dead."

"Yes," her father grunted. "Evil scum, that one. Worse than the first Ivan. At least he tried to act civilized. The other one was nothing but an animal."

"I can't believe mama's father is the leader of the Russian mafia. That's crazy!"

Her papa huffed. "She didn't have many memories of him, but she told me that ones she did remember weren't good. She said her mother was always living in fear until the day she passed."

"I wished I'd known her."

He looked at his daughter. "From everything Nadia told me, Elena was a very strong woman. I believe you get your strength from her."

It was high praise, and for once, she accepted it. It meant she had something from this courageous grandmother who defied a dangerous criminal to save herself and her daughter. That was badass in her opinion.

Moreno smiled and snuggled into her papa's side.

He leaned his head on hers.

"Tell me about your young man," he said, "since you seem to be keen on running off with him."

Moreno chuckled. It amused her how he sounded both curious and grouchy about his daughter having a man in her life, even though she was almost thirty.

For the next hour, she filled him in on Lucien Montcourt. By the end of the telling, Juan Carlos had switched his allegiance to the beleaguered French marine saying any man who would put up with what she'd put him through,

C'EST LA VIE, SOLDIER

and had saved her twice, deserved his sympathy... and his respect.

Chapter Twenty

Moreno couldn't hide her excitement. Her first sight of Paris from the window of the Boeing 787 was exactly how she'd pictured it. It was a bright blue morning and she and Lucien had only just awakened from a halfway decent slumber on the overnight flight. After quickly brushing her teeth and splashing cold water on her face in the tiny lavatory, she'd been served a hot breakfast of scrambled eggs, toast, and fruit.

Next to her, Lucien devoured his eggs, a sure sign of his recovery. Once the cabin crew cleared away the breakfast trays and the 'Fasten Seat Belts' sign lit up, Montcourt leaned over and pointed out the window just as Paris, in all her morning glory, came into view.

"I will show you everything," he whispered, then kissed the side of her neck playfully.

Moreno grinned, then reached up to touch his face. "Remember what the doctor said, Lucien," she admonished. "No getting too worked up." She cocked an eyebrow.

A slow sexy smirk slid across his lips. He lifted her hand to his lips and dropped soft, hot kisses on her fingers. "He said no such thing, Mon Amour. What he did say was to avoid stress and to rest. I have no stress with you," he smiled. "And I plan for us to *rest*... a lot."

He shot her the look that always set her lady parts on fire. It did not fail this time either. Memories of their brief encounter in the outdoor shower in Mexico flitted through her mind. That didn't help the situation. Problem was, she was caught between her desire for him and her need to protect him from harm. She definitely wanted to be with him, but what if, God forbid, they had sex and his aneurysm burst? The thought haunted her and threw cold water all over her amped-up libido.

"We'll see," she murmured.

Not only did the thought of his health cool her jets, Lucien had also mentioned they would be staying at his family home. She was a little too old for fooling around with a parent in the house. Still, he'd insisted it would be fine, but she hated the thought of intruding. Close quarters did not inspire romance no matter what city they happened to be in.

"Are you sure it's okay with your mom for me to stay? I mean, I could get a hotel room..."

Montcourt eyed Nastjia and chuckled. "Mon Amour, I already told you, there is plenty of room and it is no inconvenience. Ma Mère is very excited to meet you. You will see," he said, stroking her fingers, "you worry for nothing."

Moreno sighed. "If you say so."

"I say so," he grinned. He leaned over, looking out the window once again. As the plane touched down, Lucien kissed her cheek. "We are here!"

His excitement was contagious. Moreno laughed as they waited impatiently for the plane to pull up to the gate. It was her first time in Paris, and she was in love. It was a fairytale come true and she couldn't wait to begin exploring the city and sharing it all with Lucien.

The ride from Charles de Gaulle Airport to the neighborhood of Saint Germain in Paris was filled with much to see. Moreno marveled at the sights, the architecture, and the people going about their day. She learned the proper term for the neighborhoods comprising Paris was 'arrondissements', and the city had exactly twenty of them.

As they drew nearer Montcourt's home, the dwellings became far more upscale. Moreno's eyes widened in surprise before narrowing in suspicion as she turned to look at Lucien. When the taxi pulled through a set of gates and circled a large drive, her mouth dropped. The car stopped under a large stone portico.

She stared at Lucien. "I thought you said we were staying at your family's home. This isn't a home, it's a hotel!"

Montcourt burst out laughing before stepping out of the backseat. He offered his hand as she climbed out behind him.

They stood in the shade staring up at the four-story structure. It wasn't just one building, but seemingly three buildings joined together, built with white stone, columns, and ornate framing around more windows than Moreno could count. It was huge and intimidating and beautifully French. She pursed her lips to prevent herself from snapping at him. Somehow, he'd failed to share his family was uber-rich, an omission that left her inadequately prepared to step foot inside this Parisian mansion.

"Lucien," she began.

He pulled her close. "Do not be afraid," he said. "It is just a house. My mother will love you, just as I do."

Moreno glared at him. "You should have told me. What else do I need to know? Are you royalty or something? Do I need to curtsy, because I don't curtsy, Lucien!"

Her anger had the odd effect of amusing him, but he knew better than to laugh at her. He'd put off telling her everything fearing she would balk, and he desperately wanted to bring her here, to meet his mother and see where he came from. Montcourt shoved those insecurities to the side. It was time to come clean.

"I grew up here, Nastjia. My mother comes from an aristocratic line dating back many centuries, so yes, one might have considered the Montcourts blue bloods in the sixteenth and seventeenth centuries, but today, it's more about appearances than aristocracy. My father came from

C'EST LA VIE, SOLDIER

a more provincial family, but he was ambitious. He married my mother, and the combination of his ambition and her lineage afforded him the opportunities to succeed to the seat of power he holds today; the French ambassador to America."

"What!" Moreno sputtered. Suddenly, the absurdity of their situation hit, and she bent over, laughing hard.

Montcourt watched, surprised by her reaction. "Nastjia, what's so funny?"

She straightened and wiped the tears from her eyes.

"Us," she replied. "Look at us, Lucien." Moreno ran a hand through her hair. "You come from aristocrats and my maternal grandfather is one of the biggest, most brutal gangsters in the world. We're a hot mess!"

He smiled, relieved. "Oh, I see. Well, seems neither of us can help who we are, only who we wish to be." He turned to pay the driver who'd taken their luggage out of the trunk and set it to the side.

The front doors opened, and a gray-haired butler emerged followed by a younger man.

"Welcome home, Monsieur Fornier," said the butler. The younger man nodded to Lucien, and then proceeded to grab several suitcases and carry them inside.

"Jacques," he replied, affection and mild irritation coloring his voice as he turned to address the man. "You know I prefer to be addressed as Montcourt."

The butler raised an eyebrow, then gave a short bow. "As you wish, monsieur."

Montcourt huffed, then approached Jacques and gave the man a quick hug. "It is good to see you, old man. Where is Ma Mère?"

Jacques pointed through the doors. "In the morning room, monsieur."

"You know you can just call me Lucien, Jacques. Why do we go through this every time?" Montcourt asked, a look of amusement on his face.

The butler ignored him, but there was a telltale uptilt of his lips. "Because it annoys you to no end, monsieur."

Hazel eyes rolled as Lucien chuckled. "It's good to be home," he said, taking Moreno's hand. "Jacques, this is Nastjia Moreno. My lady," he added.

Jacques smiled at Moreno. "A pleasure to meet you, Mademoiselle Moreno."

Moreno smiled at the butler, but her eyes sought Lucien's. After Jacques left them to carry on his duties, she asked the question burning on her tongue.

"Why did Jacques call you Monsieur Fornier?"

Lucien cleared his throat. He knew now there would be many questions this day from Nastjia. He'd left much unsaid in this past year, and now it was catching up to him.

"That is my birth name. Lucien Alexandre Fornier." He took her hands in his. "I know I have much to explain, Mon Amour. For now, the short of it is that my father and I do not see eye to eye, and because of that, I took on Ma Mère's maiden name. The less connection I have to Ambassador Fornier, the better. Later, when it is just you and me, you can ask me anything you wish. For now, I would very much like to introduce you to my mother. Oui?"

It was an answer, but she knew there was more to it. Still, now wasn't the time.

"Okay," she conceded. "But I have a lot of questions, so no more keeping things to yourself. I don't want any secrets between us."

Montcourt smiled as he gazed into her eyes. He could see how serious she was being, and he wanted to answer her questions, but the idea that they would finally be alone later, with no major summoning her, and no teammates to interrupt had him thinking other thoughts. He released her hands and slid his arms around her waist, pulling her body against his own as his hands slid lower to cup her buttocks.

"I agree. No secrets between us," he whispered, his lips hovering over her mouth.

The heat his words caused sent desire zinging through her. She swallowed, then gently pushed at his chest to put a little space between them. She needed air.

"Lucien, that's not what I meant," she began.

He chuckled, then kissed her nose. "I know, Mon Amour, but you are such a temptation. How can I resist?"

"Well, try!" she insisted, even as her lady bits ached for his touch.

The flush on her cheeks was satisfying to behold, and Montcourt relished the moment before tugging her hand. "Come," he said, his voice low. "Introductions first, and then later, I am all yours."

He took the steps up to the front door and led her inside the foyer. The sheer elegance of the marble flooring, the delicate crystal chandelier hanging high above, and the grand staircase leading to the second floor stopped her in her tracks. Montcourt turned to see her reaction, and grinning, pulled her along as Moreno closed her mouth before she caught flies.

"Come, Nastjia, it is just a house. My mother awaits."

Down the hall and to the right was the 'morning' room. It was a cozy room with floor to ceiling windows facing out onto a lush garden of pale pink roses, white lavender, and periwinkle blue Forget Me Nots. The room smelled like fresh brewed coffee and croissants, which happened to be sitting on a bistro-style table near the windows. Sitting at that table reading the morning paper was a petite woman with curly brown hair piled atop her head in a classic messy bun. The sunlight caught the strands of silver shot throughout and highlighted her profile. She had the same straight nose as Lucien, but her features were soft and refined. She wore a long sleeve, cream-colored blouse with a high collar edged in lace. The top was paired with blue slacks and matching heels. To Moreno's eyes, she was the very picture of upper-class elegance.

She didn't feel intimidated at all. Nope.

"Ma Mère!" Lucien exclaimed.

His mother turned at the sound of his voice, her eyes finding her son. A smile of pure joy lit her face as she dropped the paper on the table and jumped up, running to him.

C'EST LA VIE, SOLDIER

Montcourt embraced his mother, lifting her off the ground and spinning her around.

"Lucien!" she laughed. "You are home, finally!"

He kissed her cheek and set her down. "Hello, Maman. I've missed you so."

Moreno stood back, out of the way of their reunion. She had no idea what they were saying, their French language flying from their lips. She watched as his mother cupped his face, grinning even as tears moistened her twinkling hazel eyes, so like her son's.

"You look good, but a bit pale. What have you been doing? Not taking care of yourself?"

He shrugged off her words. "I am fine, Maman. Just a small injury weeks ago. It is already healed over."

"An injury? What happened?" His mother's face fell, and concern filled her eyes. "Lucien, tell me!" Her tone changed in an instant from joyful to no-nonsense. It was instantly recognizable to the ears of anyone who'd ever been a child—which is to say, everyone.

"Maman—" he began.

She shook a slender, manicured finger at him. "Lucien Alexandre, I demand you tell me at once! What happened? What have you not told me?"

Montcourt's eyes found Moreno's over the top of his mother's head before returning his attention back to her. "I got shot in the shoulder. I am okay, though. No need to overreact—"

It was the wrong thing to say.

"Overreact? Me? The woman who gave birth to you, the one you failed to call? What in this world were you thinking? Which shoulder? How did this happen? Lucien, start talking!"

Montcourt glanced between his mother and Moreno, realizing he would not get through this day without coming clean to both the women in his life, the only two he loved. It was almost comical, and against his better judgement, he laughed. His mother looked appalled, to which he quickly replied he would answer all her questions later.

He then switched to speaking English.

"Maman, I would like to introduce you to someone."

His mother turned, suddenly aware there was another in the room. Her eyes took in Moreno from head to toe, missing nothing.

Moreno squirmed beneath her gaze.

Montcourt stepped between them. "Maman, this is Nastjia." He looked at Moreno. "Nastjia, this is my mother, Marie Fornier."

Marie glanced at her son. His eyes were on the young woman, and what she saw reflected within told her everything she needed to know. A smile tugged at the corner of her lips. She stepped closer and reached out, taking Moreno's hands.

"Welcome to my home, Nastjia. You are most welcome here." She leaned in and kissed Moreno on each cheek, then stood back and smiled at her. Marie had yet to release her hands.

C'EST LA VIE, SOLDIER

Moreno cleared her throat. "Thank you, Mrs. Fornier. It's a pleasure to meet you."

"Oh, you must call me Marie. None of this Mrs. Fornier business. So very formal," she continued. "No, no, we shall be on a first name basis. How lovely to have you and my son here. We must get you settled in, but first, please, come sit and have breakfast. I had Jacques bring the coffee and croissants in here." She tucked Moreno's arm through hers and led her to the table. "So much to talk about, I am sure. Tell me all about your flight. Is this your first time in Paris?"

Montcourt watched his mother make off with his woman, chatting away. His heart swelled. It was the happiest he'd felt in a long time.

Moreno looked over her shoulder, catching his eye. She was smiling, but obviously overwhelmed. He knew his mother could be a lot to take. Marie Fornier was a very forthright woman, but then, so was Nastjia. It was no wonder he loved her. But he couldn't leave her to his mother's onslaught of questions. He chuckled and caught up to them, pulling out their chairs in a gentlemanly fashion before joining them.

Coffee was poured. Croissants were buttered and slathered with jam, and questions were asked, answered, and stories shared, including how he got shot, and how he met Moreno. When his mother was satisfied, she rang for Jacques who escorted Lucien and Nastjia to their rooms, sending them off with the promise to see them at dinner that night.

To Lucien's delight, his mother had placed Nastjia in the room next to his in a private wing far from motherly ears and eyes. He smiled as he entered the room next to hers, glancing her way as Jacques opened the door and waited while she stepped inside. The butler pointed out where she could find the essentials and explained she need only ring the housekeeper for anything else. Then Montcourt heard Jacques inform her of the dinner hour. He left her then and stopped outside of Montcourt's door.

Lucien was standing just inside, hands in his pockets.

"I assume you remember when dinner is served, Monsieur Fornier?" Jacques inquired.

Montcourt rolled his eyes. "Yes, old man, I remember," he said, one eyebrow quirked. "Did we not already discuss how I wish to be addressed?" Mild frustration laced Montcourt's words.

Jacques's face remained neutral, but there was a twinkle in his eyes coupled with concern. He approached Montcourt and gave his arm an affectionate squeeze.

"The name does not make the man, Lucien, the man makes the name. You are a good and honorable man. Those are the qualities that you bring to the Fornier name, just as your dear mother brings to it her kindness and compassion. She knows this and does not try to hide the pain of betrayal behind denial. One day, you must forgive him, if only to free yourself from this anger you carry around on your shoulders."

Montcourt sucked in a breath and then shrugged the butler's hand away. Jacques had been a part of their family all Lucien's life, and he'd always respected the man's views. He'd never known Jacques to be wrong about anything, but in this case, he just could not allow himself to forgive the sins of his father.

"Not today, Jacques. My lady is settled in?" he asked, changing the subject.

Jacques took a step back and straightened, once again every inch the butler.

"Yes, sir. She has everything she needs and anything else is only a phone call away."

"Good. Thank you." Montcourt moved to the door prompting Jacques to do the same.

"May I say, monsieur, she seems a fine young woman." The butler moved past Montcourt into the hallway, and with a nod, left him standing in the doorway.

Pain shot through Montcourt's temples, a warning of a migraine to come. He turned and closed the door, then sought out his medicine bag. He popped two pills and laid down on the bed, rubbing his head. The past collided with the present as his thoughts ran the gamut from his father to Nastjia settling in next door. With any luck, the pills would head off the migraine as intended, and he would be functional later. More than anything, he wanted Nastjia to have a good time, and for that to happen, he needed to be whole and healthy, or as much as was possible. He just needed a nap in this quiet room to heal. Tonight, he hoped to be in a different bed, with the woman he loved.

Chapter Twenty-One

Moreno was flushed. Each of the three courses served for dinner was accompanied by a different wine. That's when she realized she was used to the lower alcohol content of beer generally enjoyed with her team versus the higher octane in good French wines. Even so, dinner was delicious, and Lucien's mother was a wonderful hostess. She shared stories of her son's early years, much to his embarrassment, that shined a light on a much different Montcourt, one who was obviously the apple of his mother's eye. One aspect of his personality, however, remained consistent from childhood to the present: unapologetic mischievousness. Apparently, Lucien had gotten up to a lot of hijinks that often landed him in hot water with his father.

Marie shared that many were the times he'd run to her to avoid punishment. Of course, in her eyes, he could do no wrong. He was just a boy doing what boys do. She felt confident he would grow beyond his wild ways into a thoughtful, confident, and competent man.

"And I was right," she laughed, her hand rubbing his arm. She looked at Moreno. "You agree, Nastjia?"

Moreno caught Montcourt's warm gaze across the table. He smiled that slow, panty-dropping smile that always did funny things to her lady bits, a glint of mischief ever-present in his hazel eyes.

"He's certainly something," she replied, a saucy smirk on her lips.

Montcourt winked, acknowledging her words. Watching the exchange, his mother chuckled and rapped her son on the back of his hand.

"Behave, Lucien."

"I am behaving, Maman," he grinned.

"You are making dear Nastjia uncomfortable," she charged.

His eyes never left Moreno's. "Her beauty makes me uncomfortable every day. It is only fair to return the favor now and again."

Moreno blushed, her dark eyes glancing quickly at his mother in embarrassment.

"Lucien Alexandre! Stop teasing the poor thing," she laughed. Marie sipped her wine, then pushed back her chair and stood. "I can see my company is no longer required, so I will excuse myself. I have an early meeting with the Société de la Rose Blanche. We're donating fifty

C'EST LA VIE, SOLDIER

Lichfield Angel rose bushes to the new children's oncology hospital."

Montcourt nodded, offering his mother a smile. "That is a worthy gesture. The children will enjoy that. Nastjia and I know well the healing power of nature. Our own teammate, Mac, is quite the gardener," he said.

"It's true," Moreno added. "Growing flowers and such helped Mac with his PTSD better than years of therapy."

Marie shook her head. "So sad, these soldiers who suffer the traumas. Perhaps I can collect some seeds for you to take back to your friend, Lucien."

"He would like that, Maman. Thank you."

"Any particular type?" she asked.

Montcourt thought for a moment, and then glanced at Moreno. "The Chantilly Cream roses," he said, eyeing her. "They remind me of Nastjia's skin," he added, his voice dropping low.

Marie rolled her eyes, then reached out and patted Moreno's shoulder. "Good luck with this one, dearest. He has a one-track mind tonight." She leaned down and kissed Nastjia's cheek. "I bid you a good night." She turned to her son. "Lucien," she began, then sighed. "Never mind. I shall see you two tomorrow afternoon."

"You will see who tomorrow afternoon?" a deep voice asked.

Montcourt stiffened, then stood, his easy expression hardening in an instant.

Moreno turned in her seat in time to see a distinguished-looking man enter the dining room. He wore a dark suit in a shade of blue complemented by a burgundy tie. The hair was gray, and the face older, but she knew immediately that this could only be Lucien's father, the ambassador.

Marie's posture changed from relaxed to wary. She looked between her son and husband, her eyes alert. Without missing a beat, she approached the man and offered the customary double-cheek kisses. This time, however, her lips never made contact as they did when she greeted Lucien and Nastjia.

"Our guests, Louie. I have a morning meeting with the society."

Montcourt glared at his father. "What are you doing here?"

Ambassador Louie Fornier eyed his son. "I live here, Lucien. Where else would I be?"

"With your lover, or lovers, perhaps? Anywhere but in Maman's house," he replied, nostrils flaring. Montcourt looked at his mother. "What is this, Maman? How could you—"

"He is my husband still, Lucien," she said, cutting him off. In a more conciliatory tone, she added, "and we have come to a mutual agreement. He keeps his own rooms, and I keep mine. I have invested too many years into this marriage to allow its ruination, and of course, for political purposes, we must maintain appearances. Louie will keep his paramours out of sight," she said, turning her laser gaze on her husband, "and never again dishonor this family."

C'EST LA VIE, SOLDIER

Her expression spoke volumes.

Moreno watched the drama unfold as she sat in awkward silence. This, obviously, was the bone of contention between Lucien and his father. The fury rolling off Montcourt crashed into her like a wave. It was exactly the kind of stress the doctor warned him to avoid.

Quickly, she stood and stuck out her hand.

"Hello, I'm Lucien's teammate and friend, Nastjia. How nice to meet you."

The ambassador broke eye contact first, turning to her. Surprise lit his eyes revealing it was the first time he'd noticed her. His hard expression smoothed over, and his face relaxed into a polite smile. He took her hand in his, patting it.

"What a lovely name, Nastjia. Russian?" he asked.

"On my mother's side. Mexican on my father's side," she added. "Or simply American." Moreno smiled, pouring on an unusual amount of charm.

Ambassador Fornier chuckled. "I see. Teammate?" his brows quirked.

"Yes," she replied, leaving it at that.

Montcourt stepped up behind her. "A Navy SEAL, the first woman to achieve the honor," he said, pride coloring his words.

Fornier eyed his son, then returned his attention to Moreno. "And what is a Navy SEAL doing with a broken French marine?"

"Father!" Montcourt interjected, storm clouds gathering in his hazel eyes.

"What does that mean, Louie?" Marie Fornier asked, confused. She looked between her husband and her son.

In that moment, Moreno understood what a bastard Lucien's father really was, and it pissed her off. The man's choice of words needled, and implied he knew more than he was letting on. Perhaps he knew about Lucien's reassignment to PATCH-COM, information he could conceivably obtain using the power of his office. But did he know why?

All the forced charm fell from her face as she pinned the ambassador with a hard look. "There isn't a thing about Lucien that's *broken*. Or perhaps I'm broken too?" she goaded. *Say something, you prick. I dare you.*

"Nastjia, no," Montcourt said, shaking his head. He then stepped between her and Fornier. "In the library. Now!" He gestured that his father should follow him.

The two men left the dining room, and the women, behind.

Marie looked at Moreno. "What was that all about? What did Louie mean?"

It was clear his mother did not know about her son's condition, and Moreno knew it was not her place to share that information. She shrugged. "I have no idea," she said.

Marie paced, looking down the hall with each turn. "This is not good, not good at all. Those two will tear each other apart, both convinced they are right. They are both stubborn as mules and Louie cannot see his own reflection in his son."

C'EST LA VIE, SOLDIER

Moreno shook her head. As far as she could tell, they shared nothing in common beyond a physical resemblance. It was also not her business if Lucien's mother had decided to let her cheating shit of a husband stay in her house, but what was painfully obvious was that she failed to inform her son, and he was blindsided by the news.

"No disrespect, Mrs. Fornier, but I disagree. In the past year that I've known Lucien, he's exhibited only the highest qualities of integrity, honor, and loyalty." She emphasized that last word. "Thank you for dinner. If you'll excuse me..." She turned to leave.

Marie watched her go, her mouth agape.

Anger nearly choked Moreno as she walked down the corridor toward the foyer. She passed the library just as furious Montcourt burst through the doors and made a beeline for the front door. He didn't even see her standing there. She spun around and came face to face with the very reason for the destruction of what otherwise had been a lovely evening.

The ambassador stood, hands in pockets, glaring at the front door as it slammed shut.

"What did you do?" Moreno asked, ready to beat the man to a raw, bloody pulp for causing Lucien so much distress. She knew any upset could be his last.

He sighed heavily and looked at her. "He will not listen to reason."

She stepped to him, her shoulders squared, fists clenched. It took everything in her not to deck him.

"What reason? You come in here and rudely insult Lucien, in front of company, no less, and you call him unreasonable?" She spat her words.

Fornier straightened, his retort sharp. "This is my house, young lady!"

"And he is your son! You treated both with contempt!"

The ambassador's nostrils flared as he opened, then closed his mouth. Suddenly, he chuckled.

"You are quite something, my dear."

His change of attitude was disconcerting.

He studied her face, then nodded to himself, seemingly satisfied. Fornier pulled a card from his coat pocket, then handed it to her.

"What's this?" she asked, staring at it like it was a snake about to strike.

He pointed at it. "My private number. I have made arrangements with the only neurosurgeon in the world who can save Lucien. He is in Stockholm."

Moreno's face reflected her confusion. "I don't understand..."

Fornier stepped closer, his gaze earnest. "He will not accept my help, Nastjia, but a moment will come when he will have only two choices. Live or die. Maybe you can get through to him," he said, his eyes assessing her in a new way. "Maybe you are his only hope. Keep the card. If the moment comes... when the moment comes, this will be his only chance."

C'EST LA VIE, SOLDIER

She heard the break in Fornier's voice before she caught the shimmer in his eyes. Lucien's father knew about his son's condition, and that information most likely did not come from Lucien. That meant the ambassador had been using his position to keep tabs on his son... and he cared. He cared enough to find the only possibility to save him. Some of her anger dissipated as she realized the old philanderer had one redeeming quality, one she shared with him. They both loved Lucien.

She nodded and wrapped her fingers around the card.

"We'll leave in the morning," she said.

Louie Fornier reached out and gently touched her shoulder. "That will not be necessary. I will leave now and stay at my apartment in town. Take care of my son, Nastjia. He needs you." He gave her shoulder a squeeze, then turned to leave.

Montcourt walked the old path around the grounds of the house, anger eating at his soul. He wasn't even sure who he was madder at, his father for his disrespect and arrogance, or his mother for being a doormat. She deserved better, and yet she'd let the bastard back in after the pain and humiliation he'd caused with his tawdry affairs, affairs conducted out in the open with women more than half his age. It was disgusting. And then there was the usual bullshit from him, his contempt for Lucien's career choice, and now his brazen prying—which was surely illegal—into his medical records and once again trying to tell him what to do instead of respecting his decisions.

He desperately wanted to punch something. His father's smug face came to mind, and with it, a pounding at the back of his skull. The sharp pain nearly blinded him and Montcourt stopped in his tracks, squatting down, and touching the gravel beneath his feet until the wave of dizziness and pain subsided.

"Lucien?"

He heard her voice in the distance and struggled to stand, not wanting her to find him like this.

"Lucien?" Moreno called out again.

He took three deep breaths, and then called out, "I am here."

The gravel crunched as she approached.

He turned to her, the moon rising at his back.

"Are you okay?" Moreno reached for him.

Montcourt kept his hands at his sides and looked beyond her to the taillights now disappearing down the driveway.

"He left?" he asked.

She glanced over her shoulder at the road. "Yeah. He's gone."

His relief was instant. "Good. I am sorry, Nastjia, for my behavior."

She turned back to him. "You don't have a thing to apologize for. I don't know what all is going on between your mom and dad, but he had no right treating you that way. He's lucky I didn't rip his damn testicles off and feed them to him!"

Montcourt laughed at that visual. He would have paid a high price to see his father introduced to the nasty side of Nastjia. He slipped his arm around her shoulders and hugged her close.

"That you defend me like this means the world to me, Mon Amour, but it is not necessary. My father cannot hurt me anymore, not since I grew to manhood."

Moreno glanced up and saw the truth in his eyes. He could speak the lies to convince himself, but she could see the hurt all over his face. And also, the pain.

"Lucien, what's wrong? Is it your head?" Her concern was immediate.

"Just a headache," he said. "To be expected after all that disagreeable nonsense."

She wrapped her arm around his waist and led him back. "Let's get you inside. You should lay down and I'll get your pills."

She'd gone into nurse mode, and he had to admit, he didn't mind. He'd wanted her for so long, and now he had her, and he could do nothing about it. Not in this condition.

They made their way inside and up the stairs. Once she'd got him into bed, she left and returned with his pills and a glass of water.

"Drink it all. You'll need it. Staying hydrated is important when your headaches flair."

"Yes ma'am," he replied, smiling as he swallowed the pills.

She took the empty glass and set it down on the nightstand, and then she kicked off her shoes and sat on the bed, scooting him over.

Surprised, he asked, "What are you doing?"

She pulled her leg up and removed the prosthetic, dropping it to the floor, and then rolled onto her side facing him.

"Keeping an eye on you."

His heart swelled. He stared into her beautiful brown eyes seeing clearly how much she cared. Reaching out, he caressed her cheek.

"Mon Amour, I am sorry tonight turned out like this. I'd planned for a much more pleasant ending to our evening."

She smiled. "Oh, you did, did you?"

Pain thrummed through his head. "Oui. At least part of my plan has been realized. You are here in my bed," he said, leaning in to kiss the tip of her nose.

"So, your plan was to get a monster migraine and lure me into bed to keep an eye on you? Well, it worked."

He chuckled, then winced. "I am nothing if not effective."

Moreno gently ran her fingers through his hair, soothing his pain.

"That feels nice," he said, his eyes closing as the pills took effect. "I will make it up to you, Nastjia," he whispered.

His face relaxed and she realized he'd fallen asleep. She watched him then, free to let her eyes roam his face. His

C'EST LA VIE, SOLDIER

dark lashes were long and his nose straight. His lips were firm and jawline perfect. He was truly a handsome man, but more than that, he possessed an inordinate amount of honor and integrity. With her, he was a gentleman, a protector, a hero even. There was nothing more attractive in a man than that. And she wanted him, even though she feared indulging those desires might kill him. He was right that the doctor never mentioned sex was off the table, only stress. Still, sex could be stressful, couldn't it?

Moreno slid her arm around him and snuggled close. While she wasn't sure about the first, cuddling couldn't do any harm, and she'd dreamed of curling up next to this gorgeous man for some time now. Being close was a good thing. She would be there if he needed her. That was her rationale, and she was sticking to it.

Montcourt awakened first. The hour was early, and the sun was not yet up. The waning light of the moon cut through a slit in the curtains, but the rest of the room was in darkness. He could feel her arm around his waist, hear the sound of her breathing next to him. Her body was warm against his and her legs were entangled with his own. The one thing he did not feel was the pounding pain of the migraine he'd had earlier. The medication had worked its magic, or maybe it was the warm, soft woman he'd awakened to find in his arms.

That last thought brought about a different kind of pounding pain, one positioned much lower, and not the least bit unpleasant.

He smiled in the darkness and pulled her closer, his hand squeezing her firm buttocks before sliding up and slipping beneath the hem of her shirt. The skin of her back was silky smooth and soft to the touch. Montcourt inhaled the fragrance of her hair, a subtle floral scent mixed with something else, something uniquely her own. He leaned closer letting the strands tickle his chin and lips.

A sleepy voice interrupted. "Lucien, what are you doing?"

He grinned and let his hand make a return trip, skimming down once again over her hip and giving it a squeeze.

"Not stressing, Mon Amour," he murmured.

Moreno swallowed hard and tried to ignore the tingling sensations dancing across her backside. She looked up and touched his cheek.

"How's your head?"

Montcourt angled his lips beneath her hand and kissed her palm. "Aching terribly," he breathed.

"What? Do you need your pills again?" she asked, alarmed.

He chuckled and fully cupped her butt, pulling her hips against his.

"Not that one, Chéri."

Moreno sucked in a breath. He was hard and throbbing against her. Her lady bits reacted swiftly, demanding closer contact.

She opened her mouth to try to slow this freight train down, but hot lips took hers in a searing kiss that stole the air from her lungs. Her body caught fire as desire, forced into dormancy for too long, broke free from its confinement and burned along every sensitive nerve ending. Before she realized what she was doing, her leg wrapped around his waist and her arms wound around his neck.

Montcourt reveled in her response. Her excitement matched his own, and all he could think was that they were alone, in his bed, in Paris. No more interruptions. It was just the two of them.

Finally.

He'd waited for this moment for so long, but he refused to rush.

He kissed her, taking his time, nibbling, tasting. His hands now roamed freely but encountered too many clothes. His fingertips needed to feel her skin again. Slowly, he let his hands slip beneath the hem of her shirt, lifting it up.

Nastjia anticipated his intention and raised her arms high letting him remove the top. A blue, satin bra greeted his greedy eyes. Navy blue, of course. He dipped his head and let his lips travel down her jaw, over the arch of her neck, and down past her collar bone to the swell just above the silky material.

She sighed, stretching like a cat as he rolled her onto her back and settled between her thighs. Still too many clothes, but the friction and pressure as their hips came together was the ultimate tease. Like a match falling on dry tinder, heat spread from their cores like wildfire.

Montcourt watched her face in the dim moonlight cast through the break in the curtains as he thrust against her. The passion between them blazed as her hips met his thrust, begging for more. He sucked in a breath as the sensations nearly unmanned him.

"Mon Amour," he murmured, burying his face in her cleavage.

Growing impatient, he tugged the straps of her bra down, revealing hardened nipples as ripe as cherries. Unable to resist the temptation, he took one into his mouth, his tongue flicking across the tip.

Moreno moaned, sinking her fingers into his hair. "Oh, my God, yes!"

Happy to oblige, Montcourt moved to the other nipple as his hands gripped her hips and pulled her legs tighter around his waist.

"Lucien, please!" she begged.

He continued to tease her breasts, driving her crazy, but there was so much more to explore. Deliberately, he licked a line down her belly and stopped at the button on her jeans. On his hands and knees now, Lucien glanced up at her.

"Nastjia, tell me what you want."

C'EST LA VIE, SOLDIER

She looked at him like he'd lost his mind. *What did she want? She wanted him. All of him. Now!* She couldn't see enough in the dim light, but she was sure that twinkle of mischief was dancing in his eyes as he regarded her. He was drawing this out, torturing her, and she didn't want to wait anymore.

She sat up, and then placed her hands on his chest, feeling the muscles beneath. She wanted to see his bare skin, all of it.

"How about I show you?" she said, and then got to her knees, flipping him onto his back like she'd learned in SEAL training self-defense classes.

When she was on top, a wide-eyed Montcourt watched with awe and male appreciation as she first undressed him with a startling efficiency, and then sat back on her knees and removed the already displaced bra, her jeans, and the matching Navy-blue satin panties.

Through hooded eyes, he watched as she straddled him, gazing at every inch of his body and letting her hands roam.

Mon Dieu, elle est incroyablement sexy!

He didn't know how much longer he could control himself.

Her attention settled on the long, hard length of him. It bobbed and twitched, reaching for her. Montcourt closed his eyes and held his breath. If she touched him, he might just explode. He tried counting sheep, then realized that wouldn't work! *Sheep? For fuck's sake!* He was just beginning to silently recite the alphabet when wet, hot lips wrapped around his painfully sensitive head, and her tongue flicked across the tip.

His hips bucked. "Mon dieu! Nastjia, I don't think..."

She took him inside her mouth and sucked.

The groan that filled her ears was the sexiest thing she'd ever heard. She slid her hand around the base of the shaft and pumped, enjoying the sounds of his pleasure. She was so wet and swollen now, she thought she'd die.

"Christ, Mon Amour, you are killing me!" he breathed. He shoved his hands behind his head, determined to let her have her way no matter how badly he wanted to bury himself inside her.

She could taste the salt on skin and feel the tension in his muscles beneath her hands. He was at her mercy. That thought was the biggest turn on ever!

Moreno couldn't wait any longer. She pulled back and repositioned herself. When she felt him at her entry, she wasted no more time and dipped her hips, taking him deep within her folds. She splayed her hands across his chest, her fingernails sinking into his skin.

Montcourt held his breath, biting his lip to keep from crying out. She was so tight, so hot, so wet, so... perfect. His body tightened with desire, and he gripped her hips. Slowly, he opened his eyes. She sat atop him, impaled on his cock, her eyes closed, and lips parted. Her body moved in a rhythm that held him spellbound even as each thrust scrambled whatever was left of his senses.

"Si beau, Mon Seul Amour," he murmured, his voice deep. *(So beautiful, my only love.)*

C'EST LA VIE, SOLDIER

Hearing his words, she gazed at him through slumberous, dark eyes. A sexy smile tugged at the corners of her lips, and she thrust harder.

"Lucien," she breathed, panting now.

"Yes, Mon Amour, take everything. Take your pleasure. I am yours." He was getting closer to the edge. The scent of her sex was the air he breathed, and the sight of her skin glistening, her breasts swaying, and her hips undulating as her body devoured his hardness was forever emblazoned in his memory. It was every sexy dream he'd ever had of her except now it was real.

"Oh, God, I'm so close, so close," she moaned.

"Come for me, Nastjia," he demanded. Montcourt thrust his hips and reached for her breast, massaging the supple skin, and tweaking her nipple between his fingertips.

"Oh, yes. Do that!" she ordered, arching her back now.

With his free hand, Montcourt slid his fingers between them and found her nub. He rubbed in hard, fast circles.

"Oh, my God! Oh, yes!" Her body spasmed and exploded like a million stars being born.

Montcourt felt every single spasm as her slick walls gripped his shaft. It was the end of him. The climax hit with extreme force robbing him of breath. He gripped her thighs and thrust home one last time, spilling inside her.

She collapsed on top of him, panting.

He wrapped his arms around her shoulders, holding her close. When he could breathe again, he turned his head and found her lips, kissing her softly, sweetly, his fingers twirling a lock of her wavy, dark hair.

"I think you have killed me, Mon Amour, for this is surely heaven."

Moreno giggled. She placed her ear over his heart and listened. "Nope. Still alive." Silently, she thanked God.

"Good. I would hate for that to be both our first and last time." He sighed, content.

"Who said there would be another time?" she teased.

Montcourt rallied and flipped her onto her back, still buried between her thighs. He drew her arms above her head and held her wrists with one hand while encircling her breast with the other.

Surprised by his sudden move, her body warmed to his touch, and deep within, she felt him twitch and harden.

He stared into her eyes. "There will not only be another time, Nastjia," he whispered low, "there will be many more times." He nipped her bottom lip, then sucked on it. "Beginning now, I think," he said, then kissed her deeply, his hips rolling and thrusting and taking her higher once again.

Moreno surrendered. It was time to admit, if only to herself, she was his woman. And he was her man. Whatever time he had left needed to be lived, not managed. At least for tonight. Tomorrow, they would figure out next steps.

Chapter Twenty-Two

Moreno soaked in the large tub, the scent of roses bubbling around her. The last few days had been a honeymoon of sorts for her and Lucien. They'd eaten great foods, drank incredible wines, and made love with abandon. The things he'd done to her! She blushed at the memories. More shocking were the things she'd done to him. Her muscles ached in forgotten and neglected places, but she was happy.

"Mon Amour, are you still soaking? We'll be late."

Montcourt's voice cut into her reminiscence. Today, they were taking a train to a guided tour of the Palace of Versailles. In all, the trip was scheduled for four and a half hours, and they had a reservation for entry to the palace. She'd been looking forward to it since he'd surprised her with the tickets yesterday.

She pulled the plug to drain the tub and lifted herself to a standing position. Balancing on one leg, she picked up the handheld shower head and rinsed off. When she finished and reached for the towel, she smiled.

"I am here to assist, mademoiselle." Twinkling hazel eyes met hers. Montcourt stood outside the tub, the towel spread between his arms. He stepped closer and wrapped the towel around her and lifted her out.

Leaning into him, Moreno kissed his lips. It was a soft kiss, meant only as a thank you, but it grew into so much more.

"You smell of roses," he said, his lips against her neck.

He set her down on her good foot and let his hands roam with the towel, drying her back, her buttocks, her breasts. He lingered over his favorite spots, a sexy smile on his lips.

She looked down at the top of his head as he knelt to dry her legs.

Montcourt worked his way down one side, and then back up the other leg, his fingers slipping free of the towel to caress the soft, sensitive skin of her inner thigh.

Heat spread where his fingers touched and she inhaled slowly, trying to calm her racing heart.

"I thought you said we were going to be late."

He glanced at his watch and grinned. "We have a few minutes to spare, I think." He stood and lifted her in his arms once again and carried her to the bed. There, he laid her down upon the duvet and pushed her legs up over his

C'EST LA VIE, SOLDIER

shoulders. With a wicked glint in his eyes, he lowered his head and licked her.

Moreno's eyes rolled back as he showed her exactly what a Frenchman can do with his tongue. Trembling, she dug her fingers into his hair and hung on for dear life.

They made it to the train station on time. Barely. Montcourt eyed Nastjia as she sat next to him in the first-class car. Her eyes were bright, and her cheeks flushed. There was a thrumming awareness between them that kept them both on edge, in the best possible way. He couldn't resist touching her, holding her hand, kissing her lips, pulling her body close. It was primal, this driving need. She was his. His love. His woman. He was absurdly happy about it and wanted to shout it out to the world.

She was so damn beautiful, inside and out.

And he wasn't the only one who noticed.

Everywhere they went, men stared at her, their desire evident. He shot eye daggers their way and snarled at two. He would beat down any man who touched her!

Warm fingers intertwined with his and he was pulled from his thoughts.

"We're almost there, aren't we?" she asked.

He looked out the window. "Oui. Just around that next bend."

As promised, the station came into view. The RER train pulled into the Versailles Chateau – Rive Gauche Train

Station. Their guide, a young woman in her late twenties, wearing a jaunty red and white striped scarf around her neck, directed their group to exit the train and wait on the platform until everyone was assembled. From there, it was a short, ten-minute walk to the palace.

Montcourt stepped out and offered his arm as Moreno followed. They moved to one side and waited.

"This is exciting," she said, looking around with excitement. "And the weather is perfect."

Montcourt smiled. There was a nip in the air. It was always chilly in springtime in Paris, and cooler the further outside the city one went. But the sun was out, and the sky was clear. They were dressed for both the weather and the walk, wearing jeans, light sweaters, jackets, and comfortable walking shoes.

"It is," he agreed.

The group of around twenty tourists milled about the platform, all eager to begin the journey. Most were families with teenage kids and young adult couples on their first trip to France. Everyone was talking amongst themselves as they followed the guide off the platform and out of the station.

Montcourt passed two men on his right who'd stood quietly while they waited on everyone else to assemble. They didn't look like tourists. Their clothing was dark, which wasn't unusual. Both looked fit, one tall and lithe, and the other brawny. They wore hoodies and kept their hands in their pockets, but it was their faces that caught his attention. No excitement, just serious, their eyes watchful. In his experience, these were the types to avoid. Petty thieves and pickpockets were a pestilence in Paris. He kept Nastjia on his left as they followed the crowd and subtly reached behind his back, under his coat and sweater. Reassured that the Sig Sauer P220 pistol was snug inside the holster clipped to his waistband, Montcourt turned his attention back to the group, and to the beautiful woman at his side determined that nothing would ruin her day.

The guide led them down the Avenue de Sceaux along a tree-lined sidewalk. Cars passed as the group moved in two lines, everyone chatting, their excitement mounting. Large buildings came into view, their architecture majestic.

"Is that it?" Moreno asked.

Montcourt chuckled. "No, not quite. They are part of the outer grounds. We still have a bit to go. Wait until you see the lines. People wait for hours to get in every day."

She held onto his arm. "Good thing we're with a group and have a reservation for our tour."

"Oui."

She glanced up at him. "I wish this was your first time too."

He smiled down at her. "My father brought us here when I was a boy. It has been a long time. But it is my first time here with you, Mon Amour."

She grinned. "Well, there's that."

"It is all that matters to me."

A family of four passed them, the two children, a boy and a girl, punching each other in the arm as they ran ahead. The father, showing frustration, sighed, and shouted at them to behave and slow down. He gave Montcourt and Moreno a comical look of apology before moving around them and tugging his wife along to catch up to the kids.

"He should put them on leashes," Moreno joked.

"Your maternal instincts are an inspiration, Nastjia," he chuckled.

"I should teach a class—"

Tires skidded to a stop on the asphalt next to them. Montcourt turned at the sound, grabbing Moreno's arm to pull her out of the way of a black van. The side door slid open and a man with a scarred face jumped out. He lunged at Moreno.

"Nastjia, get behind me!" Montcourt shouted as he thrust her back.

The scarred man turned on Montcourt just as he pulled his Sig Sauer from its holster. Behind him, Moreno screamed loudly, then cursed a blue streak.

Montcourt spun to see the two men from the train station grab her arms. She yanked one hand free and swung her fist, slamming it into the face of the tall man in the hoodie.

A fist connected with Montcourt's jaw, knocking him off balance. He stumbled, then found his footing. He tackled the man from the van and rolled him into the gutter, bringing the butt of his pistol down on the man's head re-

C'EST LA VIE, SOLDIER

peatedly until he ceased fighting. Frantic, he pushed himself up and looked for Moreno. The brawny man grabbed her around the waist lifting her off the ground. He struggled to drag her toward the van. The taller one nursed a broken nose, blood all over his hands, but he gestured for the brawny one to move fast as he pulled out a gun and pointed it over his head, firing off two rounds.

The crowd around them screamed and ran in all directions away from the scene.

Montcourt had only a split second to react. He aimed at the tall one with the gun and pulled the trigger. Three bullets tore holes in the man's torso. The man looked at Montcourt, surprise in his eyes, before he fell backwards, hitting the concrete with a thud.

The brawny one stopped moving toward the van, his eyes first on his fallen comrade, then narrowing on Montcourt.

"Let her go!" Montcourt shouted, now aiming at him.

The brawny man hesitated, looking around Montcourt at the van for help.

Tires squealed as the van took off, leaving him alone.

Their eyes locked, one man's deadly, the other's determined and now desperate.

"I said let her go!" Montcourt ordered once again, this time stepping closer.

The brawny man wrapped an arm around Moreno's neck.

"I will break her neck," the man said. "Drop your gun and move out of my way!"

Moreno's sucked in a breath. The man's accent was familiar.

Russian.

She looked at Lucien. He noticed too, his eyes glancing at her before focusing again on the thug.

"My grandfather sent you, didn't he?" Moreno asked.

"Da," the brawny one replied. "And he will kill me if I don't bring you to him."

"I will kill you now if you don't let her go," Montcourt said, a sneer on his lips. "Either way, you die."

Police sirens wailed in the distance, growing closer.

The Russian began to panic.

"Either they arrest you, and Nikolaev has you killed in prison for your failure, or I kill you now, quick and clean," said Montcourt, taking another step closer. "Your choice. I know my preference."

"Stop! I will kill her!" the Russian growled, his eyes casting about, seeking a way out.

Moreno had clawed at his arm to no avail. He held her tight, one arm around her waist, the other around her neck. Her feet didn't reach the ground. Her options were few, but she had one.

She caught Lucien's eye and then glanced down at her left foot. She held up three fingers at the same time and began a countdown.

"You won't kill Oleg Nikolaev's granddaughter," she said, then kicked her prosthetic foot hard into the Russian's shin and jammed her elbow into his ribs. When he stumbled, she twisted loose from his arms.

C'EST LA VIE, SOLDIER

"Now!" she shouted.

Montcourt fired.

A bullet tore a hole in the Russian's forehead. His big body stood for a few seconds; not yet aware it was already dead. His eyes appeared confused, then went blank. He fell face-first onto the cobbled stones, dark red blood oozing into a puddle around his head.

Sirens surrounded them. Gendarmeries jumped out of their vehicles, shouting for Montcourt to drop his weapon and put his hands up.

Moreno got up and ran to Lucien. He held out his hand to stop her.

"It is all right, Mon Amour. We will straighten this out."

"But you're not the criminal," she shouted, then turned to the French policeman. "He saved my life! These men tried to kidnap me!"

The crowd, who'd run away when the first shots were fired, began to close in, many with their cell phones out, recording.

"It's true," one of them said. "We saw it!"

"Yeah. There was a van. Someone tried to take her. She's with us!"

The officer cuffed Montcourt and placed him in the back of a police cruiser. Another began taking statements. A third approached Moreno and led her away from the crowd.

"We will have to take you both in for questioning. For now, stay here."

She leaned against the cruiser, tapping her foot in frustration.

An ambulance arrived, the EMTs moving quickly to assess, then lift the one attacker out of the street gutter onto a gurney. He was alive, but unconscious, his face a bruised and bloodied mess. One of the EMTs lifted the man's hand up and placed it along his side before securing two belts across his body, strapping him down. One of the policemen then cuffed the unconscious thug's wrists to the gurney rails. As the tech inserted an IV, Moreno noticed his hands. Tattoos littered his knuckles. Five pointed stars. Prison tats. Russian mafia tats. Her grandfather had sent hardened criminals to abduct her. Two were dead. One was now in custody. Whoever else was in that van was now in the wind. That one had two choices left. Go back and tell Oleg Nikolaev they'd failed to retrieve her or run for the rest of his life always looking over his shoulder.

The adrenaline rush from the attack began to wear off and the shakes set in. She hated the shakes. Reaching up, she stretched, and then bent at the waist to touch her toes. Stretching usually helped calm her system. Not this time. Although the shakes subsided, anger set in.

She straightened and looked over at Lucien. He was watching her from the back of the police cruiser, worry in his eyes. It hit her that Nikolaev wouldn't give up. The thug who got away wasn't the only one who would be looking over his shoulder for the rest of his life.

Motherfucker!

C'EST LA VIE, SOLDIER

Something needed to be done, and fast. But her options were limited. First off, she and Montcourt needed to squash this police investigation fast. It wouldn't do to have media attention on the two of them. Especially since Lucien killed two of the thugs. She absolutely did not want to get reamed by Major Maxwell over this. Special Operators did not draw attention to themselves, even when on leave. Second, if the first could be managed, they would need to lay low somewhere for the remainder of their vacation. If this wasn't the very definition of the type of stress Lucien needed to avoid, she didn't know what was. She didn't have much time to consider. The officer returned to the cruiser holding Montcourt and, after having a brief word with another Gendarme, drove off. She held Lucien's eye until the cruiser disappeared in traffic. The officer who put her aside began walking in her direction. Before she could talk herself out of it, she pulled out her cellphone and the card tucked away in the case.

The phone rang twice before it was picked up.

"Yes?' a deep voice answered.

"It's Nastjia. I need your help."

Chapter Twenty-Three

Moreno sipped the now cold coffee from the paper cup in her hand. She'd watched the show unfold before her tired eyes over the past four hours. Local police in Versailles were pissed when a group of suits entered their station and claimed jurisdiction, taking over the investigation of the shooting. The suits in question came from two different factions. The first was a high-ranking secretary in the French ambassador's office, a gentleman named Henri Reno, who seemed to be a one-man cleanup crew. He was both arrogant and efficient in controlling the narrative on the day's events, a narrative agreed upon by the second of two other men in this group. He'd introduced himself straight off, shocking the police officers and their captain into stunned silence.

Maurice Touchard, Director of Interpol, Paris division.

The man with Touchard was his deputy director. Moreno didn't quite catch his name. She'd waited inside a room with a glass wall, sitting at a metal table in a very uncomfortable chair. She hadn't seen Lucien since she'd arrived, but assumed he was either in a holding cell or a room much like the one she now sat in. She could hear the back and forth between Touchard, the police captain, and Henri Reno. Picking out enough words to string together the conversation was difficult. French was not one of the languages she spoke. She was limited to English, Spanish, and Russian. Still, she gleaned enough to understand the police captain was angry, and Touchard didn't give one shit about that.

When the police captain threw up his hands and stomped off, Reno and Touchard turned in her direction. Interpol's deputy director left after speaking to his boss, and the director and secretary entered the room. Moreno sat up straight, wanting answers.

"Mademoiselle Moreno, I presume?" Touchard, a man with fine features bordering on delicate, approached her, hand extended.

She shook his hand. "Where is Lucien?" she asked, looking between him and Reno.

Reno held up a hand. "Not to worry, mademoiselle," he said. "The ambassador has already taken care of the situation."

"He has? How?" Moreno eyed them, waiting for an answer.

Touchard took a seat across from her, his expression inscrutable. "Ambassador Fornier and I have devised a suitable explanation for the press over today's events. A kidnapping attempt of a minor female thwarted by an off-duty French marine. Both names can and will be withheld to protect the identity of the minor involved." He gestured toward her. "And our own serviceman as we never reveal the names of special operators." He sat back and smiled, satisfied.

It felt too easy. "That's it? What about the witnesses?"

Reno glanced at Touchard, then looked at her. "Gendarmes already rounded up those who recorded the incident. Those devices have been confiscated and their data will be wiped. The witnesses are all being informed that since this involved a minor female, every effort must be made to protect her identity."

Who would believe she was a minor? Their tour group alone knew better. Moreno fretted.

Touchard leaned forward. "Yes, I gathered from my interview with Monsieur Montcourt, that it was of the utmost importance to keep your name out of this." He stared at her, his eyes taking her in from head to toe in a curious and calculating manner. "I have met a few of your American Navy SEALs, but I must say, this is a first for me. A female SEAL," he said, as if talking to himself. He cocked his head, watching her, his hard expression easing. "Most impressive."

Moreno ignored his assessment. She wasn't sure what to make of Touchard yet. She pivoted instead.

"So now what?" she asked.

The hard look came back into his eyes. "Now we must figure out what to do about your other problem, my dear, because a man like Oleg Nikolaev will not take kindly to having his plans thwarted."

She swallowed hard. He knew. Lucien must have told him, or perhaps it was the surviving Russian thug in their custody. A third option niggled. Lucien's father knew, the same way he knew about his son's medical condition and re-assignment to PATCH-COM, and he'd shared that intel when he involved Touchard. Either way, there was no use denying the truth. She had a feeling Touchard, despite his fancy suit, lofty title, and refined features, was not a man to mess with.

He reached out and patted her hand in a grandfatherly fashion.

"Do not worry, Miss Moreno. We have an idea." He glanced at Reno.

"I'm all ears, Director," Moreno replied.

He settled back into the chair, crossing his legs, and pulled a pack of cigarettes from his coat pocket. Lighting one, he took a long drag.

"Did you know the Russian mafia have different factions, like the Italians? Familias?" he offered.

"Sure, why?"

He puffed the cigarette and exhaled, setting it down on the edge of the table. "Never an ashtray when one is needed," he mumbled. "My point is that there is more than

C'EST LA VIE, SOLDIER

one *boss*. There are several, actually. And much like the Italians or the Mexican cartels, there is much infighting."

Moreno cocked her head. "And?"

"And there is one particular boss who has reason, and perhaps with the right drip of information in his ear, the motivation to break the Vors' rules and, shall we say, take care of the problem of your unwanted family connection."

She thought about what he was saying. It sounded very much like pot stirring a mafia war. Not that she cared, but destabilizing the Bratva could have consequences beyond the underworld. And there was always the possibility that if things didn't work out as the Director hoped, it could blow back on her in the most dangerous way.

"Explain it to me, because it's my life you'll be playing with."

Touchard gave Reno a look that said, *'Get out.'* The man stood and offered a nod in Moreno's direction. Apparently, his level of 'need to know' ended here.

"I will check on the ambassador's son. He should be finished with giving his statement."

After he left and closed the door, Touchard went into details, beginning with the story of Vladimir Brezhnev, known to the underworld as *'The Butcher.'*

At the end of the telling, Moreno understood that the boss known for cutting off the heads of his enemies had a deep grudge against her grandfather dating back to when Brezhnev was just a minor drug runner on the streets of St. Petersburg. It was all related to his abusive father, a dead brother, and the mother he revered until the day she died. It sounded like a soap opera, a brutal and bloody tale.

"Brezhnev is ambitious, but not foolish. His rise in the brotherhood has been a study in cold calculation. Coercing him into breaking the Vor v Zakone's most sacred oath, to never kill a brother without the sanction of the council, will not be easy, but that is not to say it cannot be done."

"How will you do it?"

"Not I, Miss Moreno. The plan is already underway. My part has been only in clearing the path and cleaning up today's mess. Also, to advise you that soon, you will not need to worry about another kidnapping attempt. Seems you have earned favor with a powerful ally."

She thought long and hard about that, but still was not quite sure what he meant. The only name that came to mind was Louie Fornier. But how could the French ambassador to the U.S. fix her problem with the Russian mafia? It was too much to fathom, and she was sure if this was the case, she wouldn't like the answer. And why would he? The only answer that came to mind was because of Lucien. Because Fornier knew she mattered to his son. She didn't like it, didn't like the idea of being the reason someone meddled with the Russian mafia. All her own father had done was marry Nikolaev's daughter, and that hadn't worked out well for Juan Carlos Moreno. It hadn't worked out at all for her mother. But it was out of her hands now.

"So, I do nothing?" It irked. Doing nothing was not her style.

C'EST LA VIE, SOLDIER

Director Touchard picked up his cigarette, which had burned down to the butt while he spoke and took one last drag. He stubbed it out on the table and blew out smoke.

"Not nothing, I should think. You are on vacation, oui? Take young Lucien home for now. The two of you should spend a few quiet days in the country, just until the news cycle moves on." He turned to leave, then paused. "And definitely stay out of Versailles."

He walked out, passing Henri Reno in the hall, who was leading Montcourt to the interrogation room.

He rushed ahead of the secretary, to her side.

"Mon Amour, are you all right?" His concern warmed her.

"I'm fine. What about you?" she asked, her hands reaching up to touch his face.

He placed his hand over hers and kissed her palm.

"I'm fine. Ready to get out of here."

He offered his arm.

Reno stood just outside the door leaning on the glass. Moreno glanced at the ambassador's assistant, then looked at Montcourt.

"I can explain..."

Montcourt sighed. "I won't even ask how you managed to get hold of him, but I do not blame you, Nastjia. Under the circumstances, it was the right call."

She nodded, relieved. "I'm glad you think so. I didn't know what else to do. Maxwell would have killed us both."

"We can talk about it later. Let's just get out of here, please." He took her hand and led them both past Reno.

"Tell my father..." he began. Montcourt stopped, his eyes filled with conflict. "His help was appreciated, for Nastjia's sake."

Henri Reno stood, hands in pockets. "I will relay your gratitude to the ambassador."

Montcourt eyed the man, then shook his head as he led Moreno out the back of the station house. A black sedan with official plates idled outside. The driver stepped out and opened the back door.

Moreno cringed. She felt Lucien's hand squeeze her fingers tighter the moment he saw the car. He may have spoken the words only moments ago, but it was obvious that calling his father for help was not fine. Not at all. She bit her tongue and waited quietly.

He snorted like an angry bull once, then headed to the car. For Moreno, it was a long, uncomfortable ride back to the house. She just hoped by the time they arrived, Lucien managed to calm down, before the stress killed him.

It was just past three in the afternoon and Moreno was already tired. Montcourt hadn't spoken a word since giving the driver the order to take them back to the Fornier residence. He covered his eyes while massaging his forehead as he leaned back into the leather seat. She knew that was a sign another migraine was coming on and there wasn't anything she could do to help. He needed his pills, which were back at the house.

C'EST LA VIE, SOLDIER

That didn't stop her from thinking through the events of the morning, but it was ultimately a waste of time. She couldn't change what had happened, and Touchard made it clear that whatever plan had hatched between him and the ambassador, she had no say in. Her thoughts turned back to Lucien. She felt the need to apologize for involving his father, but at the same time, she wasn't really sorry. Like he'd said, under the circumstance, it was, if not the right call, the only call. It fixed one problem but created another.

Montcourt got out on his side and went directly into the house, leaving her to exit the vehicle on her own. It was a sure sign he was pissed, even if he wouldn't admit it.

Moreno followed at a slower pace, passing Jacques in the hallway.

"Which way did he go?" she asked.

The butler pointed her toward the sitting room.

She sucked in a deep breath, then entered the room.

Montcourt stood in front of the bar, pouring bourbon into a tumbler. He knocked it back and poured a second.

"You might want to slow down on that," she said.

He ignored her and finished off the second shot before turning to look at her.

"I think after killing two damned Russian bastards, causing an international incident, and nearly losing you again, I deserve a drink, Nastjia!"

Her mouth dropped. The entire car ride back she'd been wallowing in self-pity thinking he was both angry with her and suffering the pain of another migraine because of the choice she made to involve his father. It never occurred to her what he'd gone through, that he'd been scared.

Tears pricked her eyes, and she ran to him, throwing her arms around his neck and hanging on for dear life.

"I'm sorry!"

Montcourt dropped the tumbler, letting it shatter on the floor, and wrapped his arms tightly around her. He buried his face in her neck and lifted her off her feet, holding her high.

"I cannot lose you, Mon Amour! Don't you understand?"

The catch in his voice sent hot tears streaming down her face.

"I thought you were angry with me," she cried.

He kissed her cheeks, then claimed her lips. Frantic and desperate, their tongues tangled, tasted, caressed. Montcourt's hand slid down beneath her butt and hitched her higher, encouraging her to wrap her legs around his waist. He carried her to the nearest sofa, a peacock-blue velvet-covered loveseat, and settled them both, keeping her straddled across his lap.

"I could never be angry with you, my Nastjia," he breathed between kisses. "Never! You are the love of my life."

Her heart nearly burst from her chest.

"I love you," she whispered.

Lucien pressed his forehead to hers, his mouth hovering over her lips. "I think I have always loved you, that I was born to love you, Nastjia Moreno." His hands roamed her back, then slid up into her hair. He held her face still.

"And I will always love you no matter what. No one and nothing will change that, and no one and nothing will take you from me."

Time stood still. It was just the two of them, and nothing else outside the room existed.

She leaned in, touching her lips to his. Once, twice, and then deeply, pouring every ounce of love she felt for this man into a sizzling kiss. The fire between them quickly blazed out of control.

Montcourt unbuttoned and unzipped her jeans, tugging them down past her hips. He flipped her onto her back, pulling off her boots, then the pants and panties, before yanking her back onto his lap. Moreno had already made short work of his belt, and fly, freeing his cock.

They came together, hard and fast. Montcourt gripped her hips and thrust deep, his body claiming hers.

Each stroke sent her higher and higher. His lips left hers and traveled to her neck, biting and sucking, and a hand cupped her breast through her sweater, pinching her nipple.

"Yes, yes," she panted.

"Come with me, Mon Amour," he growled, his breath hot against her ear.

He ground her hips down on his, pounding harder.

"Lucien, please," she begged.

He grinned. "I love to hear your pleasure. Come for me, Chéri." He sucked her earlobe and bit her neck.

"Oh!"

Nastjia's body tightened with every stroke of his thick, hard shaft. Tingles ran down her spine and pleasure shot straight to her core with every tweak of her nipple. Her slick walls spasmed and the climax sent her tumbling over the edge.

He felt it happen, the moment she came. Montcourt slammed into her one last time and spilled his seed. He was drowning in ecstasy, so overwhelming, tears fell down his cheeks. He buried his face in her neck, inhaling the familiar scent of her soft, silky hair.

They remained entwined, each catching their breath.

Montcourt wiped his tears away before pulling back to look at her.

Her cheeks were flushed, and her lips swollen from his kisses. There was a glow about her and a softness to her lovely brown eyes. She'd never looked more beautiful.

Gently, he pushed a lock of hair back from her face and smiled.

"This is how I would have you always."

She grinned. "Well, I can't spend all my time bottomless in your mother's sitting room."

He gave her naked ass a light slap and chuckled. "I suppose not, but seeing you safe, and naked, and loved is all I wish."

She ran her fingers through his hair and kissed his nose, then his forehead, and cheeks.

"That sounds nice," she murmured.

Their lips met in a sweet kiss.

C'EST LA VIE, SOLDIER

"Maybe if we changed your name, we could keep you off Nikolaev's radar. If he cannot find you, he cannot harm you."

She gave him a wry look.

"I don't think the Navy, or our commanders would be up for a name change. My entire record is under Nastjia Moreno. I don't think the military does witness protection for granddaughters of Russian mafia bosses."

Montcourt ran his hands up and down her back in a soothing gesture.

"I didn't mean your first name, Mon Amour, only your last name."

"Well, how's that—" She stopped and looked at him.

Montcourt grinned, then his expression turned serious.

"Marry me, Nastjia. Marry me and make me the happiest man in this world."

"Lucien..." Tears filled her eyes as her lips parted in surprise.

"My love, this is where we belong, with each other. Forever, or for however long I—"

"Shush!" She placed a finger over his lips. "Yes. Yes, Lucien, I'll marry you."

This time, it was his jaw that dropped. His hazel eyes widened, and a smile pulled at his lips.

"Yes?"

She laughed. "Yes!"

He kissed her then, frantically, joyfully.

Moreno felt herself tumble backwards onto the sofa. Montcourt stood and hastily pulled up his pants before grabbing her discarded clothes and scooping her up in his arms.

"We will continue this in our room," he said, laughing as he snuck them both out of the sitting room and up the stairs before Jacques or any of the house staff discovered them in flagrante delicto.

As Lucien struggled not to drop her or her boots, making her laugh hysterically, a niggling thought intruded. He did not know what the Director of Interpol and his father had planned to keep her safe from her biological grandfather. Truth was, she didn't quite know, either. It seemed a bad idea to bring up anything related to his father at the moment. But the question that nagged was would it work, this mafia war they planned to ignite, and would Lucien still want to marry her if there was no longer a need to protect her?

As he laid her on his bed, his hazel eyes filled with love, she knew she couldn't live without him, not anymore. He'd chased her down since day one, and now she was well and truly caught. She loved him. In this moment, neither her own insecurities, nor the ticking time bomb in his head mattered. All that mattered was right now.

They made love again, this time slow and gentle. Lucien worshipped every inch of her body and whispered words that filled her heart to bursting. It was their own little paradise, a safehouse created by love, one where nothing and no one could harm them.

They ordered room service from the kitchen staff and ate fruits and cheeses and drank wine. They took a long soak in the large tub with lots of bubbles, and when they exhausted themselves, they curled up under the covers and fell asleep, wrapped in each other's arms.

It was the perfect night and the perfect beginning to their life together.

Nastjia peeked up at him admiring the way his lashes fanned out at the top of his cheeks, and the straight line of his nose.

He shifted closer, murmuring, "I can feel you watching me, Mon Amour."

She giggled. "Can't help it, Lucien. I love you," she whispered.

He smiled, his eyes closed. "I love you too. Now sleep," he said, his hand caressing her back. "I have plans for you in the morning."

Chapter Twenty-Four

Faint light filtered through the gap in the curtains creating a pattern on the carpet. Moreno cracked open an eye and stared at the beam illuminating tiny particles of dust floating in the air. It was quiet, peaceful. She smiled to herself and snuggled closer to Montcourt, her back against his chest, and his arm around her waist. She wiggled her butt as she settled in and waited for his response. If it was anything like the night before, he'd be making good on his promise for the *plans* he mentioned he had for her in the morning.

Nothing. He slept on.

Disappointed, Moreno slipped from beneath the covers and went to the bathroom. She took care of business and then brushed her teeth. Catching sight of her reflection in the mirror, she shuddered. Her hair was a mess, and she had mascara smudged beneath her eyes. She scrubbed her face and ran a comb through her hair. It was an improvement.

There was a nip in the air this morning, and she borrowed Lucien's blue robe, slipping into it as she exited the bathroom. The plush material was warm, but he was warmer. Moreno walked to her side of the bed and began to climb back in. He was as she'd left him, his arm stretched out across the covers where she'd slid out from beneath earlier. Lifting his arm, she rolled back in, facing him this time. His face was in shadows as she leaned in for a soft, morning kiss.

Something wet and sticky smeared her lips.

Pulling back, she wiped the back of her hand across her mouth. A dark substance coated her skin, and her gut clenched in alarm.

"Lucien, wake up. You're bleeding!"

Moreno shook his shoulder.

"Lucien!" she called out again.

He didn't move or respond.

Panicked, she pushed him over onto his back and laid her head on his chest. Tears pricked her eyes as she listened, concentrating hard.

"No," she moaned, swallowing the lump in her throat. "No, no, no, no..."

Thump, thump thump.

It was there, his heartbeat, but it was weak and slow.

Her own heart rate accelerated.

"Don't you dare, Lucien! Don't you dare!" she cried, staring down into his face, her hands shaking. Moreno jumped off the bed and ran to the door, throwing it open. She stepped out into the hall and screamed.

"Help! Help!"

Below, a door opened, and footsteps pounded up the stairs.

She ran back into the room and turned on the lamp in time for Jacques to enter.

"Lucien won't wake up! Help me! Please!" She was screaming wildly now, tears flooding her eyes.

Jacques shouted orders to someone in the hall and then ran to the bedside. Marie came running in next, still in her pajamas.

"What is it? What's happening?" she demanded. And then her eyes landed on her son lying in the bed with Jacques leaning over him, checking his breathing. When the butler straightened, Marie saw the blood on her son's face, trickling out of his nose and across his cheek.

"Lucien! Lucien!" She ran to the side of the bed.

Moreno's blood ran cold. More people came into the room. Some were house staff, next came the paramedics. She was shoved aside as they assessed the patient, all the while firing off questions to Marie that she couldn't answer.

Jacques looked at her, seeing her wide-eyed panic.

"Do you know anything, mademoiselle? Was he drinking? Did he take anything?"

His voice sounded a million miles away.

"What? No! He has an aneurysm. I think it burst."

"An aneurysm? Did you say aneurysm?" Marie asked, shocked. "Since when? How?"

Moreno looked at his mother. "Since I first met him. It's why he was sent to America, to my unit."

"I don't understand," she said, confused. "Why did he not tell me?"

"Madam, now isn't the time," Jacques said, stepping in. He turned quickly and relayed the information to the paramedics.

It all went fast then. They moved Lucien to a gurney and wheeled him out, already hooked up to an IV pole with an oxygen mask over his face.

Marie Fornier ran from the room, leaving Moreno behind.

The butler followed, then the few house staff gawkers removed themselves, and once again, the room was quiet, but not peaceful. Moreno crumpled to the floor, sobs wracking her body. Lucien was dying. Her Lucien, her love. It was happening, and she couldn't stop it.

"Why! Why!" she moaned. "Please, God, help him. Please!"

She was doubled over, her face to the floor, pain gripping her heart. She couldn't breathe, couldn't get enough air.

"Mademoiselle." Hands gently gripped her shoulders. "You must get dressed. You need to go to the hospital. He needs you. Madam Fornier needs you."

Moreno heard Jacques's words, but she couldn't make herself move. He helped her up.

C'EST LA VIE, SOLDIER

"I will send in someone to assist you," he said, his old eyes filled with compassion.

She stared at the older man. Old man. That's what Lucien called him. He'd known Jacques all his life, since he was just a small boy. He'd told her some stories, and all of them shared with great affection for the butler. Jacques was more than just a butler, he was a family friend, maybe even a pseudo-father figure to Lucien. The butler's grip trembled as he held her shoulders. Jacques had defaulted to his familiar role, but he, too, was distraught.

"I don't know where to go," she began, swiping at her eyes.

Jacques patted her shoulder. "I will take care of everything. Just get yourself together. I will send in Aileen to help."

Moreno shook her head. "No. I can do it." She sucked in a breath, striving for calm.

He nodded. "There will be a car ready to take you and Madam Fornier in fifteen minutes. Hurry, Mademoiselle Moreno."

He left her then to make arrangements.

Moreno shook herself and slapped her face, blinking back the tears.

"He needs me. He needs me," she repeated over and over as she rushed to get dressed and get downstairs. At the last moment, she stopped and grabbed her purse, pulling out her wallet. With her cellphone in hand, she pulled out the card the ambassador gave her and dialed the number for a second time. As the phone rang, she prayed he was right about the Swedish surgeon, and that it was not too late.

Four hours passed in the slowest of increments. Moreno leaned her head on the window staring out across the hospital parking lot. She stood there in the surgical waiting area, numb. Since they'd arrived in the emergency room, Lucien had undergone multiple tests including a CT scan that confirmed a subarachnoid hemorrhage—a direct result of a burst aneurysm. The only good news was that he wasn't already dead. The doctor on call explained to Madam Fornier and the ambassador, who'd arrived shortly after them, that sixty percent of such cases resulted in instant death.

By the third hour, Doctor Emil Blom, the world's leading neurosurgeon, arrived at the hospital from Stockholm. After conferring with the ER physician, studying the test results, and reviewing Montcourt's medical record, he then pulled the ambassador aside, speaking low.

Moreno could see their heads bent together and the somber expression on Louie Fornier's face. Marie stood next to him, leaning heavily upon her husband's arm, tears in her eyes. She desperately wanted to know what was being said, but she didn't want to intrude. She wasn't family.

When Doctor Blom walked back through the double doors leading into the emergency department, the ambassador approached, explaining that Lucien would be going into surgery, and it would be hours before they knew anything more.

"You did the right thing, my dear," he said, patting her arm.

Moreno stared at the now closed doors. "Is there anything I can do?" she asked, a wobble in her voice.

Fornier blinked, a world of worry in his eyes. "Pray," he said.

That had been more than an hour ago. She glanced at the clock. It was almost 11:30 a.m. With nothing else to do, she pulled out her cellphone, and calculating the time in her head, hit dial.

"Hello?"

"Connie? It's Nasty. Is my father awake?" Her voice broke.

"Nasty? What's wrong?" Connie asked.

Hearing the instant concern in Connie Wheeler's voice, the tears burst their dam. She needed her friends. She needed her papa. She couldn't handle this alone.

"It's Lucien..." she cried. "He's...he's dying."

"What? Oh, my God. Nasty, hold on!"

She could hear the urgency in Connie's words and the sounds of her rushing through the house, and then muffled voices in the background before he came on the line.

"Mija! Mija, what's wrong? Where are you?" Juan Carlos asked, panicked.

This was the voice that mattered, that had been absent from her life for so long. She'd suffered more than she realized not having him around when she needed him most. Her knees buckled and she slid to the floor, broken.

"Papa, papa, I need you. Please, can you come? I need you! Please," she cried.

"Breathe, baby. Breathe! Tell me where you are." She could hear him whispering to Connie in the background. *"I need something to write on!"*

Through a wave of tears, Moreno told him everything from the attempted kidnapping to finding Lucien unresponsive. Her father said something about calling her back once plans were made, and Connie came back on the line to reassure her she'd let Mac and the others know and do everything she could to get Juan Carlos on a flight out to Paris. By the end of the phone call, she was all cried out, miserable, and exhausted.

All she could do now was wait. And it was hell.

The sun had long since set by the time the double doors to the surgical suites opened. Doctor Blom entered the waiting room and found the Forniers sitting in the far corner near the coffee machine. Moreno had taken over a couch on the opposite wall, curling up and closing her eyes, but sleep would not come. She'd survived the day on caffeine, vending machine donuts, and a sandwich picked up at the cafeteria mid-afternoon. It hadn't been much better for Lucien's parents.

C'EST LA VIE, SOLDIER

She'd watched as the ambassador made sure Marie ate something and drank water. She'd given him a lot of guff at first, insisting she was fine, but he was not having it. Moreno saw him slip cash to a passing orderly, speaking quietly to the young man. The orderly left and came back with a loaded tray of food. Marie had picked at it, and Louie sat down next to her, picking up the fork and offering her bites. They shared the meal, and drank coffee, but they were all exhausted by the time Doctor Blom came out.

Louie Fornier stood, facing the doctor. Marie jumped up behind him, clutching at her husband's hand.

Moreno turned and sat forward but didn't dare approach. As desperate as she was for news of Lucien, she was keenly aware she was not family. She was barely the girlfriend. At least, it was all new.

The doctor spoke too low for her to hear. The ambassador's face remained neutral, but Marie quickly covered her mouth and cried, burying her face in her husband's chest.

Blom touched her shoulder, speaking directly to her now. Marie nodded, and the doctor left, disappearing once again through the double doors.

Moreno felt the bottom fall out of her world. She stopped breathing and gripped the armrest.

Fornier looked her way and seeing her pale face and the naked terror in her eyes, waved her over.

She stood on rubbery legs and walked to them.

"I am sorry, Nastjia," he said. "I should have called you over sooner. He is out of surgery. Doctor Blom said the procedure was difficult, but a success..."

Moreno released the breath she'd been holding, her body shaking with relief.

"But," he added, taking a beat.

Her pulse ratcheted up again. "But... what?"

Next to Fornier, Marie hiccupped, a cry escaping her lips.

The ambassador pulled his wife into his arms and continued. "But we will not know the extent of the damage until he wakes up," he said, his eyes downcast. "*If* he wakes up."

Moreno swallowed hard. The implications were dire. Lucien may have survived the surgery, but perhaps not fully intact. Worse, he might not ever awaken again.

"When will they let you see him?" she asked, hoping with everything she had that she might, too, get the chance. She had so much to tell him, even if he couldn't hear her.

"Soon," Fornier said. "Doctor Blom says Lucien is in recovery, and perhaps in another hour we can go in," he added, looking at Marie.

Just his parents. Moreno nodded and backed away.

"I think I'll take a walk and stretch my legs a bit," she murmured.

She didn't know where she was going, not knowing the layout of the hospital. All she knew was she needed some fresh air, needed to get out of that waiting room. When she turned the corner, she found another long hall and no helpful signs. She slowed, looking left and right. Near the end of the hall was a door marked with a familiar symbol, one she hadn't sought out since her mother died. But it was here now, in this unfamiliar place, when she was so lost. Moreno opened the door and stepped inside the small chapel.

After hours, it was dimly lit, with no one inside. There were six pews, three on each side, and an altar on a small dais at the end of the short aisle. Behind the altar, affixed to the wall, was a simple cross, backlit in a soft, white light.

She took a seat in the back pew and stared at the cross, her thoughts all over the map.

"Why?" she whispered.

Her question was a single word yet asked so much. *Why did this happen? Why Lucien, who was a good and kind man? Why now? Why bring love into her life and rip it away when she'd already lost so much? Why give her hope at all if he might never wake up? Why, God, why?*

She leaned forward, resting her arms on the back of the pew in front of her, her head bent. Moreno had learned to believe in only what she could see, could touch. Nothing else mattered. But now, she couldn't see Lucien, couldn't touch him, but she believed in him. It was all his fault. He'd been there for her when no one else was, and he'd promised he always would be, even when she wished he would just go away. She chuckled through her tears, thinking of those early days. Still, until this moment, he'd kept that promise.

She sniffed and dug her fingers in her hair, tugging until she felt pain. She needed that. Pain meant she was still alive. If she was still alive, the fight wasn't over. He'd been there for her. Strong, stalwart. Maybe it was time to be there for him, to fight for him. But she needed to see him, to touch him, to tell him she loved him. Lucien had told her she was the love of his life. His life couldn't be over.

She looked up at the cross again.

"You can't have him. Not yet!"

She got up and left the chapel, walking with purpose back to the waiting room. One way or the other, she was going to see him. He needed to know she was not giving up on him, on them. And he needed to fight.

She marched right up to the Forniers, her posture resolute.

The ambassador looked up from scrolling through his cellphone.

"What is it, Nastjia?" He'd taken to addressing her informally.

"When the doctor okays it, I want to see him." She spoke the words quietly, respectfully, but with conviction.

Louie Fornier glanced at his wife, who'd opened her mouth to speak. Fornier shook his head, stopping Marie from saying whatever it was she was about to say, and turned to Moreno. He gave a single nod.

"Of course. Lucien wouldn't even have this chance had you not called me. I am," he began, then looked at his wife, taking her hand in his, "*we are* forever grateful. When it is allowed, his mother and I will check in on him. Then, I will let the nursing staff know you are to be admitted."

Moreno exhaled. "Thank you."

The ambassador got up and faced her. "No, my dear, thank you." He embraced her, patting her back. "I am happy he has you in his life."

She stood there, awkwardly held in the arms of Lucien's father. It occurred to her how odd it was that he'd gone from arrogant philanderer and for-shit father to this humble individual in such a short period of time.

She pulled away and nodded, unable to find the appropriate words. Tossing a quick glance at Marie, Moreno sat back down on the couch to wait. She owed Lucien's mother an apology later for snapping at her last night. It was uncalled for, no matter how she'd felt at the time about the comparison between father and son. Although it was true that the ambassador was a cheater, she could see now the similarities between them when it came to loyalty of a different stripe, and deep caring. Fornier had gone above and beyond to keep tabs on the son he often found himself at odds with, to the point of researching and securing the best surgeon in the world to save Lucien. His methods were undoubtedly intrusive and conducted knowing his son would not welcome the help, but his intentions were pure. Love. And he'd been right here, right by Marie's side the entire time. It spoke well of the man, and for Moreno, it counted.

She looked up at the clock on the wall, wondering how much longer before she could see him. Time ticked by slowly, and before she knew it, another three hours passed. Three hours! Didn't the doctor tell them it would be about an hour two hours ago? Something was wrong. Something had to be wrong!

Feeling anxious, she got up and walked the room.

"Nastjia, it will be okay." The ambassador watched her pace. "If anything was amiss, someone would have come out by now to inform us."

She wrung her hands.

"You think? What if they're too busy in an emergency?" she asked.

"Mija."

Moreno swung around, and then seeing a familiar face, ran.

"Papa!" She flung herself into his waiting arms.

Juan Carlos lifted his daughter off the ground, holding her tight.

Tears flooded her tired eyes as she clung to his neck. He was here.

A hand reached out and patted her back. She twisted around and saw Mac, Connie, Harry, and Griz through a wet blur.

"You all came?" she asked, surprised.

"Oh, hon, I couldn't stop them," Connie said, reaching out to hug her. "And I couldn't leave you with just the boys," she chuckled, sniffing back her own tears.

Moreno's heart soared. After Connie, she hugged Harry, then Griz, and finally, Mac.

"I can't believe you're all here."

C'EST LA VIE, SOLDIER

Mac shrugged, never one comfortable with the emotional stuff.

"We don't leave our own alone," he said.

Harry laughed. "Don't let him downplay it, Nasty. Mac was the one that got all our leave granted with Maxwell. Hell, the rest of the team would've been here if she'd let them. They send their love, by the way."

Moreno sniffled. "I can't tell you how much this means," she began.

Griz patted her back. "We're happy to help any way we can. Any news?"

She took a deep breath and then caught them up.

"Now we're just waiting to see him," she said.

"We?" Mac asked.

"Yeah, me and Lucien's parents," she replied, pointing at the couple seated near the coffee machine. "Come on, I'll introduce you."

She led them over and made the introductions.

The ambassador shook everyone's hands and spoke briefly with Juan Carlos. Marie Fornier eyed the others with curiosity. She turned to Mac.

"You know my son? You work with him?"

Mac nodded. "Yes, ma'am."

When he said no more, she turned to Harry and Griz. "All of you?"

"All of us, and more," Harry added. "He's a great guy."

Montcourt's mother reminded Griz of his own mom. She was clearly distressed and talking about him with those who know him, work with him, might help ease the pain she was going through.

"Montcourt is well respected in our unit. He's proven time and again to be dependable in a moment of crisis. He's tenacious, for sure. I have no doubt he'll come through this. There's no quit in him," Griz said.

"Plus, he's one hundred percent in love with Moreno," Harry added. "No way he'd leave her now after finally getting the girl."

Mac punched Harry in the arm, clearing his throat.

"Ow! What was that for?"

Griz rolled his eyes and then glanced at Mrs. Fornier who was dissolving into tears before their eyes. "What it's usually for, Tyler."

Seeing Montcourt's mom start to cry, Harry's gut clenched. "Shit. Sorry, ma'am." Then he bit his tongue and began again. "Sorry for saying shit. Sorry for whatever I said to upset you," he rambled.

Moreno stepped in. "He was raised by wolves, Marie. But while we're on the subject of saying the wrong thing, I need to apologize for the other night. I'm so sorry. I overstepped."

Marie Fornier shook her head and wiped her eyes. Then, she began to laugh.

The ambassador turned to look at his wife and the team stood around her, dumbfounded.

Finally, she got herself together and looked at each of them, a motherly smile on her face.

C'EST LA VIE, SOLDIER

"It is so good to meet you all, and to have you here. Lucien was such a scamp as a child, and a charming rogue as an adult. He is headstrong and sometimes foolhardy, but I see a little bit of him in each of you," she said. Then she turned to Moreno. "And if what your Harry says is true, you, Nastjia, will be the reason my son gets through this. Thank you." Marie gathered Moreno in her arms and kissed her cheeks before hugging her tightly. "Thank you."

The double doors opened, and a nurse came into the waiting room.

Everyone turned, suddenly alert.

"Ambassador and Madam Fornier?" she called.

Montcourt's parents sobered and looked to each other for support. Fornier took his wife's hand, giving it a squeeze. He glanced at Moreno, nodding.

"We'll be back soon," he promised.

When they left, Mac moved next to Moreno. "They gonna let you see him?"

She nodded. "Yeah."

"Good."

Griz joined them, flanking her. "He's going to be okay, Moreno."

Her father came up behind her, wrapping his arms around her shoulders. Connie and Harry closed the circle. She was surrounded by family, protected by their support and love.

"He has to be," she whispered, "because I can't live without him."

Chapter Twenty-Five

Moreno stood inside the white room and looked at Montcourt. All around him were monitors and machines beeping and pumping air. There were IV lines giving him life-sustaining fluids and wires attached to electrodes taped to his chest. His head was wrapped in white gauze and there was a drain tube coming out the back somewhere beneath the material. More tubing ran across his handsome face from the nasal canula providing oxygen.

Her chest tightened and she rubbed the spot to ease the pain.

The ambassador had warned her before she went through the double doors, but the reality of seeing Lucien like this hit hard. She focused on breathing and swallowed her fear.

There was already a chair next to his bed. She approached and gently curled her fingers around his. His skin was warm, a reminder he was still alive. She looked at his hand, remembering that only twenty-four hours ago, he was holding her with those hands, stroking her hair, touching her everywhere. He'd been so bold, and confident, and sexy, and animated, and whole. But now...

She sat next to him, settling into the chair, still holding his hand.

"Hi," she whispered. "I'm here, Lucien." She stroked the back of his hand.

The monitors beeped and whooshed.

Moreno struggled to find words.

"The doctor told your parents that the surgery was a success. Hear that? You thought it was impossible, remember? Turns out you just needed the right doctor for the job. Damned military doctors told you it couldn't be done safely, made you worry for nothing," she said, her voice catching on a sob.

She swallowed it down.

"Please don't be mad at me for calling for help, Lucien. I know you said you'd accepted your fate, but dammit, then you made me fall in love with you. Did you really just expect I'd be okay with you leaving me after that? You promised me, Lucien. You promised to be here for me, and I'm holding you to it. You have to fight. You have to heal and wake up, because I need you. I need you," she cried, the tears slipping down her cheeks. "Please wake up, baby. I love you so much!"

Moreno held his hand to her cheek, her tears now a veritable flood. She'd come in with a plan, to fight for him,

C'EST LA VIE, SOLDIER

and to encourage him to fight for his life. But seeing him lying in this hospital bed, unmoving, had ripped her plan to shreds. This wasn't a battle she knew how to win. It was out of her control.

"Come back to me, Lucien. Please come back to me," she whispered hoarsely. All she could do now was repeat the words like some magical incantation. She'd never felt more helpless.

It had been a long day, and a longer night. Moreno was beyond exhausted and weary to her soul. She clung to his hand, laying her head beside it. The chair wasn't the most comfortable, but she'd been in worse conditions., and she'd suffer any discomfort gladly to be with him.

Memories flooded in of the first time she'd met Lucien in the conference room. He'd been cheeky in that annoying way of all men hellbent on getting a woman's attention. She'd ignored him, hoping he'd go away. She was also aware that the guys had a bet going to see how long it would take before she walloped the impudent Frenchman. Knowing the odds were against him was what saved him from her wrath. It confounded her that she had kind-of felt sorry for him. Plus, despite how much he annoyed her, he was attractive. She just wasn't willing to admit it. So, she'd given him the cold shoulder, which led to the betting pool growing. When she didn't put the poor man in his place, the bet changed. She knew about that one too. Mac might be able to keep a secret, but Harry and Diaz seemed unaware that people with ears could actually hear them when they thought they were whispering. They made a mistake talking about the bet a little too close to Natalie Janeway, their comms liaison. Moreno knew all about Natalie's little crush on Diaz and used that to gain information. She could be devious with the best of them.

Meanwhile, Montcourt was wearing her down with his charm, his kindness, and his loyalty. Then, somewhere along the way, he'd slipped right past the walls she'd carefully built. It was the Honey Hole mission. That was the moment she realized she cared. Things got a bit awkward after that. Every minute they spent together seemed to bond them closer, and the closer they got, the more she noticed other things about him, things that set her lady parts on fire.

He began as a teammate. He became a friend. Then he turned into a lover, and finally, the man she loved. There was no one else now, could never be anyone else.

"You're mine, you know," she said absently. "And I'm yours. I think we were always meant to be."

"Haven't I already said so, Mon Amour?" a weak voice replied.

Moreno sat up and stared, her mouth hanging wide.

"Lucien, you're awake!" She stood, leaning over him, still holding his hand.

He opened his eyes, trying to focus.

"Where am I? What happened?"

Relief and joy flooded her body.

"In the hospital, baby."

"Hospital?"

C'EST LA VIE, SOLDIER

"Yeah. Your aneurysm..." she began. "I need to get the doctor... Oh, and your parents," she added.

"Mon Amour, don't go," he said, panic in his hazel eyes.

She turned back to him, smiling through tears. "It's going to be okay, Lucien. You had surgery and it worked. It was a success."

Confusion marred his face. "But the doctors said—"

"They were wrong, baby. Turns out you just needed the right doctor, the best neurosurgeon. Your dad found him. He had the man on standby, but that's a story for another time. He cares about you, Lucien. He's been here the entire time, he and your mom."

Montcourt stared at Moreno trying to take it all in. "Sounds like I missed a lot. I am sorry, Nastjia."

She cupped his cheek. "For what?"

"For worrying you."

She leaned down and placed a gentle kiss on his lips. "You'll make it up to me... by getting better."

"The surgery truly worked?" he asked, fear and hope warring in his eyes.

"Yes, it worked. No more aneurysm. The doctor will explain it all, but no more ticking time bomb."

A smile tugged at his lips. "So, we have time?"

"All the time in the world," she said, smiling back.

Tears pricked his eyes. "I love you with all my heart, Nastjia. I was yours the moment you walked into that conference room," he whispered.

"And here I thought you were just playing games with me," she parried, her voice wobbling.

He grinned. "Never, Mon Amour."

She kissed him then, softly, carefully.

"I'm going to get the doctor now, and your parents. Oh, and Mac, Harry, and Griz are here, too. Plus, my dad and Connie."

"They all came?"

"They all love you. Of course, they came. If Maxwell had been more generous with leave, all of them would be here. Everyone sends their love."

"I am a blessed man to have such wonderful friends, and such an amazing lady in my life." He held her hand and stared into her big, brown eyes.

He didn't want to let her go, but he had something now he didn't have before. Time, the biggest blessing of all.

"Go, then. Go get this doctor. I owe him many thanks."

She straightened and turned to leave. He watched her go, admiring, as always, the view of her backside.

Moreno paused at the door, glancing over her shoulder.

"I can feel you watching me."

He chuckled. "When I am better, we have much catching up to do, Mon Amour."

She laughed, happy to hear the familiar Montcourt she knew so well.

"I love you, Lucien."

"I know, Nastjia," he replied. Despite the monitors and tubes and gauze bandaging, Lucien Montcourt smiled slowly, deliberately at the woman he loved, and winked.

Epilogue

Six Months Later

Clouds rolled in, darkening the sky, and threatening rain. Mac cursed as the wind whipped up, sending the smoke from the barbecue pit billowing into his eyes. He flipped the burgers and chicken onto platters and handed one off to Ben Holiday, and then followed him inside the house.

Mac joined Connie in the kitchen, setting the burger platter on the kitchen island with all the other food prepared for their Labor Day get together.

Moreno sat next to Montcourt on the patio swing watching her teammates enjoy the day. Irina and Jessica were helping Connie in the kitchen, one placing a large bowl of cold potato salad near the burgers and grilled chicken, and the other arranging plates and utensils. The buffet was looking good and smelling better.

Ben had come back out with Mac to bank the fire in the pit before the storm arrived. Griz, Harry, Jackson, Moses, and Matt were playing a game of poker at the kitchen table, and Joely watched them from the comfort of the couch with her feet propped up. She was nine months pregnant and due any day now. No one could wipe the smile from Harry's face.

Griz, thanks to help from Jessica, was once again a brunette, his bad bleach job now remembered only jokingly out loud by those brave enough to poke the bear. Namely, Harry.

Across from where she sat, Art, Woody, and Natalie Janeway sat in lawn chairs, a cold drink in hand, and deep in conversation. Poor Woody was, as usual, completely oblivious to the unspoken communication happening between Art and Natalie as he kept up a steady stream of chatter.

The doorbell rang, and Moreno knew that it had to be the major and Dr. Delaney. Syd and Lila's relationship was going strong, enough so that Major Maxwell brought her partner to all the team's off-duty gatherings now.

The only one not at Mac's house was her dad. He had to work.

Juan Carlos had secured a new job at the local whole food's grocery store as their assistant manager a month after arriving back from Paris. Having been out of work for a significant period of time set him back just a bit and downgraded him from full management, but he was happy and thriving in their little corner of Las Vegas. Two

C'EST LA VIE, SOLDIER

months after that, he'd found an apartment and moved in. She'd helped him pick out furniture, and Joely helped set things up and decorate. Mac took her dad to a car lot where he purchased a used pickup truck.

Things had worked out well, all in all. There was even talk of a road trip to New Mexico, to their old house to retrieve the family photo albums hidden beneath the kitchen floorboards... when it was safe to do so.

She turned her attention to the man beside her.

Lucien sat with his arms outstretched across the back of the swing and his legs crossed at the ankles as they swayed with the strong breeze. Wind ruffled his hair, grown back out now from surgery. It covered the scar at the back of his head, hiding the evidence of how close he'd come to death. Rehab began for him in that hospital in Paris, and when he was strong enough and stable enough to travel, they'd flown back here and continued his care at Camp Lazarus. Joely kept in contact with Doctor Blom, updating him on Montcourt's progress. He was now off all blood thinners and his migraines were a thing of the past, much to his relief.

He turned to her, a lazy smile on his handsome face.

"What are you thinking about, Mon Amour?"

Moreno reached up to push a lock of his brown hair back from his forehead, the platinum diamond ring on her third finger catching the light. The twinkle of the gem reminded her of the magical night a few months back when he slipped the ring onto her hand while dancing under the bright light of the moon. They'd had a dinner date and were enjoying live music on the patio of a popular restaurant. As the band sang a song about a great love beating all odds, he'd kissed her breathless. And while she was distracted, the ring slid into place. He'd asked again, and again, she said yes. Only now, it was official.

She gazed at him, filled with love and sheer wonder that they'd survived the worst and found each other.

"I'm thinking I need to cut your hair. It's getting long again."

He turned his face into her hand and kissed her palm. "You take such good care of me."

She leaned closer and rested her chin on his shoulder.

"Sure, because I love you," she said, grinning.

His eyes twinkled. "A thinly veiled excuse to get your hands on me and have your way, I think."

"Do I need an excuse?" she asked, beginning to feel the heat he was sending her way. It was that damned panty-dropper look, the one that always got her.

His free hand slid around the back of her neck, his fingers caressing the sensitive skin of her nape.

"You need only ask, Mon Amour, and I am your willing body servant."

She laughed out loud, catching everyone's attention. Blushing at their knowing looks, she cleared her throat.

"Lucien Montcourt, stop teasing me," she chided.

He leaned in and snaked a quick kiss. "Never," he murmured, his voice husky. "I enjoy it too much," he said, then whispered in her ear, "and so do you."

Her cheeks flamed again, and her body tightened as it always did in response to this amazing, sexy man.

"Nasty, did you see this?"

Moreno turned at the mention of her name, grateful for the interruption.

Mac approached, his cellphone in hand. Ben was right behind him.

"What?" she asked.

Mac handed her the phone. She looked at the screen displaying a feed of international news. The first headline grabbed her full attention.

RUSSIAN MAFIA BOSS FOUND DECAPITATED IN ST. PETERSBURG PARK.

She read through the article, which was one day old.

"What is it, Mon Amour?" Montcourt looked over her shoulder.

"It says Nikolaev was found dead. Well, his body was found. They haven't found his head yet. It goes on to say a war between Bratva factions has terrorized surrounding communities and exposed deep corruption within the politsiya and the FSB over the past six months. Their primary suspect is Vladimir Brezhnev, known as *The Butcher*." She finished reading the article in silence, her mind drifting to the conversation inside an interrogation room in Versailles with Director Touchard. He'd mentioned a plan, something cooked up between himself and Ambassador Fornier. So much had happened after that, she'd forgotten about it, and never once spoke of it with Lucien.

The article was harsh proof something seedy had gone down. Whatever leverage Louie Fornier had cashed in with this Brezhnev had surely tilted the scale. Mafia bosses never did anyone a favor without getting something in return. Lucien's father had put himself in debt to a brutal killer. For her. For his son's happiness. That thought weighed heavy upon her conscience. Her mind screamed, *"Tell him!"* Her heart disagreed. Following his surgery, Lucien and his father had begun to rebuild their relationship. It was fragile, at best. Telling him what his dad had done might not cause harm to their tenuous reunion, but it could possibly destroy it.

Making a decision, she handed the cellphone back to Mac.

"Looks like I don't have to worry about that anymore."

"Guess not," Mac agreed. "Still, that's a fucking brutal way to die."

"Live by the sword, die by the sword," she said.

Montcourt pulled her close to his side and kissed her cheek. "Well, I for one am glad you are out of danger. And I am hungry," he added, looking at Mac and Ben.

Mac turned to look inside at the women in the kitchen.

"Looks like they're ready for us. Let's eat." He waved at everyone and ushered them inside just as the first drops of rain hit the ground. "Don't let the cat out!" Mac groused, rushing to shoo the giant, orange beast away from the screen door.

Moreno and Montcourt got up last and waited as first Woody ambled inside on his cane, followed by Natalie

C'EST LA VIE, SOLDIER

Janeway wearing her cute short shorts. Behind her, Art Diaz stared at her backside, a silly grin on his face.

Montcourt held her hand as they watched the two.

"The betting pool went up by a thousand dollars after Mac and Jackson shared that Natalie was teaching young Art to waltz," he said.

Moreno grinned. "I think after today, it's going to go up again. Just look at the way he's eyeballing her. Those two will be doing it before this month is out," she said, chuckling.

Montcourt laughed, then pulled her into his arms. He stared into her big, brown eyes, his lips twitching with merriment. "I am betting you and I will be *doing it* before this night is through."

Moreno wound her arms around his neck, rubbing her chest against his. Montcourt sucked in a breath.

"Your odds are very good, but you should know, the house always wins."

He squeezed her butt, his eyes twinkling. "I've already won, Mon Amour. You are all mine."

She sighed, her heart full. "And we have all the time in the world."

GET A **FREE** BOOK!

Did you know you can get a FREE book on my website? Visit micheleegwynnauthor.com and pick one of two available FREE books as a gift from me to you for signing up for my newsletter. Just click the GET A FREE BOOK tab at the top of the page. Be the first to know when a new book publishes, and also be eligible for my sporadic (holiday) giveaways. Your information is never shared, and you will not be spammed. You can unsubscribe at any time by clicking the "unsubscribe" button at the bottom of my newsletter. You have nothing to lose and everything to gain. Come join my list and grab your FREE book today!

Also By Michele E. Gwynn

Did you miss books I-V in the Green Beret Series? Grab them now! Rescuing Emma, Loving Leisl, Freeing Fatima, Saving Christmas, and Loving Freddie, newly remastered and re-edited with bonus scenes. The Green Beret series was previously written as part of the special force's world created by NYT Bestselling Author Susan Stoker. The series is now re-edited outside of Stoker's world with an all-new SEAL teams as a point of contact/support team to Outlaw's Green Berets: Visit micheleegwynnauthor.com. The Soldiers of PATCH-COM is the spinoff series from Gwynn's Green Beret series. Secondhand Soldier is the debut book. Keep up with new releases in this series by signing up for my newsletter.

Checkpoint Novels (18+)
Exposed: The Education of Sarah Brown (novel)

MICHELE E. GWYNN

The Evolution of Elsa Kreiss (novel)
The Redemption of Joseph Heinz (novel)
The Making of Herman Faust (prequel novella)

Green Beret Series (18+)
Rescuing Emma
Loving Leisl
Freeing Fatima
Saving Christmas
Loving Freddie
Saving Major Morgan (A Green Beret Series prequel novella)

The Soldiers of PATCH-COM (18+)
Secondhand Soldier
Second Chance Soldier
Second Breath Soldier
Silent Night Soldier
C'est la Vie, Soldier

The Harvest Trilogy (18+)
Harvest
Hybrids
Census

Section 5 (A Harvest Trilogy Spinoff) (18+)

Angelic Hosts Series (18+)
(Now Exclusively Available for FREE on Michele E. Gwynn's Substack)

C'EST LA VIE, SOLDIER

Camael's Gift
Camael's Battle
Sophie's Wish
Nephilim Rising

<u>Stand Alones</u>
Darkest Communion (Paranormal Romance, 18+)
Waiting a Lifetime (Contemporary Romance, Mystical)(16+)
Hiring John (Romantic Comedy 18+)

www.ingramcontent.com/pod-product-compliance
Lightning Source LLC
LaVergne TN
LVHW041621060526
838200LV00040B/1371